Excuse Me While I Ugly Cry

'A sweet, romantic debut that celebrates the joy of being your authentic self. I loved it.' – Alexandra Sheppard, author of *Oh My Gods*

'A hilarious and swoonworthy story about friendship, family, overcoming your fears and falling in love. The chemistry between Quinn and Carter is electric, and this debut left me completely charmed.' – Kristina Forest, author of *Now That I've Found You*

'A fun, emotionally rich romance that explores themes of bravery, friendship and race, with a sweet, imperfect character who will win your heart.' – Liara Tamani, author of *All the Things We Never Knew*

'At its heart, this is a story about finding the courage to be honest and take risks and the freedom that follows from embracing authenticity. A perfect mix of humour and romance – and a source of inspiration for being brave.' – Kirkus, starred review

'Goffney's important debut novel navigates the messy feelings Black teens may experience. This authentic look at the teen years will undou̶̶̶̶̶̶̶̶̶̶̶̶̶̶̶̶̶̶̶̶klist, starred review

Excuse Me While I Ugly Cry

Excuse Me While I Ugly Cry

JOYA GOFFNEY

HOT
KEY
BOOKS

First published in Great Britain in 2021 by
HOT KEY BOOKS
An imprint of Bonnier Books UK
80–81 Wimpole St, London W1G 9RE
Owned by Bonnier Books
Sveavägen 56, Stockholm, Sweden
www.hotkeybooks.com

A CIP catalogue record for this book is available from
the British Library.

ISBN: 978-1-4714-1011-6
Also available as an ebook and in audio

1

Typography by Molly Fehr
Printed and bound by Clays Ltd, Elcograf S.p.A.

Hot Key Books is an imprint of Bonnier Books UK
www.bonnierbooks.co.uk

For A-May, whose given name I thought was
literally A-hyphen-May until an embarrassingly
old age. You deserve all the love. I give you
all my love and all these words.

contents

chapter 1

DAYS I'VE LOST MY
LIST JOURNAL

"FRANK SINATRA."

"Which song?" Auden asks.

"Just write *Frank Sinatra*."

"But Mr. Green wants us to be specific."

Carter sighs. He's sitting in the grass across from me, his arms hugging his kneecaps, arguing with Auden. I'm too distracted to pay attention, watching Carter roll up the sleeves of his T-shirt, the white fabric contrasting against his dark skin. I've never been grouped with him before, but now that we're here, I can't seem to concentrate on anything outside his physicality.

When he moved here sophomore year, I remember thinking he looked different from the rich white boys I'd always been surrounded by—them and their Bermuda shorts and collared shirts, him and his dingy T-shirts and baggy basketball shorts. I couldn't look away. But when he finally met my gaze, he instantly dropped it. I don't know. For some reason I thought he'd see me, really *see* me, considering we have the same dark complexion, but no. He looked at me just as apathetically as he looked at everyone else.

"Huh, Quinn?"

I look up from the stubble on Carter's chin to find him staring back at me, his brows pinched, like he's wondering if I'm mental.

My cheeks warm as I cover my mouth with my fingertips. "What was the question?" I ask Auden, too afraid to look at Carter again. This is the third time he's caught me gawking today.

Auden shifts his eyes impatiently. "Any soundtrack suggestions for our JFK screenplay? The project we've been working on for hours now."

I lower my hand to the base of my throat. *Right.* I swallow and look for answers in the cloudless sky. "What songs do we have so far?" I stall, plucking a few blades of grass.

Auden checks the list in his lap with an exasperated sigh. That's the thing about Auden: he's sweet, but he has absolutely no chill. I've been grouped with him before, and the second we got our assignment, he started dishing out commands. He's also the type to do all the work in a group, because no one ever follows his orders just right. People tend to take advantage of that. I'm trying my best to not become one of those people, but Carter . . .

Get ahold of yourself, Quinn!

While Auden continues reading songs from our soundtrack list, I pull my red spiral out of my backpack, then flip past my to-do lists and my how-tos, all the way to the back section for miscellaneous lists. If I can get my thoughts about Carter all out at once, then maybe I can focus on JFK's assassination.

CARTER IS . . .

1. Cool. In every respect of the word.
2. Attractive. As. Hell.
3. A "real Black guy," as I've heard it put around the halls of our predominantly white private school, which makes me wonder about the authenticity of my own Blackness. I've never heard anyone call me a "real Black girl." In fact, I've only ever heard the opposite. I bet he never has to deal with white people telling Black jokes around him. Must be nice.
4. A back-of-the-classroom, forehead-perpetually-glued-to-his-desk kind of student—really adds to his mystique. He never shares his thoughts in class, so suddenly having access to them must be why I'm so shell-shocked right now.
5. Not materialistic, like the other boys at our school. He couldn't care less about brand names. If it still works, it's good enough for him. I like that. I consider myself pretty low-maintenance too.

6. Conscientious of how he smells. I can smell him from here, and it's nothing like the obnoxious colognes the other boys wear. Carter simply smells clean.

7. Unwilling to date girls from our school, which is quite disheartening.

8. A player? I've heard rumors about him and Emily Hayes getting busy at a party last year. It's never been confirmed, though.

9. Kinda antisocial. He doesn't typically hang around the white kids at school, which means he doesn't have many friends. I only see him talk to Olivia Thomas. Every time I see them laughing together, it makes me wish I had Black friends too.

"Hilary." I peek up from my list into Carter's curious eyes. "You know we can only turn in one list for the group, right?"

He can't see my journal, but it feels like he knows I'm writing about him. Cheeks on fire, I slam it shut. "That's not what I'm doing." I drop my gaze to the glossy red cover. "And please stop calling me that. I'm nothing like her."

He's been calling me Hilary ever since he got to my house today. He stepped out of Auden's Nissan Versa, looked up at my house like he was Will in *The Fresh Prince of Bel-Air*, and said, "Yoooo, I didn't know you lived like this. Over here living like Hilary Banks and shit."

I think I'm at least an *Ashley*.

4

He looks at me, amused, his arms resting on his knees. "I guess you're smarter than Hilary. But I bet you're just as spoiled as her. All you gotta do to get your way is cry 'Daddy.'"

"Excuse me?" I say, taken aback. "I am not spoiled."

"And you sound just like her, too!" He laughs, throwing his head back.

"I do not!" I lower my voice. "I don't sound anything like her."

He shakes his head, playfully tsk-tsking. "It's nothing to be ashamed of, Hilary."

I roll my eyes like I'm annoyed, but honestly, I'm buzzing off his attention. I'm not used to Carter doing much more than glancing at me and immediately looking away.

"Who's Hilary?" Auden asks, reminding us that we're not alone.

"That's way before your time, buddy." Carter stands up, pulling his white tee down over the band of his black basketball shorts. He steps toward me, his body blocking my sun. "I need to use your restroom real quick. Show me where it is?"

I could easily give him directions (through the foyer and living room, it'll be the first door on the right), but he's offering me an opportunity to be alone with him. How could I refuse?

My pulse blares in my ears as he follows me to the back door.

"Excuse me. Where are you going?" my mom asks from her chair on the patio. She's been scrolling through her phone, "chaperoning," as if we're not all seniors in high school, two months away from graduating.

"Just showing Carter to the bathroom."

She turns back to her phone. "Okay. Come right back, Quinn."

I stop myself from sighing. I mean, I get it. She's not used to me having a boy in the house who isn't our neighbor, Matt. Especially not a tall, dark, and handsome Black boy.

When the door shuts behind him, I'm acutely aware of how big and empty the kitchen is. How we're completely alone. How, as I lead him into the living room, I have no idea where his eyes are. I run my hair from the back of my neck over my shoulder.

"Nice house you got here, Hilary."

I turn around and walk backward past the spotless white couch and the wooden end tables. "Why are you still calling me that? Didn't we establish that I'm smarter than her?" I'm smirking, playing his little game.

But then he says, "Are you, though?"

My back hits the doorframe of the half bath. "Is that a joke?"

"I mean"—he shrugs, making his way toward me, gazing at the living room furniture—"getting into Columbia doesn't mean you're smart. It just means you're rich."

My stomach twists at the mention of Columbia. His tone isn't playful anymore, and neither is his expression. My smirk wanes as he joins me in the doorway, so close I can smell his clean scent.

He says, "Which, obviously, you're very rich," motioning to the multi-thousand-dollar vase on the mantel and the sixty-inch landscape electric fireplace. He sounds bitter about it. Then he eyes me from my flip-flops to the top of my poofy hair. "Girls like you ain't gotta work nearly as hard as somebody like me."

My jaw tightens. He has no idea what I've had to work for. And even if I am rich, I'm still one of only five Black kids at our school. I have to deal with the same racist bullshit he does.

"You don't know anything about me."

He hums in thought, holding up his index finger. "I know you got into Columbia."

Another pang in my stomach.

He narrows his eyes and lowers his voice. "But I also know you're struggling in all your classes."

My brows shoot up. "How do you know that?" I ask before I even consider hiding the fact that he's right.

"It's obvious." He smiles. "And I'm observant."

It's obvious that I'm struggling? It's not like I advertise my less-than-spectacular grades, so what the hell does he know about my struggle? And, anyway, who is he to talk? He never says a word in class, much less picks up a pen to take notes. I doubt his grades are much better than mine.

He nods while taking inventory of all our furniture. "I bet your dad donated a library or something." His condescending eyes land on me. "That's the only way I figure *you* could've gotten into Columbia."

He says *you* like he knows exactly how unimpressive I am. His presumption crawls under my skin and nests there.

"You know what? The toilet's right there." I nudge my head to the left. "Help yourself." Then I shoulder past him.

Who does he think he is? I've said all of two words to this guy, and he thinks he knows everything about me. Did I say he was attractive? My mistake. He looks like the dirt beneath my shoes. That's about as much as he interests me now.

I slam the patio door, rattling the back windows. My mom's head snaps up. Her eyes ask me if I've lost my damn mind.

"Sorry," I say preemptively.

Auden's got his head down, studying the soundtrack list, when I walk up. I grab my list journal and flip to the new list about Carter.

"Everything okay?" Auden asks.

"Perfect."

CARTER IS . . .
10. A judgmental asshole.
11. A know-it-all, holier-than-thou, pretentious bas-
    tard.
12. Not as great as he looks. I wish I never got a peek
    into his ugly thoughts.

I'm thinking of more insults when he waltzes through the back door with a smug smile. I don't acknowledge him as he sits in the grass.

"Your dad's home," he says, smiling, but then his smile falters, like he's having a hard time holding it up. "When he saw me, he thought I was a burglar." Carter drops his eyes, pressing his lips tight. "Guess he's not used to seeing a real nigga in his house."

My stomach squeezes, a cold sweat washing over me. Auden looks up.

"So, I'm gonna go." Carter nods, angry and disappointed and hurt. He looks like he's way past saying *I told you so. I told you I know exactly who you are.* But he's mistaken. This has to be a mistake.

I drop my journal in the grass and rush back to the patio. Mom notices the hurricane winds beneath my arms. "Quinn, what's wrong?"

I catch my dad in the kitchen, as he's taking the first step up the stairs, work shoes in hand. "What did you say to Carter?"

He looks at me over his shoulder, eyebrows raised. "Who is Carter?" He's playing dumb, and I don't have time for it.

I point behind me. "The boy who just walked through that door. He's under the impression you thought he was a burglar."

"Desmond, really?" Mom hisses, closing the back door behind her.

"I did *not* think he was a burglar." He scrunches his face. "My entire house was empty except for a stranger coming out of my bathroom. All I did was ask what business he had in my house."

I roll my eyes, shaking my head. I can just imagine it now: Carter comes out of the bathroom as my dad walks through the foyer, having already taken his shoes off at the door. When they see each other, my dad's voice booms, *What are you doing in my house?*, the accusation clear in his eyes. But he won't admit it, and he won't apologize for it. He never apologizes for anything.

"You asked him why he was in our house? Obviously, he's my classmate," I say.

"I've met a lot of your classmates, but I've never seen that boy before."

"I can't believe you, Desmond," Mom says.

His eyes snap to hers. "Wendy, you're one to talk."

"Excuse me? I would never assume he's a criminal. Based on what? The way he looks? I'm from Chicago—"

My dad throws his arms up, letting his shoes drop to the floor. "Here we go. You're from Chicago. We know, Wendy! How about you not bring it up every chance you get?"

Great. They've found an excuse to fight.

But the kitchen falls silent when the patio door opens. Carter and Auden walk inside with their backpacks on their backs, entirely aware of what they're interrupting. I'm standing between my parents, mortified.

Mom says with her charming hostess smile, "You're leaving already?"

"Yes, ma'am," Auden says. "Thanks for having us."

"Would you like anything for the road? Carter?" She asks

him specifically, trying to smooth over the debacle with my father.

"No, ma'am," he says, glancing over his shoulder. Then he walks past me, disgusted.

"See you at school, Quinn," Auden calls. Carter says nothing.

Then the front door closes, and there's nothing I can do to change his mind about me or my rich, entitled family.

Mom zeroes in on Dad. "You insulted that boy. You ought to apologize."

"I'm not apologizing. If he thinks I assumed he was a criminal, then I think that says more about him than it does about me."

Mom laughs, walking past me to the bar. "You *never* take responsibility for how you make people feel."

"I'm not responsible for other people's screwed-up perceptions. All I did was ask him what he was doing in my house. I did nothing wrong!"

"You never do anything wrong, Desmond!"

This fight isn't about Carter anymore.

Having heard enough, I go outside and try to extract the disgust in Carter's eyes out of my head. What must he think of us? I don't even know what I think of us. I don't know exactly what happened, but it's shameful that he had to experience that in a Black home. *My* home.

Even from the patio, I can hear them screaming. It's never enough to just go outside, so I leave. I go to Matt's house next door and climb onto his trampoline, doing all I can to keep my dress down in the process. I text him: **I'm on base. Where are you?**

After a few seconds he texts back: **Omw.**

I stretch my legs in front of me and wait, flexing my calves and scrutinizing the polish on my toenails. Every second adds weight to the thump of my heartbeat.

Then his back door opens. He steps outside wearing a red-and-black Hayworth Private School shirt and bright-yellow board shorts, no shoes. Then he takes off in a sprint, his perfect brown hair flopping in the wind. When he reaches the edge of the trampoline, he springs up and over the side, bouncing me up, forcing me to hold my dress down around my legs. I laugh against my will.

He sits at my toes, spread-eagling his legs. "Quinnly." He smiles, and my spirit soars at the sight of him.

"Mattly," I say, my smile not nearly as bright.

He picks up on it, his lips falling. "What's wrong?" Then he grabs my feet and pulls himself closer. He leans down, crossing his arms over my shins.

We like to play this seesaw game, where I push back on his chest with my toes, and he pushes down on my feet with his chest. He says it's a good way to exercise my calves, while at the same time, he gets to stretch his thighs. He's a soccer player, after all, and his body shows it.

I have no need to condition my calves—I *hate* soccer—but this game we play always makes me feel lighter. "My parents are at it again," I say, losing myself in the softness and the warmth of his shirt, the rigidity of his chest beneath.

"What's it about this time?"

"The usual." I really don't want to get into the Carter thing. "Dad can never admit when he's wrong, but clearly my mom yelling at him doesn't work."

"It's better that they yell, though." He looks up, his blue eyes catching a ray of sunlight. His parents don't fight—or, rather, they fight silently. It's just as intense, if not more, than my parents' shouting. "It's when they stop fighting that you should worry." He's smiling a sad kind of smile.

"Worry about what?"

"Divorce."

I push my toes into his chest, digging my heels into the trampoline. "Are your parents—"

He shakes his head, tousling his hair onto his forehead, then runs his fingers through it, combing it back in place. "Not until after I move out."

"How do you know that?"

"I heard them talking about it when they thought I wasn't around."

I release my calf muscles, letting the weight of his chest push against the balls of my feet. "I'm sorry, Matt."

He shrugs. "I guess it sucks, but I won't be around to see it happen."

"What about when you come home for Thanksgiving and Christmas break?"

His brow furrows. "I didn't think about that." Then he meets my eye, frowning. "Thanks, Quinnly."

I laugh. "I'm sorry!"

"Way to ruin my perspective." He laughs too.

I rest my hands behind me, angling my face to the sky. "They'll feel so guilty about it, you'll get twice the amount of Christmas presents and double the Thanksgiving dinner."

"That's not how my house works. Christmas gifts stopped being a thing after about fourteen."

"Really?" I ask absentmindedly. The sky is so blue and empty. I take a deep breath, the air just as hot coming into my nostrils as it is going out.

"We ain't got that Columbia money," he teases.

I stiffen, pulling my eyes from the sky.

"Better yet, we ain't got that brand-new-Mercedes-as-a-congratulatory-gift kind of money."

I cringe, breaking under the guilt. "God, I wish they hadn't done that."

"You don't love the 'Cedes?" I roll my eyes, giving his chest a forceful push with my toes. He laughs, leaning in farther. "What's wrong with it?"

"I just . . ." I sigh and lie all the way back. My mom will kill me if she finds out I laid my head on this dirty trampoline. "I feel like I don't deserve it."

"Quinn, you got into Columbia, for Christ's sake. Of course you deserve it."

I close my eyes and squeeze them shut. "No, I don't." I whisper it to the wind, afraid to admit exactly why I don't deserve it. If only he knew. If only my *parents* knew. They'd trade in that Mercedes so fast.

"And, by the way, I still haven't gotten a chance to ride in it."

"No one has."

"Lies. When your parents surprised you, Destany was the first person to ride in it."

My whole body turns to stone at the mention of her name. *Please don't ask.*

"Speaking of . . ."

Oh God, here we go.

"What's going on between you two? What happened at Chase's party last weekend?"

I don't speak. My eyes are wide open, filled to their capacity with the big blue Texas sky.

"Quinn," he says, patting the tops of my shins.

"I don't want to talk about that, Matt." I don't even want to think about it.

"I've heard some crazy shit." He hisses the swear word. Matt doesn't curse unless he means business.

"What have you heard?" I ask, like I don't already know.

"That you two are fighting over *me*."

My eyes flutter closed.

Matt releases my shins and removes his chest from my feet. They feel cold now, and my ankles feel weightless. He crawls around me and sits cross-legged beside my cheek. "Is it true?" he asks.

I roll my neck over and look up into his concerned eyes.

"We're not fighting over you. We're not even fighting, at this point. Our divorce is finalized."

He meets my gaze, somber. "If you had a problem with me asking her out, you would have told me, right?"

"Matt, you and I are friends. You can date whoever you want."

I close my eyes again. Can we just go back to playing seesaw and talking about anything else? Because as much as I may have "had a problem" with Matt asking Destany out, I'm not petty enough to let that ruin a ten-year friendship.

He lifts his legs, gathers a chunk of my hair and plays with it in his lap. I get nervous about the amount of moisturizer I slathered in it this morning and whether he feels it. I pull my hair out of his hands and run it over my other shoulder.

It doesn't go unnoticed. He lets his hands drop, dejected. "Well, I can't exactly ask her out *now*. Not if I want to keep you as a friend."

I roll over on my side, facing him with my elbow propped up on the trampoline. "That's true."

"That's why I deserve to know." His blue eyes sweep over my face, down to my hand resting in front of my abdomen. He grabs my fingers within his.

Then the back door creaks open. His mom's head pops out. "Matt?"

I pull my hand out of his.

"Oh, Quinn." Her eyes take us in. She smiles. "Hi, sweetie."

"Hi, Mrs. Radd." I sit up, straightening my dress.

"Dinner's ready." She rests her head against the door. "You're welcome to join us."

"Thank you, but I should get going. I'm sure my mom's cooking something."

That's a total lie. My mom hasn't cooked for me in ages. But I definitely don't want to stay for dinner, not with Matt asking all these questions about my feelings for him and about Destany—none of which I'm ready to discuss.

"Tell Wendy I said hi."

I nod, smiling. Then I glance at Matt. He says, "I'll be right in, Mom."

"All right." She lifts her head off the doorframe. "Good seeing you, Quinn."

"You too."

Matt turns to me with tired eyes. "You really could stay. I know your mom isn't cooking."

I smile. "I should go check on the house to make sure it's still intact."

"Could you at least tell me why it's a secret?"

"It's for your own good that you don't know." And with that I stand up and walk to the edge of the trampoline.

"That just makes me wanna know more."

I look at him over my shoulder. "I'm wearing a dress. Do you mind turning away?"

He glances down at my bare legs, then sighs and closes his eyes.

I hurry over the edge, phone in hand, doing my best to keep my skirt down in case his mom is watching through the window. When I've got my flip-flops back on, I say, "Bye, Mattly. Thanks for meeting me."

"See ya at school."

There are so many reasons I can't tell him what happened between me and Destany. All of which are filling my head as I make my way back to my house, making it hard to think— making it hard to *not* think.

Like, for one, telling him will make me relive last weekend.

Two, telling him will make him realize who she really is, and that will ruin her for him.

Three, if what I tell him *doesn't* ruin her for him, then that will ruin him for me.

Four, he might not think it's as big a deal as I'm making it.

Five, if he ends up hurting me, too, then I'll seriously be alone.

I need to write these down, so I can stop obsessing, and so I'll stop feeling this incessant need to turn around and tell him everything, because maybe he *will* understand.

Six, he could never fully understand why I feel the way I do, because he's white.

When I get back to my backyard, I search for my journal in the grass. It's sitting off to the side of my backpack. When I pick it up, my eyes inspect the stray black ink all over my red cover, and for a few seconds I stare down at it, confused.

Where did all this ink come from? I flip to the back cover where I expect to find my name written on the cardboard, only to find random grease splotches.

This is not my journal.

My stomach plummets into my intestines. Impossible. Of course this is my journal. It *has* to be my journal. I mean, I had it two seconds ago. Didn't I? I was writing that list about Carter, then I laid it in the grass before I stomped in the house, and here it is. Somehow the front cover must have gotten inked up. My lists are safe inside. They have to be.

But when I open the spiral, I find Carter's illegible notes . . . and not my lists.

chapter 2

THINGS THAT I WOULD
NEVER ADMIT OUT LOUD

I RIP OPEN MY BACKPACK: HISTORY NOTEBOOK, BIOLOGY, calculus, everything except my list journal. My eyes cloud over.

This isn't about someone reading my to-do lists, or my how-to on changing a tire, or my list of days I've ugly cried. This is about the list of boys I've kissed, the list of reasons I'm in love with Matt, and this:

THINGS THAT I WOULD NEVER ADMIT OUT LOUD

1. My dad told me when Grandma Hattie dies, she's leaving me a sizable inheritance. I actually allowed myself to wonder how much longer it'd be before she dies.
2. I didn't get a 34 on my ACT. I got a 24.
3. My acceptance letter to Columbia was fake. I created it in Microsoft Word.
4. I never wanted to go to Columbia. That was my

parents' dream, not mine.

5. I'm in love with Matthew Radd.

6. I was there when Olivia Thomas's photographs got vandalized. I drove the getaway car.

7. I used to embrace being called an Oreo (white on the inside, Black on the outside), until I realized the implications—I realized far too late.

These are the things I don't voice even when I'm alone, because admitting them could change my life forever. And then it dawns on me—Carter could change my life forever.

I open my phone and text him: **Hey, I have your journal. I think you might have mine? It looks like yours, and it's extremely personal, so please don't flip through it. Just look for my name on the back cover.**

Hopefully, he doesn't read it. Please don't let him read it.

Then I text Auden. He replies: **I don't have it, sorry.**

I go back to Carter's thread, and nothing. When I finally go inside, Mom's sitting at the bar with a glass of wine. I guess Dad left again, back to the hospital, or to Gold's Gym, or wherever he's always disappearing to. She asks me, "Where'd you go? To Matt's?"

"Yeah. Mrs. Radd said hello." I head upstairs, staring at the unread message, like I can will Carter to see it.

His name comes up several times in my journal. First, in my *fuck/marry/kill* trials, where I typically choose to fuck him, on the hot side of my *Hot or Not* list, on my *Boys with Whom I Wouldn't Mind Repopulating the Earth after the Apocalypse* list, which, I admit, is basically a replica of the hot side of my *Hot or Not* list. Then there's the list from this afternoon, with his name as the title. I can't imagine what Carter would do with that information. Actually, I can imagine so many different scenarios, especially after his run-in with my dad today, but I try to think positively.

If Carter has my spiral, he'll notice the difference in the condition of our red covers. He'll be like, *Wow, this is way too intact to be mine.* He'll search for his own journal, realize the mistake, and finally read my message.

That's the best-case scenario.

My mind keeps taking apart the worst-case scenario: Carter won't notice a damn thing about the condition of my red cover. He'll open to the last section, the most personal section of my journal, because the last section of *his* journal is history, and the first list that will pop out at him will be:

IF I COULD KISS ANYONE
1. Matthew Radd ♡
2. Michael B. Jordan
3. Bryson Tiller
4. Zayn Malik
5. Diggy Simmons
6. Quincy Brown
7. Ryan Reynolds
8. Noah Centineo
9. Carter Bennett

Which isn't all that embarrassing, but it *is* interesting, especially with his freaking name tacked on at the end. From there, he'll curiously flip the page and end up reading the entire thing.

My body slips to the carpet like a silk gown after a long night at the ball, waiting, but I get nothing from Carter. I take a long shower, come back, and nothing. I open *Crime and Punishment*, pretend to read for English for a half hour, and still nothing.

If only I knew where he lived.

Maybe a movie will help distract me. If I had my journal, I'd check my list of movies with intense rewatchability and rewatch one of those. But let's be honest, I know it by heart.

MOVIES WITH INTENSE REWATCHABILITY

1. Love and Basketball
2. ATL
3. This Christmas
4. Identity Thief
5. Deadpool
6. Friday
7. Girls Trip
8. Black Panther
9. Love, Simon
10. Little

Destany helped me build this list. She was the only person who could rewatch movies as many times as me. Mom and

Dad have a strict one-watch rule, and I'd be lucky to get Hattie to sit through the first, but Destany? She understood that some movies are good enough to become a favorite but are way too heavy to watch over and over.

I flop onto my bed and turn on *Love and Basketball*. I get under my covers and attempt to sink my mind into the story, but there's this gnawing in my brain, this constant vibration beneath my skin, drawing my eyes to my phone every other second. Where is he? What could he possibly be doing that would prevent him from looking at his phone for *two hours*?

My mom opens my door. She checks my TV screen and sighs, seeing that I'm watching this movie yet again. "Food is here."

I stop it in the middle of the breakup scene, then follow her downstairs. I only take two bites of my sub sandwich. That's all I can stomach. On my way back to my room, Mom asks, "That's all you're gonna eat?"

"I don't have an appetite." I keep going up the stairs.

"Is everything okay?"

I pause and look over my shoulder, left hand on the banister, right hand clutching my phone. She looks worried. She looks like me, but her hair is much tamer, and her body too. Same round eyes, though, and same plump lips.

"I'm okay," I say, then I turn and head back upstairs.

"Wait, Quinn. Your father called from work. He wants you to call him on his cell."

I pause, agitated. "I don't exactly want to talk to him right now."

"I know, but it's important."

"Mom, I'm not in the mood to get yelled at about finding an apartment right now."

"It's about Hattie."

The Earth halts spinning on its axis. My back starts to ache from standing so still. "What about her?"

"She's okay," Mom says quickly, putting out the fire before it can spread.

"Then what about her?"

"Just call him."

I hurry up the stairs, calling my father, but I get his voice mail. So I call again, closing my bedroom door. And again, landing face-first on my bed. When, finally, he answers. "Quinn, are you okay?"

"Mom told me to call you about Hattie. What happened? Is she okay?"

"Quinn." He breathes my name as if he can breathe air back into my lungs. He can't. "She had a minor accident, but she's okay. I checked her out myself to make sure."

"What happened?" My voice is turning into mush as I roll over onto my back. "What kind of accident?"

"She fell."

"What?" People her age shouldn't fall. Falling could turn her to dust—all of her, not just her brain. I imagine her writhing on a tiled floor, wrinkled up, bones frail and fractured. "Oh my God, Dad."

"She's okay. Nothing's broken. She's just a little sore."

I wonder if she was alone when it happened, or if she

cried. I've never seen Hattie cry. Did she rock on the cold floor until someone came to turn her right-side up? How long did it take for someone to find her? I wonder how much pain she can handle now, if her numbing brain numbs her body too. If maybe she's forgotten how to feel pain. I hope she has. I hope that was the first thing she forgot.

I try to push down the sob building in my chest. "You have to move her! Those people are incompetent!"

"Quinn, I promise you, she's in good hands. Listen to me." His voice jiggles like he's walking. "Come with me to see her this weekend. I haven't forced you because I know you have a hard time—"

"No."

"When you go to Columbia you won't get to see her. Don't make the same mistake I made with your granddad. You don't want to regret all this time you could have spent with Hattie before she—"

"Don't say that to me!"

He sighs. "We'll talk about this later. Just think about it."

Just think about it, as if I have a choice in the matter. Hattie lives like static in my mind, sometimes in the background, sometimes snowing me in completely.

I go outside and stand before Hattie's porch swing on the patio. I remember when I found it last summer, among our chaise lounge chairs, as if it were just another piece of furniture. But it still smells like her porch, like freshly chopped oak for the fireplace, and a little bit of pine to get the fire started.

According to Hattie, being outside is an activity in and of itself. She and I used to sit on her porch swing, watching the birds and trees and clouds, sometimes talking, sometimes not. We could do that for hours, sipping lemonade or tea or both.

I sit and swing in the dark, watching the half-moon slowly bury itself behind the trees, thinking of her. Worrying. If I had my journal, I'd make a list of all my worries.

I'm worried that she was alone when she fell.

I'm worried that it hurt.

I'm worried that she cried.

I'm worried that she didn't.

I'm worried that she's pissed at me for never coming to see her.

I'm worried that she's nothing at all like I remember her.

I'm worried that when I finally go see her, she won't recognize me.

I'm worried that she'll be gone before I get the courage to go see her.

All this worrying is stealing my breath, and it's slowly morphing into gut-crushing guilt and soul-sucking fear. If I don't write these down, my fear's going to do a lot more than just steal my breath. I need my journal *now*.

Then my phone chimes in my lap, like clockwork. It's after eleven p.m. I scramble to pick it up, and my eyes can barely focus on Carter's one-word reply: **Yeah.**

So he has it, but there's no indication that he read it. I respond, retyping ten times before sending: **I need that**

journal back. You haven't read it, right?

I watch his reply bubbles appear, and then disappear. I'm on the verge of imploding when he finally answers after another ten minutes: **We can switch back tomorrow. Meet me at my locker in the morning.**

He didn't answer my question. Why didn't he answer my question?

My skin prickles, going numb. Maybe he's like my mom—when I text her multiple questions at once, she only ever answers one. Maybe he simply *forgot* to answer that extremely important question. So I text back: **Okay. Where's your locker?**

chapter 3

TO DO BEFORE I GRADUATE

HIS LOCKER IS IN B HALL, NUMBER 177. I'M STANDING against it in my brown chunky-heel boots and my off-the-shoulder yellow dress. I've got my unruly hair in a topknot, makeup done, my dark brown skin shining with baby oil, perfume light and free. No, I didn't dress up because I knew I'd be meeting him, and no I'm not "posing" against his locker with my legs crossed. This is how I always look.

But if my appearance inspires him to be a little nicer to me, who am I to complain?

He didn't answer my question last night, and I couldn't sleep for pondering why. He couldn't have possibly read my journal, right? He wouldn't blatantly invade my privacy like that. But what if he did? He'd know everything I've lied about. He'd know how much of a monster I am. I bite my bottom lip, getting nervous, because then maybe he'll tell people.

Students push their way down the hall. I search the crowd, lockers opening and closing, but no sign of Carter. And he's usually easy to spot, taller than most, skin way darker, but all

I see are average-height, white faces.

Then, in my search, I accidentally make eye contact with Destany. I've been careful to not let our gazes meet all week.

She's strutting down the hall wearing a white lace blouse showing off the tan she got over spring break, tight jeans, and red pointed-toe heels. She's bumping hips with Gia Teller, who's wearing basically the same thing.

They're coming my way. I avert my eyes, looking down at the screen of my phone, but then they stop in front of me. Gia opens locker number 176, right next to Carter's. *You've got to be kidding me.* She says, "Look who's finally ready to talk."

I take a tiny step back.

Gia looks me up and down, then smiles. "You look really pretty." I know her well enough to know she doesn't mean it kindly.

Destany steps between me and Gia, her eyes big and round. "Quinn, I'm so glad you're here. I've been spinning out without you."

I take another step back. My heart clenches because I've been spinning out, too. I've been needing our after-school trips to Starbucks to fill up on unnecessary caffeine and purge our day. She would get her coffee, take a quick sip, then spread her arms wide and say, "Go, Quinn. Purge." I haven't been able to purge all week.

I would tell her about yesterday with Matt, how he held my hand on the trampoline. That's a major development on the Matt front. She'd be so excited for me.

I could just forgive her. We could have a sleepover this weekend, just me and her. No Gia. No drama. God, that sounds good. Being alone has truly sucked. At least when we were friends, I had someone to walk down the hallway with, to eat lunch with, to text in class. It's only been four days, and I'm already cracking.

Then she says, "I'm sorry about Matt and the party. He was flirting with me, and I should have never engaged. Not even a little bit—"

Gia cuts in, "It's not Dessie's fault that Matt likes her."

My blood bubbles. I despise hearing Gia use the nickname I gave Destany. I realize that I'm not ready to have this conversation, especially not with Gia around. I look around the girls, hoping Carter will come save me from this dreadful interaction.

Destany says, "Let's just forget about the whole thing. I know sometimes we get in our feelings and make rash decisions. We can go back to normal. Pretend it never—"

I walk away.

"Quinn!"

Gia snickers. "I told you, Dessie. Real friends don't walk away because of a guy. Let her go." She must yell it at my back, because there's no way I should be able to hear her from this distance, what with the fact that I'm practically running. A few heads turn. They heard what she said too. And now they're judging me.

I get to psychology without my journal. I get to psychology and wish like hell that I had my journal. The night of

Chase's party comes pouring back to me. The ride home was the worst part. I had to sit alone in the back seat and attempt to not break down.

I was stunned. I was disgusted. I was hurt beyond reason. Destany and Gia were cackling in the front seat, and when I didn't join in, Destany turned. "Quinn, what's wrong?"

I couldn't speak. I knew that if I tried, I would burst, so I kept quiet, and I kept my eyes on my window.

Carter texts me after the bell rings. **Did you forget? I'll meet you after first.**

Mrs. Henderson closes the door and turns on her favorite guided breath meditation video. And for once, I'm thankful for the routine. "Bring your attention to your breath. Take a deep breath in . . . and out. If your mind wanders, that's perfectly fine. Acknowledge the thought, then come right back to your breath."

My mind runs rampant, but I do as the soft-spoken lady says, except I don't acknowledge the wild thoughts. I snap my attention back to my breath. No thinking. No worrying. Just breathing.

But as soon as the ten minutes are up, everything I've been holding down comes flooding back. I need that journal. I can't keep doing this. I don't care if Gia and Destany are stalking Carter's locker. I'm getting my journal back one way or another.

I sweat through all fifty minutes of class, then the bell finally rings. I get back to B hall, my feet crying out, feeling ridiculous in this dress and all this makeup. I spot Carter at his locker. Gia and Destany are nowhere to be found, thankfully. His backpack is open and swung around his chest. He's wearing simple black sweatpants, a bicep-hugging blue T-shirt, and those old tennis shoes. My mouth dries, and my steps slow. Seeing him does something to my body. It feels like I swallowed Icy Hot.

I think these are nerves. I have so many reasons to be nervous right now, but way too many lists are already sitting in my head.

When I approach, his eyes quickly take me in, then drop back to the inside of his backpack. I lean against Gia's locker with his nearly identical journal in my hand. "Hi."

"What up," he says casually, grabbing the journal from me and throwing it in his locker.

I falter, not sure how to start. "So . . . did you read it?" Might as well come out with it. He sure isn't making it easy.

Carter looks up, his eyes arresting me. He holds my gaze for a silent second, then finally, he shakes his head. "Nah." My breath audibly whooshes from between my lips. "Not past the first page."

I tense up again. Wait. The first page is a to-do list, but not just any to-do list, my *To Do Before I Graduate* list. It's practically a road map of all my lies.

TO DO BEFORE I GRADUATE
1. Visit the two universities I got accepted into.
2. Admit my love for Matthew Radd.
3. Experience Austin's supposedly incredible nightlife.

4. Tell my parents I didn't get into Columbia.
5. Visit Grandma Hattie.
6. Tell Destany the real reason I ghosted her.
7. Save for last. You know what you have to do.

Eyes wide, I ask, "But you did in fact read the first page? In its entirety?"

He's still shuffling through his backpack. "Yeah."

My mind is racing, standing in the middle of this awkward realization. Then he has the audacity to say, "You know we only got two months left before we graduate, right?" He smiles at me. "When are you planning to tell your parents you didn't get into Columbia?"

Before I can stop myself, I point my finger in his face. "That's none of your business."

"I'm just saying, you got seven items and only eight weeks left."

I hold my hand out. "I came for my journal, not your input."

He smirks, going back to his backpack. "My bad."

"And I'd appreciate it if you kept your mouth shut about it."

Maybe I should ask nicer? I'm technically still at his mercy, but I can't stop myself when he looks at me like that, like I'm a pathetic rich girl who couldn't get into an Ivy League even if her dad donated a library.

"No problem. I mean, you obviously don't need my help in making yourself look bad."

"What's that supposed to mean?"

He laughs, infuriating me further. "Nothing, Hilary. Nothing."

I clench my fists by my sides. "Can I have my journal back now?" I have absolutely no patience left. As soon as I get my journal, I'm adding his name to my *Mankind Would Be Better Off Without* list, right under ranch dressing and Nickelback.

He says, "Yep."

But he's still shuffling through his backpack. Why hasn't he found it yet? Then I look at his face and his brows are pinched. "Um," I say.

"Just a sec." He gives up on his backpack and looks in his locker. His hands are sifting frantically, and my heartbeat is speeding up exponentially.

He looks back and forward and back again. My eyes are starting to water. "Do you have it?" I ask, hoping he has a hidden shelf or deeper pockets than I thought. He stops and turns to me, his eyes distraught. My gut drops ten stories.

"I know I had it in first period," he says, slamming his locker shut.

"Who do you have first period?"

He doesn't answer me. He takes off, zipping his backpack along the way. I jog, unable to keep up with him. "Wait!"

He doesn't. But he's so tall that I can see his head above everyone else's. I see him cut into the hallway that connects B hall to C hall—BC, as they call it. Once I get in the alley, I see him duck into a classroom on the right, Mrs. Yates's bio lab.

By the time I hobble to the classroom, the desks are already filled by her second-period class. Carter's in the middle of the doorway. I can barely see around him. Mrs. Yates is standing at the front, writing on the dry-erase board. She says, "I haven't picked anything up. Class, did any of you see a journal when you walked in?"

Nobody's paying attention or cares enough to answer. "Which desk was yours?" I ask between huffs, still trying to catch my breath.

Again, he doesn't answer me. He goes to the third row toward the back, and stops beside Timothy O'Malley, who looks up at him with the fear of God in his eyes. Carter places a hand on the desktop, crowding Timmy's space.

My heart is pounding, drowning out the sound of the classroom. When Carter comes back empty-handed, I ask, "So? Where is it?"

"I swear I had it on the bus." His eyes beg me to believe him. "I thought I had it first period, but . . ." He shakes his head, like he's trying to shake out his uncertainty. "That must have been my bio notebook."

"So?" I ask, my voice a shaky mess. I'm careful to keep my facial muscles under control. I cannot let him see me ugly cry. He'd never let me live that down.

Carter lowers his chin to look me in the eye. "I think I left it on the bus."

chapter 4

PLACES I IMAGINE MY
JOURNAL MIGHT BE

THE TARDY BELL RINGS. I'M LATE.

"You *what*?"

"That's a good thing," he says.

"How is that a good thing?"

"Excuse me," Mrs. Yates says, hands on her hips. "You two need to get to class."

Carter rolls his eyes, grabs my shoulders, and guides me out of the classroom. Mrs. Yates closes the door behind us.

"How is it good that you lost my journal?"

"Not that I lost it, but that I lost it on the bus. You don't know anybody who rides the city bus," he assumes. "So whoever finds your journal, anything they read won't mean shit to them."

That's true. "But I still don't have it."

"Yeah, but . . ." He shrugs.

"That journal has every detail about me. I don't know who I am without it."

He looks at me like I'm insane. "You're you. Why do you need a manual for being you?"

"It's not a manual. It's a . . ." I try to think of a better word for my lists. "It's like my foundation. It doesn't tell me where I'm going. It tells me where I've been."

"Okay. So make a new one."

I look at him, baffled. "I can't just make a new one."

"What's going on here?" Principal Falcon says from behind us.

"Just getting to class, sir." Carter takes a step backward, his eyes on me. "I'll see you later." Then he turns and hurries to C hall.

My lips press tight. This whole thing has been a complete waste of time. My journal is gone, lost forever. I hadn't prepared myself for this possibility. I always thought that by the time I was crazy enough to get rid of it, I'd have coping methods in place.

I turn around, fighting a wave of tears. Principal Falcon looks at my face and his expression softens. "Everything okay, Miss Jackson?"

"Yes, sir." I hurry past him to calculus, where I collect my late slip and a subsequent eye roll from Mr. Foster, then sit down and neglect to take notes.

Carter thinks I can create another list journal. I mentally flip through all my lists: *To Do Before I Graduate*, *To Buy for My College Dorm/Apartment*, *To Toss Out When I Move Out*. Then my how-tos: *How to Read Body Language*, *How to Make New Friends*, *How to Forgive and Forget*. Haven't quite mastered any of those. My favorite books, favorite movies, favorite foods, favorite streets to speed through with the windows down. The best and worst and most memorable days of my life. And then there's my last section: miscellaneous. It's probably the most irreplaceable.

I wonder where my journal is right now. Maybe it's sitting abandoned in Carter's bus seat because no one's interested enough to touch it. Maybe at the end of the route, the bus driver will find it and throw it in the trash. Or maybe they'll take it to the lost and found.

But what if someone *is* interested enough to touch it? Maybe he's a smoking-hot college guy. He'll read the seven things I need to do before I graduate. He'll know that I'm in love with some guy named Matt. And he'll know I didn't get into Columbia, and that my parents don't know yet. He'll see that I've ghosted some girl named Destany. He'll see that I'm a disaster.

Then maybe he'll grow bored of my to-do lists and leave them for the next bus rider. Maybe a slew of strangers will read my lists. Maybe no one will.

PLACES I IMAGINE MY JOURNAL MIGHT BE
1. The bus seat where Carter sat.
2. The bus terminal lost and found box.
3. A passenger's home.
4. Maybe the passenger is the hot college guy, and after reading my journal, he's fallen in love with me. Now he's on his way to find me.

5. The coffee shop where the hot college guy is ordering a tall soy double-shot vanilla latte with caramel drizzle because he read my list of favorite coffee combos, from best to meh.
6. Carter's backpack, because he's the devil, and he wants to see my world burn.

My phone vibrates on my desk. Mr. Foster's pointing to unintelligible symbols on his Smart Board, his back turned to me. I open the DM under my desk. Then everything around me fades out of focus and into the four words on my screen: **I have your journal.**

I gasp and cover my mouth.

Mr. Foster turns to stare at me. So does the rest of the class. "Is there a problem, Miss Jackson?" he asks.

I shake my head, my lips clamped shut. He turns back to his scribbles on the board. I really should be taking notes. I'm already so lost in this class, but I can't look away from the hand-drawn smiley-face profile picture. Who is this? Someone who found my journal on the bus? Hot college guy of my dreams? Carter?

I type: **Can I get it back, please? Where can we meet?**

I nibble my bottom lip and wait, glancing at the bald spot on the back of Mr. Foster's head. Reply bubbles dance. **Not just yet. I have a condition first.**

What kind of condition? My hands fly across my keyboard: **Who is this, and what do you want?**

I place both elbows on my desk, waffling my fingers and balancing my chin.

When my phone vibrates again, I nearly drop it trying to grab it out of my lap. **I want you to do this list.** Then a picture of my own handwriting appears:

TO DO BEFORE I GRADUATE

1. Visit the two universities I got accepted into.
2. Admit my love for Matthew Radd.
3. Experience Austin's supposedly incredible nightlife.
4. Tell my parents I didn't get into Columbia.
5. Visit Grandma Hattie.
6. Tell Destany the real reason I ghosted her.
7. Save for last. You know what you have to do.

My mouth slowly drops open. *Carter.* The way he kept pushing me to complete this list. *You got seven items and only eight weeks left.* My breath speeds. I am going to kill him. No, I'm going to destroy everything he loves. **Give me back my journal, you stupid asshat. You think I don't know this is you, Carter?**

I watch the reply bubbles dance. **Complete this list, or your journal is going public.**

Do it. I dare you. I will destroy you.

I'm going straight to Principal Falcon's office when the bell rings. Carter's going to wish he never touched my journal. Doesn't he know my mother is a lawyer? If anything from my journal goes public, his future is over.

My phone vibrates in my lap. **You shouldn't tempt me like that.** Then it vibrates again, but not from a message. I've been tagged in a new picture.

chapter 5

FIVE LIES PEOPLE
BELIEVE ABOUT ME

FIVE LIES PEOPLE BELIEVE ABOUT ME

1. I'm cool with my white friends saying the N-word around me.
2. I ghosted Destany because Matthew Radd flirted with her.
3. I only got into Columbia because of affirmative action.
4. It was "easier" to drop Destany because I got into Columbia and she didn't.
5. That I got into Columbia in the first place.

I'm not the only person tagged in the photo. Everyone in the class, everyone in the *school*, was tagged. I hear their phones vibrate at the same time, and I watch as they read my list under their desks.

Then their heads come up, one by one. Kaide, Lucy, Macy,

and Trish look at me like I'm their breakfast. Yesterday I was one of them—an Ivy Leaguer. Now I'm just a lying failure.

When the bell rings, I know I should run to the principal's office, but I'm glued to my seat. They swarm me like a pack of hyenas.

"So, is it true?" Harvard-going Kaide asks. "Did you seriously not get into Columbia?"

My lips tremble. I didn't wake up prepared to admit this today. I've barely admitted it to myself. All these months of lying must have somehow made me believe that I got accepted. That, plus the years my parents have been preparing for my life in New York, as if I'd been accepted at birth.

Princeton Lucy shakes her head, while Dartmouth Macy and Trish snicker.

"What happened?" Kaide asks. "Affirmative action couldn't save you?"

I freeze. The two Dartmouth girls laugh, but Lucy's taken aback. "That's racist."

"How is it racist? It's just a question. Isn't that what affirmative action is for? To give a pass to people who aren't white, for not being white?"

I don't know what I feel right now. Embarrassed, sure, but more ashamed than anything. Ashamed that I don't open my mouth and tell him how much harder my parents had to work just to be *considered* alongside less qualified white people.

No. I let them walk away with those ideas in their heads,

like always. Speaking out against racism when you're the only Black kid in class sounds like a bad idea to me, especially given the circumstances: that they all got accepted into Ivy League schools while I'm the Black girl who lied about it.

My phone vibrates in my lap. I'm scared to see what else Carter has in store for me. **If you go to the principal about this, I'll send this list to your parents.**

You know what? No. Forget going to the principal. I'll handle this myself. My palm has been itching to slap the shit out of him since he "lost" my journal.

I hurry out of Mr. Foster's classroom into a sea of judgmental stares. Mannequin heads watch me race down the hallway, my eyes searching for Carter. When I get to C hall, I spot his head above everyone else's. My eyes narrow and, unfortunately, water again. I'm so mad. And when I get this mad, I cry. And if I let it get too far, I ugly cry. It's truly, truly unfortunate.

When I'm within reach, I snatch his arm and pull him around to face me. His mouth is wide open as I curl my fingers around the collar of his shirt, pulling his face down to my level.

"Yo, what the fuh—"

"Give me back my journal before I ruin your life." I grind the words through my teeth.

"What are you talking about?" He searches my eyes, his face only inches from mine.

"I know you're the one blackmailing me!"

People are staring at us, but I don't care.

Carter pries my fingers from his collar and straightens his spine, standing much taller than me. "Blackmailing you?"

I hate that he won't just admit it. He's already exposed my Columbia rejection to the whole school. Hasn't he done enough?

My hands press against my sternum. "What have I done to deserve this?"

He looks around the hallway, then lowers his chin and his voice. "Tell me what you're talking about."

I pull out my phone and shove the post in his face.

He looks at my list of lies like it's his first time seeing it. "Who posted this?" He grabs his phone from his pocket. "Wait, is that what everyone was looking at in class?"

"Like you don't know!"

He opens his own notification from the post.

"Hey, Miss Columbia," Darla Mason says with a smirk as she passes me and Carter.

My heart doubles in speed. Everyone knows about Columbia, and they undoubtedly will tell their parents. It won't be long before my own parents find out.

"Quinn," he says, regaining my attention, "you think I did this?"

"I know you did." I laugh. "Just give me back my journal and leave me the hell alone."

The tardy bell rings. I'm late again.

"Look, I need to get to class." He steps backward. "I didn't do this, okay? I swear, I didn't do this." Then he turns and leaves me alone in this disaster.

Like hell he didn't do this. If he didn't, then some anonymous barbarian has read everything about me, is holding my secrets over my head, and is forcing me to pull the trigger before they do. Some anonymous barbarian is a lot more intimidating than Carter, so I don't consider it an option. This is Carter. This has to be Carter. Please let this be Carter.

I share third period with Destany. I bet she and Gia are eating this up. She may have hurt me last weekend, but I've been lying for months about Columbia. I can't face her like this. So I run out of the school, to the back of the building.

The doors open to a grassy hill with an oak tree planted at the bottom of the incline. In the distance, the pasture is lined by a wooden fence surrounded entirely by trees and dense brush, and at the moment, it's filled with low, thick fog. I go to it and imagine myself climbing the fence, carving a path through the brush like the trails at Hattie's house, and riding the trails in her Gator with her sitting right beside me.

I look up at the gray sky. A small part of me wishes it'd rain, but most of me knows that would be hell for my hair. Back then, it didn't stop me, and it sure as hell didn't stop Hattie.

When I was fifteen, I was driving to the creek buried deep in the woods behind her house. The clouds were filling up, gray and black. I asked her, "What if it rains while we're out here? What if the Gator gets stuck and we get stranded with no food and no water and no cell phones?"

"If we get stuck, then I'll show you how to get unstuck."

But, at that point, her body hunched when she stood, and she had to use the handrail when she walked down the steps. I couldn't help but wonder how the hell she would show me how to get a Gator out of the mud when she could barely get down the porch by herself.

I whined as sprinkles dotted the windshield. "Hattie, we should go back."

"Come on here, li'l girl," she said, calling me little even after I'd grown taller and thicker than her. "You the one said you wanted to go swimming today, now, ain't you?"

"Yes, but I was just saying that. I didn't mean let's risk everything to go swimming."

She rubbed her thumb across my cheek as I turned down the trail that led to the swimming hole. "Chile, you too young to be so careful."

"And you're too old to be so careless," I muttered.

She pinched my arm. "I heard that." She laughed as I scowled, rubbing my arm where she pinched me. "If I can still move, what I'm gon' be still for?" That was always her rationalization when my parents and I tried to slow her down.

I think to myself, *If I can still move, what I'm gon' be still for?* Maybe because I'm too scared to move. Because if I move, people might see me. Because staying still is easier.

Hattie didn't do things the easy way. If someone stole her journal and blackmailed her with all her secrets, she would . . . Hell, Hattie didn't keep secrets. And if she had, she wouldn't let anyone hold them against her. She'd shout the truth down the halls, then she'd destroy Carter Bennett for all he is.

But I don't have that kind of courage. When the bell rings for fourth period, I don't move. I stay outside and allow the humidity to take my hair to hell. And I know I shouldn't, but I can't help it. I peek at the post on Instagram.

Gia commented first: **Soooo this bitch didn't even get into Columbia? That's hilarious.** The comment has thirty-five likes.

Harvard Kaide commented below that: **I should probably stop singing along to Drake and Vontae and DaBaby and literally every rapper ever when I'm around you? What makes you so special?**

Apparently, you have to run all your music choices by her, because she's black.

Not even affirmative action can make up for how much you suck.

Nothing from Destany.

The grass is wet, so I'm sitting on my backpack. I'm leaning back on my hands with my legs crossed in front of me, staring through the wooden fence. I could stay out here forever, skip my graduation, never go to college, never have to face my parents, Destany, or Hattie.

My phone vibrates during lunch period. I don't want to look at it, not while I'm in my safe space, but I can't stop myself. Carter asks, **Where u at?**

I put my phone down. I'm tired. Hopeless. I'm seriously considering jumping the fence and running away forever.

But I pick it back up and text: **Out back.**

A minute later, I hear the door shut behind me. The fog has dissipated, the afternoon heating up, burning my skin.

"Hey," he says, leaning his back against the fence, facing me. I don't look up at him.

"I ain't the one who posted your list."

I roll my neck up. "Is that right?" I smile. Then I grab my phone and open the thread between me and my blackmailer. "So this isn't you?"

He bends down and grabs my phone, then he's reading through the messages, his brow furrowing by the second.

"You were so persistent in encouraging me to complete that list." I laugh. "You're telling me this is all just a coincidence?"

"Yes! Hell, it's barely a coincidence."

"If it's not you, then who is it?" I ask.

"I don't know! I thought I left your journal on the bus, but I guess not. It's somebody in Mrs. Yates's first-period class."

I turn my eyes back to the forest because I'm still thinking about jumping the fence. This is all too much.

"You don't believe me, do you?" he asks.

"No. I think you have someone working for you."

"Quinn, why would I do this?"

"Because!" I spit. "You had so much to say about my acceptance into Columbia, and about how I'm rich, and how I don't have to work as hard as you. And now that you know the truth . . ."

His expression softens. "Look, I would never do something

this crazy. I don't care that much about you or your future."

That stings. It's supposed to comfort me, but it stings.

My phone vibrates in his hand. His face grows somber as he looks down at it. "Clearly," he says, handing it back to me, "there's no way I could have sent that text."

I take my phone, reading the new message: **If you don't do something on the to-do list by midnight tomorrow, another one of your lists is going public.**

Tears surface to my eyes, lips trembling. "Please call off your man," I beg him. "What did I do to you? Please, Carter."

"I'm trying to tell you, it ain't me." He digs his hands into his pockets. "Believe what you want to believe." Then he pushes off the fence. "Have fun being blackmailed."

He leaves, and with blurry eyes I look back down to the message. When I made that to-do list, I made it as an attempt to release some pressure. It was everything eating away at me. I had no intention of ever actually completing it, because I literally *can't*.

And now I'm being forced to.

It feels like a balloon is inflating inside me, taking all my air. It feels like no matter where I turn, everything is on fire in every direction, and I have no one to help me. It's too much. My hands fly up to my face, barely catching the stream of tears that spurts from my eyes.

Some girls cry and it's easy to feel sorry for them. Their eyelids flutter like cute little butterflies, and the tears sprinkle down. But not me. My ugly cry is especially ugly. My tears spurt out like a broken fire hydrant. My thick lips stretch thin and wide across my face, saliva trickling out of the sides. My skin wrinkles and puckers, my round eyes puffing up. It'd be a sin for anyone to see me like this.

I sit for a while, skipping a few more classes, letting the wind dry my face. I don't attempt to eat the lunch I packed. I don't think I can stomach food right now.

If Grandma Hattie were still at home, I'd jump in my car and drive the forty-five minutes to her house. I'd change out of this stupid outfit into my work pants and my work boots. I'd help her plant seeds in her garden and help her pick out the weeds. That always used to settle everything—my mind, my stomach, and my heart. What I wouldn't give to be able to do that right now.

When the bell rings signaling seventh period, I take one last look at the surrounding trees, then I stand up.

chapter 6

IF I COULD CHANGE ONE
THING ABOUT TODAY

I SHARE MR. GREEN'S HISTORY CLASS WITH DESTANY AND Matt and, of course, Carter. It's a recipe for disaster. I go to the restroom, take a makeup wipe, and clean my face of the runny colors. I look like myself. I look *pissed off*.

When I walk in the door, Auden's already seated, but Carter's chair is empty. Then my eyes crash into Destany's. She looks confused. She's wondering if this Columbia thing has anything to do with my current behavior. She's relieved that I'm not innocent in our situation.

Before I can sit down, Mr. Green stops me. "Are you okay, Quinn?" His face looks troubled.

I shift my eyes to the tiled floor, then back up. "Yeah, I'm fine." Wait, does he know about Columbia too?

"You look like you've been crying," he says quietly.

Oh, thank God. He's so close to my parents, he practically has them on speed dial. "It's just PMS," I assure him.

He narrows his eyes, unconvinced.

"I'm fine." I nod, taking my seat with a thousand eyes on my back, and attempt to get my sweating under control. Not even two seconds later, a body sits in the desk beside me, but I know immediately that it's not Carter.

I look up into Matt's blue eyes. "Quinnly," he says, "where have you been today?"

Has he been looking for me? "Hiding."

"Are you okay?"

Having him next to me, and the fact that he's still talking to me after the Columbia sitch makes me feel better. I nod, nibbling on my bottom lip.

He's studying me like he's trying to figure out why I lied, and what else I might have lied about. "When were you planning to tell me?" He frowns and pinches my cheek.

I smile. "Never."

But then a throat clears behind us. Carter stares at Matt's fingers on my cheek. He looks mildly pissed off, but not as pissed off as I feel.

"Oh, I'm sorry, Carter." Matt releases my face and hurries out of Carter's desk, but he holds my gaze. "Meet me on base tonight?"

"'Kay," I say, grateful. He's my only ally in this godforsaken school.

Carter sits beside me, but he doesn't look at me.

"The quiz will begin when the bell rings," Mr. Green says.

My heart stops. I never studied last night. I was too busy freaking out about whether Carter had my journal. I open my textbook and attempt to cram every word into my head, but I can feel the details slipping through my brain like sand. Then the bell rings.

"Hey, you good?" Carter's looking at me with his brows crinkled, as if he actually gives a shit.

"What do you care? I'm struggling in all my classes, right? What's another F?" But my grade in this class is the highest of all my grades, and it's not even that high. I do not need this right now.

Mr. Green passes out the quizzes, then sets his timer. Once I flip mine over, the dread sets in. I don't know any of this stuff. My three minutes fly past without pause, and when the buzzer goes off, I have three questions unanswered—automatic seventy, not to mention if I got any of the other seven wrong.

I've never scored less than perfect on one of these quizzes. It's amazing how Carter walked into my life and screwed everything up in less than twenty-four hours.

Once the tests are in hand, Mr. Green picks up our assignment from yesterday and passes out our assignment for today. "This is a list of JFK movies, including a short summary about each of them. At the end of class, I'll draw numbers, and each group will get to choose three DVDs to take home and watch over the weekend."

"Mr. Green, what if we break your DVDs?" someone in the back asks.

"You break it, you buy it."

"Mr. Green, what if we don't have anything that plays DVDs because it's such an ancient form of technology?"

The whole class laughs, including Mr. Green. "Mikey, I'm sure someone in your group has a DVD player."

Mikey groans. "I don't think that's a safe assumption."

"All right! No more questions. Get to work."

I immediately look at Auden and say, "I want to be Kennedy, but I think"—I point to Carter—"he should play Oswald."

Carter scoffs. "Really, Quinn?"

"What conspiracy should we use for our screenplay?" I ask Auden and Auden alone.

"I think it was the CIA."

"Really? I think it was Cuba."

Carter says, "I think it was Johnson."

"So it's between Cuba and the CIA," I say, ignoring him again.

Carter turns and glares at me. "It'll be easier to find evidence for the Johnson theory."

"That's probably true," Auden says.

I sit back in my chair, crossing my arms over my chest. "I disagree."

"Do you, Quinn? Or are you just mad about your journal?"

"I'm furious about my journal. *And* I think you're wrong."

"You're not about to destroy my GPA over some dumb shit."

"Me destroy your GPA?" I turn to him. "All I ever see you do is sit in class with your head down."

"You really want to go there, Miss Columbia?" He smirks at me, and I narrow my eyes. "Just stop. I'm not gonna deal with this all month."

"So get a group change," I say.

"I already tried. Mr. Green won't let us switch."

I close my mouth. He already requested it?

"Guys," Auden says. "Is everything all right?"

We ignore him.

"I'm the one who should get a group change. I'm the one having to work with the person ruining my life."

Carter exhales out of his nose. "For God's sake, Quinn, I was standing right there when the text came through. How could that possibly have been me?"

"You have someone working for you."

He shakes his head at me, then a smile cracks across his lips. "I'm flattered that you think I'm so calculating, but, like I said, I don't care about you or your problems."

"If you don't care, then why'd you feel the need to stick your nose in my business, saying I couldn't possibly get into Columbia without my dad donating a library?"

He laughs. "Clearly, I was right."

"But it was none of your business!"

"Guys," Auden hisses.

Neither of us looks away.

"So now you're publicizing my journal and blackmailing me into telling my parents about Columbia. You're a cruel man, Carter Bennett."

"Oh my God." He claps his hands in frustration. "What do I have to do for you to stop acting like this?"

I scoff. "Oh, I don't know. Give me my journal back?"

"How I'm gon' do that, if I ain't got it!"

"Hey!" Auden slaps his hand on the desk. We turn to look at him, aghast. "I don't know what's going on between you two, but ever since we started working together it's been nothing but drama." He props his fingers up on the movie list. "After class, you can chew each other's heads off, I don't care, but while we're here, can we *please focus*?" He hisses the last part, like a mom scolding her four-year-old in H-E-B.

Carter rubs his hand over his forehead and sighs. Then he looks at me with his eyebrows raised, silently asking if I'm ready to behave, as if *I'm* the problem here. And it pisses me off, because what am I supposed to do? Forget that my life is crumbling before my eyes?

Air filters in and out of my nostrils, never quite getting down to my lungs. I'm so angry and inconsolable, I can feel my tear ducts warming up again. Without my journal to write down all the reasons I'm upset, I feel like I'm going to explode.

"You lost my journal." The words spurt out, and I can't stop them. "Because of *you*, some lunatic has access to all my most personal lists. And you can't even apologize for it! Now everyone knows about Columbia. Now someone is blackmailing me into telling my parents. And maybe that someone isn't you, but if it's not you, then I have no idea where to start with trying to find out who it is. So I blame *you*," I spit. "I blame you because I don't know what else to do. My entire life is going to shit—"

"I'm sorry," Carter says.

I freeze, stunned. *Wait, what?*

"You're right, I did lose your journal. None of this would have happened if I had kept up with it." He drops his gaze and sighs. *"Jesus."* Then he glances at Auden before looking at me. "How about I help you find it? Then you'll know for sure that it's not me, and we can put this whole thing to bed."

I clamp my lips shut, surprised that I exposed myself like that. But even more surprised that he actually apologized. I clasp my hands on my desk, not wanting to admit how much I would like for him to help me, how relieved I would be.

He holds out his hand, catching me off guard. "Deal?" he asks.

I ponder, biting my bottom lip. I want his help, but what if he *is* my blackmailer? I suppose there's no reason I can't work with him while still suspecting him. Keep your enemies close, right? So I place my hand in his. "This doesn't mean I trust you."

He says, "You don't have to."

Then we both turn to face Auden.

"So . . ." He's looking between us tentatively, unsure of what he just witnessed. "If we're going with the Johnson theory, I think we should prioritize the 1991 *JFK* film."

IF I COULD CHANGE ONE THING ABOUT TODAY, FROM LEAST DESIRED TO MOST

1. That I wore this uselessly extravagant dress and these painful shoes.
2. That I skipped so many classes.
3. That I let Destany and Gia keep me from getting my journal before first period.
4. That I didn't bombard Carter the second he stepped on campus to retrieve my journal.
5. That I didn't think to meet him at his bus stop. Or to drive him to school this morning.
6. That I provoked the blackmailer into exposing my list.
7. That I got out of bed and came to school in the first place.

chapter 7

HOW TO SOLVE THE CASE OF
THE MISSING JOURNAL

I LEAD CARTER TO MY MERCEDES IN THE PARKING LOT. After tossing my bag in the back, I slide in next to him. His smell is already filling my car, teasing the wires in my brain that control attraction and rationality. I press-start the engine, blast the AC, hoping to blow his smell away from me, and let the windows all the way down as an added measure.

He marvels at my central touch screen. "Yo, this is . . ." He goes through my Apple Music app, but he doesn't play anything. "Must be nice to get a car like this at eighteen." He looks at me, completely serious. No sarcasm. No joking.

I turn away, rubbing the back of my neck. "It was a gift for getting into Columbia."

He's quiet for a moment, then he says, "That's rough."

"Yeah." I glance at him. "Seat belt, please."

He adjusts the levels of his seat so that he's not cramped against the dashboard and so his head isn't hitting the roof. It reminds me that the last person to ever sit there was Destany, when we went to the public library after school last week "to check out books." In actuality, she just wanted to flirt with the guy who works the front desk.

Carter finally buckles up. The parking lot is still bustling when I pull out of my space. Matt is climbing onto the running board of his diesel pickup truck as I'm driving past. He looks over the top of his door at Carter in the passenger seat of my car, and I nearly rear-end the car in front of me, watching him watch us.

When I slam on my brakes, Carter turns to me, eyes wide. "If you're planning to kill me—"

"I'm not."

"Maybe not even kill me, but just scare me a little."

"You're in my car for one reason, so let's get to it."

Matt pulls out behind me. I can hear the rumble of his truck. I can feel it. When I glance in my rearview, it feels like he's watching me, but I know he can't see through my tint. I pull out onto the highway, letting up the windows. Matt follows closely behind.

"A'ight, let's look at this profile," Carter says.

Matt isn't leaving much space between my car and his truck. He has no intention of allowing anyone to squeeze between us. I come to the first stoplight on this long highway, then I watch him in my rearview. He's got his visor down, so I can barely see his face.

"The picture is blacked out except for a smiley face. You ever seen this before?"

Matt puts up his visor a hair, like he's trying to get a better view into my car.

"Huh, Quinn?" Carter asks, turning to me.

I drop my eyes from the rearview. "What?"

"What are you—?" Carter turns to look out the back windshield, then he faces me with a frown. "I see your boyfriend's behind us."

"He's not my boyfriend."

"You should tell him how you feel," Carter teases. "I saw how he was all up on you in Mr. Green's class. He obviously likes you too."

I sigh, pressing the gas when the light turns green. "That's how Matt is. He flirts with me one day, and the next, he has a new girlfriend."

"That just means you're too available." He rests an elbow on my center console. "You need to hang out with other dudes. Let him see that you have options. Make him jealous."

I look at Carter sitting in my front seat, then I glance at Matt behind us and consider the fact that he's been tailing us since we left the parking lot.

"But not with me, though," Carter says. "I'm here for one thing. Remember?"

"I never *suggested* you."

"I saw it in your eyes, Jackson." He smiles. "I'm sorry, I'm just not into you like that."

"I'm not into you, either."

"You sure about that?"

"Yes. Not one bit," I say. Although there are plenty of lists

in my journal that would suggest otherwise. Then I realize—
my eyes widen—if Carter's my blackmailer, he's read those
lists, and he knows exactly how sexy I think he is.

So I test him. "Do you have any reason to believe I'm
lying?"

He smirks. Then he points to the green light ahead. "Just
maybe the fact that I caught you staring at me about ten times
yesterday."

My cheeks catch fire. I stomp on the gas, jerking us forward. "I wasn't—" Not ten times. Maybe three and a half.
Four at most. "There was something on your face."

He laughs, throwing his head back. "Something on my
face?"

"Yes. There was . . . something."

"Yeah. This sexy all over my face."

Cocky bastard. "Why are we even talking about this? The
only reason I let you in my car was to figure out who my
blackmailer is."

"I was trying to! I asked you a question, but you were too
busy stalking your bae."

"Okay, go ahead," I say as we pass the street to my neighborhood. I watch Matt's truck slow down and turn in. I
wonder if he's thinking about where Carter and I are going.
Maybe Carter's right. Maybe it's not a bad thing for Matt to
think I have options, even though Carter is definitely not
one of them.

"Huh, Quinn?" Carter asks, turning to me.

"What?"

"Seriously? You get onto *me* about focusing, but I can't get you to answer this one question."

"I'm sorry! I was distracted."

"No shit."

"This time I'm listening, I swear."

He sighs, then shoves his phone in my face. "Does this profile picture mean anything to you?" I glance at the road, then at the white smiley face.

"No."

He pulls his arm away. "Okay, so it's probably anonymous." He looks down at the screen. "The profile name is just a bunch of numbers. Do you think it could be a date?"

I had thought so earlier, when I exiled myself to the back of the school, but now that he's suggesting it, I'm thinking otherwise. "No. That's too obvious."

"Yeah," he says. "But there's a twenty-twenty one in here. Don't you think that's too big of a coincidence to ignore?"

"I think the fact that you were the last person to have my journal is too big of a coincidence to ignore, but here we are, ignoring it."

He turns and glares at me. "Do you want my help or not?"

I roll my eyes. "I'm just saying."

"Maybe you've got this figured out on your own, or maybe you're prepared to have your journal posted online. I don't know."

My lips press tight.

"All I know is, whether I'm your blackmailer or not, time's a-ticking, Quinn. Do you want my help or not?"

"Fine! Yes! You're right, I've got until midnight tomorrow. So how do we figure this out?"

He sits up in his seat. "We need suspects, we need motives . . ."

HOW TO SOLVE THE CASE OF THE MISSING JOURNAL (ACCORDING TO CARTER)

1.   List all possible places the journal could have been stolen.
2.   List all people present in each domain.
3.   Assign motives to each person.
4.   Investigate compelling suspects.
5.   Find journal.

He continues, "But I don't know if we have enough time to figure this out before midnight tomorrow. I need to get home right after we watch this movie at Auden's."

I ask him, "Why?" without thinking.

He looks at me like I've stepped all the way out of line. "Because I have things to do. Duties. Responsibilities. Those things you've never had to worry about in your cushy life."

"Hey!" I point my finger at him. "My life is not *cushy*."

He looks at me like he wants to argue. Instead he says, "Maybe you should think about doing something from the to-do list to buy us some time."

I feel the tension rise in my chest. "I can't do anything on that list. That's why the blackmailer is using it against me. Because they know I can't do it."

"Whoa, calm down. We'll do the easiest thing."

"What *easy* thing?"

"There's gotta be something. Let me see the list again."

I grab my phone from the middle console and hand it to him.

He goes to my Instagram DMs. "Okay, here we go. Tomorrow we'll go visit a college you got accepted to."

"We?" I glance at him, then back at the road. "You'll come with me?"

"Yeah," he says, like it's obvious.

"Oh. Okay, cool." I realize that being alone has been the hardest part of this item. No one knew I'd gotten rejected by Columbia, and I've never been brave enough to visit new places alone. Now I don't have to be alone. The idea of going is *easy.*

"Exit up here," Carter says. Then he asks, "What schools did you get into?"

"The University of Houston and Sam Houston State."

"Are those both in Houston?"

"Sam Houston's in Huntsville."

He looks at me, confused. "Where is that?" Before I can try to explain, he shakes his head. "Nah, let's just go to U of H." He points out of the windshield. "Turn left at this light."

"Kinda sucks that the only schools I got into are both infested by crime."

He looks at me. "What do you mean?"

"Houston is one of the most dangerous cities in America. And Huntsville, if you didn't know," I say glancing at him, "is a prison city."

"First of all," Carter says, clearly offended, "every city is dangerous in its own way. Second, U of H is in central Houston. Just don't go south and you'll be fine."

I roll my eyes. "That makes me feel better. And anyway, what even is U of H? Like, what programs are they known for?"

"I don't know, Quinn. Maybe you should research it since you have a good chance of actually going there."

I scoff.

"Why are you shitting on it before you've even visited the campus?"

"I'm not shitting on it."

"You are. I mean, I know it's not up to Columbia's standards, but . . . neither are you."

Ouch. I mean, it's true, but damn. "That was cruel," I say.

"Sorry, but you had it coming. Give Houston a chance. Who knows? You might like it even more than Columbia."

I twist my mouth. Maybe he's right. I always felt intimidated on Columbia's campus, what with the prestige and all the stock my parents put into it. Maybe I'll feel more at home on a campus like U of H.

chapter 8

IF CARTER HAS MY JOURNAL,

HE KNOWS...

WE GET TO AUDEN'S HOUSE IN PFLUGERVILLE, RIGHT outside of Austin. Two Nissan Versas are parked in the drive-way, Auden's black one, and another that's white. I park along the curb, looking out Carter's window at the perfect yard, with bird feeders and rosebushes lining the house.

As we walk up the driveway, the front door opens, and Auden comes hustling down the steps. "Listen, guys, I need to warn you about my mom."

Carter immediately asks, "Does she not like Black people?"

Funny. That's where my mind went too.

Auden shakes his head. "No, she loves Black people." We both raise our eyebrows at him. "I mean, she doesn't *love*—she loves Black people the same amount that she loves other races."

I smile, trying not to laugh.

"So what's the problem?" Carter asks.

"She can be a little much. Just don't accept any food she offers."

My eyebrows furrow. "Why not? Is it poisoned?"

"No." Auden sighs. "It'll just encourage her. Just please—"

Then the front door bursts open. A lady wearing a mom bun, a gray T-shirt tucked into mom jeans, and clean white sneakers steps out and exclaims, "Hello! Are you Auden's friends from school? Quinn and Carter, right? Please come in! I'm making cookies!"

Auden turns. "Be right there, Mom." Then he looks at us over his shoulder, his eyes swimming in discomfort. "I'm so sorry."

She goes back inside, leaving Auden tense, and me and Carter just a little uneasy.

Inside smells like vanilla and patchouli and cookies. We pass a dark sitting room and the kitchen across from it, going down a dark hallway. Auden's mom follows behind, chirping nonstop. "Do any of you want anything to drink?"

Simultaneous "No, ma'am."

"What about you, Auden?"

"That's okay, Mom."

"What about cookies? They're still warm."

I look over my shoulder, tempted to accept one. Cookies sound amazing right now. But Auden gives me a look and says, "No thanks, Mom."

The hallway opens into a foyer with white tile, white walls, and three closed doors. Each wall is occupied by shelves full of trinkets and photos. Auden and Carter continue to the right through a vinyl accordion door. But I get caught up looking at the pictures of young Auden, his curly brown hair out of control, wearing glasses since forever.

The photos start out with a family of three, but as Auden gets older, the photos are only of him and his mother. I stare at the largest photo on the wall, of his father in a military uniform, with a yellow ribbon tacked to the bottom of the frame. My heart splits open.

"You ready, Quinn?" Auden asks from behind me. When I meet his gaze, I can see how much he doesn't want me to ask about his father, so I don't.

I follow Auden down three stone steps into a cozy den. There's a wicker love seat covered in rose-petal cushions, and a matching chair. My breath catches. It looks just like the set in Hattie's living room. I can almost see Hattie's tiny body being swallowed up in that chair. Then Auden plops down, and I gasp.

He looks up, opening Mr. Green's DVD case. "Everything okay?"

Carter sits on the love seat, glancing back at me too.

"Yeah, I'm fine." I walk into the room, looking at the flower print rug on the floor. "This furniture set," I say, trying to sound nonchalant. "Is it new?"

"Not really." He's crouching in front of the modest plasma, turning on his DVD player. "My mom got it at a yard sale a few months ago."

My eyes flutter closed. My parents wouldn't sell Hattie's stuff, right? They'd never do that. One day she's going to get better. One day she'll come back home.

"Where was the yard sale?" I ask.

"Honestly, I just came home one day, and we had new furniture." He looks at me curiously. He can see my next move in my eyes. "Please don't ask her. She'll never stop. Please don't."

"I won't." I don't want to know the answer anyway.

I sit beside Carter on the two-seater, telling myself that it doesn't smell like Hattie. I'm sure Auden's mom purchased this furniture from an old dusty house where everything smelled like peppermint and tobacco, just like Hattie's. This is just a coincidence. This is not Hattie's furniture. It's not. Because if it is, I'll lose my shit, so it's not.

As the movie starts, we all get out our pens and paper. Mr. Green's requesting a page of notes from each of us—insurance that no single person is doing all the group work.

I stare at the television screen, watching the colors, but not seeing, and hearing the voices, but not listening. Instead, my mind plays a different scene: me getting out of my dad's car and walking up the steps to Hattie's house. Opening the door because it was never locked. Hattie sitting in that rose-petal armchair. "Hey, li'l girl." Glasses on her nose, she wouldn't smile. But her unchanged expression was welcoming, like the sight of me coming through her front door was nothing new. I was just coming home.

By the end of the movie, I only have half a page of notes.

Carter glances down at my paper. He looks like he wants to offer help but decides against it.

"Can I take that DVD home with me?" I ask Auden.

"Sure thing."

As I'm heading to the doorway, Carter announces, "Olivia's coming with us tomorrow."

"Olivia Thomas?" I ask, whipping around.

"Yes," he says, like it was obvious. Auden perks up.

"Why?" I ask, unable to control myself. But I already know they're friends, and it's not that I don't like Olivia. It's just that, ever since the vandalism incident, when I see her, my whole body becomes this silent apology that I will never be able to voice aloud.

"Because," Carter says, shifting his eyes. "She's from Houston. She can be our tour guide. And because I want her to."

"How am I supposed to get my parents to let me go tomorrow?"

He looks at me like I'm insane. "Don't tell them."

"Just skip?"

"Take a college day."

"So you two won't be in class tomorrow?" Auden asks.

I look at him thoughtfully. "We're visiting the University of Houston. You should totally come with us." I figure inviting more people might act as a buffer between me and Olivia. And I don't want him to feel like he's doing all the work for our group. So far, Carter and I have been nothing but unhelpful.

Auden looks surprised at my invitation. "Oh. Okay." He nods. "Maybe I will."

When we emerge from the foyer, Auden's mom meets us in the hallway, standing in the dark like a ghoul. Thankfully, Carter is ahead of me. She can take him first.

We end up taking baggies of cookies, a round of hugs, and consequently another look of pity from Auden before we trek down the driveway together.

"She was really nice," I say as we get in the car. "Auden shouldn't be so embarrassed of her."

"I don't think he has a lot of people over," Carter says.

I think about that, trying to place Auden in the social strata of our school. I have no idea who his friends are, or if he has any.

When we get downtown, we hit evening traffic on I-35. Carter's silent, while my head is whirling with conflicting emotions: contentment, anger, anxiety. We're sitting at a standstill for five minutes straight when he breaks the silence. "I got a question."

It catches me off guard. "Oh?" I raise my eyebrows.

"What's the last thing on your to-do list?"

I glance at him, then shake my head. "No."

"Still don't trust me."

"I have no reason to. It's a cold, hard fact that you were the last person with my journal."

"What's up with this journal, anyway?" Carter turns to me. I can feel his gaze on my cheek, but I can't turn to meet it. "It's a journal full of lists? What kind of lists?"

"Extremely private ones."

"Like what?" he presses. "I wanna help you, but I need to know why this journal's so important." I don't answer him. And just as I think he's about to press me again, he says, "Please, tell me."

It's not what I expect from him—to ask nicely, to be so curious in the first place.

"I have a list of my most horrifying memories."

"Tell me one."

"No," I say. "I have a list of everything I swore I'd never say out loud. I have a list of all the moments I've ever had with Matt—"

"Wait. You keep a log of all your moments with Matt?" He draws back. "Damn, you've really got it bad for him. That's stalker-level shit."

I toss him my side eye. "I'm not a stalker. Okay? I'm just organized."

He laughs. "Spoken like a true stalker!"

I can't believe I'm talking about this with him. I never thought I'd share my lists with anyone, much less Carter Bennett. But honestly, this feels good, like finally I have someone I can be completely real with. It's just surprising that that someone is him.

He's quiet for a second, facing his window. Then he turns back to me. "What other kinds of lists?"

"I have a list of all the days I've ugly cried."

He looks at me with his face scrunched up. "You keep a list of all the days you cry? That's depressing as shit."

"*Ugly* cry. There's a difference."

"Would you have written today's date?"

I scoff. "Yeah."

"Would you have started a list about me?"

If he had my journal, he'd know that I already have a list about him. "Probably," I say.

"About how much you hate me?"

"About how much I don't trust you."

He looks at the side of my face for a while, then turns back to his window, not asking any more questions.

IF CARTER HAS MY JOURNAL, HE KNOWS . . .

1. I think he's attractive.
2. There was a time when I wanted to kiss him.
3. I think he's more fuck material than marriage or murder.
4. I also think he's a pretentious bastard.
5. How intricately I write about fantasy sex with Matt.
6. How often I ugly cry (like once a week).
7. How involved I was in the smear campaign against Olivia Thomas a few months ago—and by involved, I mean that I waited in my car while her photos got vandalized.

Carter lives on the east side of Austin. Panhandlers stand at stoplights with cardboard signs and dirty faces, daring me to make eye contact, and when I do, they take it as an invitation to scratch on my window, begging for spare change.

He tells me to keep straight, that his complex is on the right, two lights ahead. Then his phone rings. I accidentally look at it, sitting in his lap. Olivia Thomas's beautiful face fills his screen.

"Hey," he answers. Then his voice gets softer and sweeter, a side of him I didn't think existed. "Hey, baby."

My hands tighten around the steering wheel as I fill up with something sour and bitter. I had no idea that they were dating. I thought Carter didn't date girls from Hayworth. I try to appear like I'm not listening to his conversation, but we're stuck at a red light, so there's not much to focus on.

"I'm almost home." He points to a complex with a gate code. "Three thousand, then pound," he says to me, then into the phone, "I'm pulling up now. See you in a sec." Then he hangs up.

I don't know why I feel disappointed. There's a good chance he's my blackmailer. And if he's not, he's the reason my journal is lost in the first place. Not to mention that up until this point he hasn't been very nice to me. I do not like him. Sure, he's fine as hell, but that's it. I've already established that his mind is ugly and so are his words.

I punch in the code and drive through the gate. He points out Olivia's building. When I pull around, I see her standing at the bottom of the stairs, waiting for him, but Carter doesn't get out. When I turn to him, he's studying me. He asks, "When are you gonna tell me what the last thing on the list is?"

"Never."

He nudges his chin up. "When are you gonna trust me?"

"When I get my journal back, and not a second sooner."

He nods, looking me over like he's trying to commit me to memory. "That's fair, I guess." Then he gets out and jogs to his girlfriend waiting on the steps for him. Olivia stands at his approach. They look good together, her tiny stature making Carter's look that much stronger. My body would only serve to drown his out.

Then Carter nudges his head toward my car. Olivia looks right at me and waves with a half smile. My heart races. I wonder what she thinks of me, or if she suspects that I had anything to do with the vandalism. I guess I'll find out tomorrow when we road-trip to Houston.

I wave back, then hurry and reverse out of my spot.

chapter 9

WHAT I KNOW ABOUT
MY MOTHER

WHAT I KNOW ABOUT MY MOTHER

1. She grew up in inner-city Chicago.
2. She doesn't talk about her childhood.
3. Her big brother was her best friend and her protector.
4. She had a teacher who helped her get out of the ghetto and into Columbia.
5. When she met Dad, she thought he was pretentious.
6. It bothers her when Dad and I don't finish all the food on our plates.
7. Her mom died from heart disease.
8. We didn't go to the funeral.
9. She doesn't know the whereabouts of her father.
10. Her brother was killed in a drive-by before I was born.

11. The rest of her family doesn't acknowledge her existence.
12. Dad and I are the only family she has left.

When I get to the kitchen, she's sitting at the bar, staring at her iPad with a glass full of red wine. "Excuse me. Where were you?"

"Oh, sorry, Mom. I was at Auden's. I—"

"You neglected to let me know where you were," she says. "I know you're moving to New York in a few months, but while you're still here, I need you to respect our rules. Now come eat. Your food's getting cold."

At the mention of food, my stomach growls. It's been twenty-four hours since I've had an actual meal. I want to eat *everything*.

I sit at the bar next to her, digging into my loaded baked potato from Jason's Deli, and she says, "Speaking of Columbia, I got an interesting call today."

I freeze, my heart icing over, my mouth stuffed with potato. Is it already happening? Why would the blackmailer jump the gun?

"You failed your history quiz."

I release my breath, spraying bits of potato on the counter. That shouldn't be a relief, but it is. "Mom—"

"Do you know Columbia can rescind your admission if your GPA falls between the time they accept you and the end of the year?"

"Yes."

"Do you? Because you just failed a major quiz." She looks at me with a stupefied expression.

"I'll do better. I've just had a crazy day."

"A crazy day?" she says, turning to me, rage in her eyes. "I almost want to take your car back after that phone call with Mr. Green."

Please do.

"He's letting you retake that quiz tomorrow morning, but you better understand that you won't get many chances like this, especially not with skin as dark as ours. You have to work twice as hard as everyone else."

"I know."

"Do you know how hard I *still* have to work for people to take me seriously as an attorney?"

I nod.

"Figure out what you want to do in life, Quinn. Pick a major. Pick an apartment. This undecided mess is just"—she waves her hand dismissively—"a luxury only rich white boys can afford. You are not that. You have to be better than that if you want to compete."

I am not that. And I am not better than that. There's no way I can compete. How can I possibly tell her that? How can I tell her that this quiz isn't the first I've failed since I've been at Hayworth? And worse, that I didn't make it into Columbia?

Once I've finished my food, she says, "Get to studying before your father gets home."

"He's coming home?" I ask, grabbing my backpack and

heading to the patio door. I haven't seen him since the Carter incident. I don't think I *want* to see him.

"He'll be here in a little bit. You need to go study in your room." Which means she'd rather I not be around when he gets here, because they are definitely fighting tonight.

"I study better out here."

"Quinn."

I hurry outside, peeking my head back in. "Just until he gets here."

I sit on Hattie's swing, study for my makeup quiz, and text Carter about booking the U of H tour tomorrow.

Night falls over the backyard. The neighborhood is quiet—nothing like Hattie's house. At Hattie's, the night would sound like a chorus of owls, crickets, the occasional coyote howl, and Hattie's voice singing me to sleep. *Don't you fear, I'm right here.* Hattie's voice singing in the garden. Hattie's voice singing in the passenger seat of the Gator, getting carried away by the wind. Hattie's voice echoing in my mind.

Dad used to take me to Hattie's when he and Mom would fight, but once I got there, I could only worry about what was happening at home. Whether, when I got back, they'd both still be there. I never said it in words, but Hattie knew. She'd see it in my eyes.

I'd follow her into the kitchen, sit at the table while she cooked a pot of white rice, and I'd tell her about my day, all the way up to the point of my parents fighting. When I'd get to that part, my eyes would swim back and forth, so as not to drip on her tabletop.

Hattie would fill the silence with her voice: *Don't you fear, I'm right here.* That's all I could ever count on, Hattie always being there. And now she's not. Now her home is empty. Now her mind is full of memories that don't include me. Now all I have left of her is this porch swing.

The patio door opens. I jump out of my memories. "Quinn?" Dad steps around the chaise lounge chairs and smiles down at me. His brown skin looks tired, especially below his eyes, and his beard looks grayer. He leans down and attempts to kiss my forehead, but I pull away from him, avoiding eye contact.

He pauses, stunned. "Is something wrong?" He says it in an accusatory way, like if something *is* wrong it must be of my doing.

I shake my head. "It's fine."

You made a Black boy feel unsafe in our home.

My skin is as black as his, so I can't be sure what you think of me. Am I a criminal too?

You haven't talked to me about it, and I really need you to, because I feel like I don't know who you are.

And I feel like I can't trust you.

And I feel like I'm going to explode if we keep skirting the issue.

He says, "You should probably go study upstairs."

I close my textbook, grab my phone and my backpack, all without looking at him. "Actually, I'm going to Matt's."

"It's a little late to just pop in."

I stalk past him with my backpack on my shoulder. "I was invited."

"How do your parents not know? How did you possibly keep a secret that huge?" Matt shakes his head, staring at the screen of his Nintendo Switch.

"I'm really good at it."

He's sitting in his beanbag chair across the room with wet hair, pajama pants, and no shirt. I'm lying on my back in his bed staring at the popcorn on his ceiling, so as not to stare at the wispy hair on his bare chest.

"Didn't they ask to see your acceptance letter?"

"Yeah. They framed it and everything."

"What?" He looks up, astounded. "Did you make it yourself?"

"In Word."

He scoffs. "Wow. So when are you gonna tell them the truth?"

"I hadn't planned on ever telling them."

He sets his Switch down in the beanbag chair and scoots to the edge. "How?" He has no other words.

"I'll just . . . I'll tell them I don't want to go to New York, then pivot."

He clasps his hands together and presses his pointer fingers against his lips. "That's the craziest thing I've ever heard. I know your parents—"

"I just haven't figured it out yet. But the last thing I need is for someone else to tell them before I find a way to do it myself."

He sighs, picking his Switch back up. And just as he says, "Well, I can make sure my parents don't find out," his mom walks through the open door with an armful of folded towels.

"Make sure your parents don't find out what?" she asks, looking between the two of us with one eyebrow cocked.

I sit up on my elbows, with my mouth and eyes wide open. Matt looks over the screen of his Switch with the exact same expression. We're both trying to think of a lie, and I don't know about Matt, but I can't think of anything except the truth.

"Somebody better tell me something," she says, setting the towels on his bed and putting her hands on her hips.

Matt shifts his eyes to me. "It's a secret, Mom."

She purses her lips. Then she throws her hands up and turns. "Whatever. It's not like I won't find out anyway." And she walks out confidently.

Matt and I look at each other, our faces full of silent horror. That was too, too close. He mouths to me, *This isn't safe*.

I mouth back, *Obviously*.

Then he nudges his head and stands up, Switch in hand. I climb out of his bed and follow him to the door, but we run into his mom standing with her ear against the wall. She looks just as caught as us.

"Mom, what are you doing?" Matt asks, astounded.

"I was just coming to bring you . . ."

Her hands are empty.

"Bring me what?" he asks.

She looks around the dark hallway. "To bring you good news: We're having steak for dinner tomorrow. You're welcome to join us, Quinn."

Matt shakes his head and walks past his mom. "She's a vegetarian." I follow, playfully shaking my head at her too.

"So no steak?" she calls after us.

We head down the stairs, past the deer mounts on the walls and the cowhides on the floor, through the kitchen to the back door. He doesn't bother putting on a shirt, and neither of us bothers putting on shoes. We run across the yard to the trampoline. He hops on without pause, like the athlete he is. I stop and climb on slowly and carefully. Then we get in position to play ankle seesaw, but I don't think we've ever played while he's been shirtless.

"Okay," he says, leaning his skin against my toes, resting his arms on my shins, still playing his Switch like he was never interrupted.

His chest is warm, the hair scratchy on the bottoms of my feet. I throw my hands back and look up at the empty night sky. "I feel like I don't know my dad anymore." It kind of comes out of nowhere for me *and* for Matt. I hadn't planned on saying that, but now that I have, I can feel a stream rushing up my esophagus.

"Why not?" he asks, glancing up fast, then back down to his game.

"I always thought that he was conscious . . . you know?"

"No, I don't know what you mean."

"Like, conscious of race issues and stuff."

Matt's face folds and stays folded. The mention of race makes him uncomfortable.

"I feel like maybe he doesn't love his skin color as much as I thought, and maybe—"

"Wait, why would you think that?" He looks up. "That's crazy. I've known your dad for a long time. I know he prides himself on being the first Black chief surgeon at his hospital. It's like the second thing he tells people, behind his name. Then after that is the fact that he went to Columbia." Matt laughs and goes back to playing his game. "I think you just miss him," he says. "I know he's gone a lot."

I twist my mouth, looking up at the night sky. "Yeah," I say. "Maybe."

He doesn't get it. None of that matters. My dad can be proud that he's the first Black chief surgeon, but that doesn't mean he's proud to be Black.

When I get back home, my parents are still fighting, but it's not like I can run back to Matt's, so I sit on the porch swing and wait it out.

She screams, "Do you know your daughter visits your closet when she misses you?"

I didn't know *she* knew that.

"This is what happens when I'm here. This isn't better for her."

"Your relationship with your daughter shouldn't be long-distance when you live in the same house."

"What about our relationship, Wendy? Why don't you care about us?"

"I'm the only one who cares about us. You're too busy to care."

"It's hard to remember why we keep doing this."

"Quinn is why we keep doing this."

So, when I leave for college, they won't have a reason to keep fighting.

SEVEN THINGS THAT ARE ALWAYS MOVING AROUND DAD'S CLOSET

1. The silver wristwatch his father gave him—the one with his name, Desmond Jackson, engraved on the underside.
2. The cap to his favorite cologne—the one my mother gave him for their anniversary three years ago.
3. His black tie.
4. His work sneakers.
5. His endless supply of scrubs.
6. Me.
7. Mom.

chapter 10

TEN RULES OLIVIA THOMAS
BREAKS DAILY

THE SECOND I WAKE UP I PEEK OUT MY WINDOW. DAD'S car is still parked beside Mom's. My stomach twists and knots.

I get dressed, and as I make my way downstairs, I hear pots and pans clacking. When I get to the kitchen, I find Dad reading a box of pancake mix. Mom's in her robe, clinging to his back. The sight gives me conflicting emotions.

"Morning."

They both whirl around as I grab an apple from the bowl and my lunch kit from the counter.

"Put that down, Quinn. I'm making breakfast," Dad says. Mom hops up on the tips of her toes and kisses his cheek. Dad grins, turning into her lips.

"I don't want to be late." For my makeup quiz.

Dad sighs, holding Mom against his side. "Aren't those shorts a little short?"

"Dad." I roll my eyes. He doesn't get to wake up one

morning, decide to see me off to school for the first time in months, and then try to tell me how to dress.

"I'm just saying. The dress code at that school is nonexistent."

"For a reason," I say, walking to the foyer. "They realize that what I'm wearing doesn't affect my education in the least."

"Quinn, come home right after school today," Mom says. "We're going to dinner."

I look back at them and the hearts in their eyes. "All of us?"

Dad nods, then turns back to his doting wife.

And the cycle begins again. Dad will come home right after work, as will Mom. They'll do what they do together. But tonight, or maybe tomorrow, depending on the strength of this love spell, their old fights will resurface.

Dad will leave and not come back. They'll ignore each other until the tension rises. The fighting will end in a huge blowup like last night. And somewhere amid the anger, they'll fall into each other again. It's like they can't love each other without anger as a precursor. It's confusing and frightening, because their relationship feels like a ticking time bomb, and I don't want to be the one to set it off.

In the driveway, I spot Matt walking to his truck. We see each other at the same time. He waves, and I wave back, opening the door of my Mercedes. As I'm starting my car, I hear his truck rumble to life. Then I get a text: **Everything go okay last night?**

Yeah, it was fine. Thanks for the talk.

Anytime, Quinnly. You know I'm always here for you

Then he backs out of his driveway and speeds out of our neighborhood. It's the winking emoji that does it for me. I gaze after him, sitting in a puddle of the same goo my parents must have stepped in.

Cars are scattered about the student parking lot. When I pull in, Matt's getting out of his truck. Before I can turn my car off, my passenger door opens. Carter slides in.

"Where the hell did you come from?" I screech.

"The bus stop." He points to the stop a few feet behind us. "You ready to skip school, Jackson?"

I watch Matt cross the parking lot, looking at my car over his shoulder. "I need to see Mr. Green before we go."

Carter follows my gaze. "Damn. I'm making the white boy jealous."

I turn to Carter and shrug with a sly smile.

"That ain't why I'm here, Jackson."

"Two birds with one stone," I say, opening my door.

"Hey," he says. With one foot out the door, I glance at him, really getting a good look. His expression looks contemplative. "I was thinking about what you said yesterday."

I instantly brace myself.

He blinks down to the console. "You said your journal is like your foundation, that it tells you who you are." He meets my gaze again, and I nod. "Would it be so bad to make a new foundation? To redefine yourself?"

I bring my foot back inside. "Are you saying that I need to redefine myself, because I'm a shitty person?"

He looks baffled, then he laughs. "No." A dazed smile is still on his lips when he scratches the side of his jaw. "I'm just saying it's a little hard to change when you have a journal telling you who to be." He drops his eyes, his right hand stroking the inside of his left wrist. But then he looks up again, like he's nervous about my reaction. He shrugs. "I was just thinking about it last night."

My skin sizzles. I feel like I'm glowing, like all the parts of me that I try so hard to hide are visible to him. I clear my throat and get out of the car, leaving the engine running. "I'll be back."

I walk to Mr. Green's room, my head in the clouds. He was thinking about me and my journal last night? I wonder how late last night. And I'm stunned that his thoughts weren't ugly. *It's a little hard to change when you have a journal telling you who to be.* Well, that's kind of the point. But, for the first time, I'm considering how toxic it might be, writing in stone who I am, and who I should be.

I'm still deep in thought when I enter Mr. Green's room. "Quinn, hey. You ready?"

I nod, taking a seat up front. "Thank you for the second chance."

"No problem." He turns my makeup quiz facedown. "I noticed how upset you looked yesterday. I figured you were distracted by something."

I nod, avoiding eye contact. I know he wants me to talk about it with him, but I can't. He's too close to my parents. If he finds out I didn't get into Columbia, I'm a goner.

I breeze through the new set of questions and finish with one minute to spare. "Thank you," I say sincerely.

He takes it, going back to the paperwork on his desk. "If you need to talk, I'm here."

"Thanks," I say, speed-walking out of his classroom—*But no thanks.*

I walk out of the building, feeling like a rebel, like someone might come running after me any second now.

When I get to the parking lot, the sun is blazing. I spot Carter and Olivia standing outside my car, Carter in his knee-length black athletic shorts and gray T-shirt, Olivia in her deep, *deep* V-neck crop top and baggy blue jeans. She looks like a model. Olivia always looks like a model.

Looking at her, I'm afraid of how this trip is going to play out. I feel like every time we make eye contact, there's blame in her eyes, like she knows that I was involved in her smear campaign.

I never thought I'd encounter her like this. I thought I would graduate, never see her, never think about her, never feel this guilt again. And she'd forget, too. That's what college is for—forgetting the horrors of high school.

But here we are, about to be trapped in a car together for two hours to Houston, and another two hours back.

She throws her hands up to the sky, and Carter shrugs

helplessly in response. They look like they're arguing. I have this irrational fear that it's about me.

Thing is, Olivia may be tiny, but I know for a fact that she'd win in a fight against me.

TEN RULES OLIVIA THOMAS BREAKS DAILY

1. She's a mixed girl, but according to my old friends she acts "Blacker" than me.

2. She has beautiful mixed-girl curls, but she always keeps them hidden in long microbraids.

3. She wears a silver hoop through her septum, during school hours, studs all up her ears, and a belly-button ring, blatantly exposed by her endless supply of crop tops.

4. She's had tattoos on her arms since she was sixteen.

5. She calls teachers by their first names. Only Mr. Green (Edward) has stopped correcting her.

6. She's gotten into several fights over our four years at Hayworth, all of them with white boys she's claimed were racist, entitled pricks.

7. She won all of them. Somehow, she manages to hold on to her scholarship.

8. She's very forthright about the fact that she's on scholarship. Everyone knows how poor she is, and she doesn't give two shits.

9. She's open and chatty about her sexual feats. I know more about Olivia's sexual history than I

think I should, especially since I haven't said more than two words to the girl.

10. All her friends are boys . . . but, honestly, that might be a result of the smear campaign.

When I walk up, I'm grasping the straps on my backpack tight. Carter looks at me and says, "He's lame. Ain't that right, Quinn?"

Olivia looks at me. I grow still because her gaze is so pointed.

"What? Who?" I ask, stopping ten feet away from them, keeping my eyes on Carter's. His gaze feels safer.

"Vontae."

"Oh." So this isn't about me at all. This is about music. Really bad music.

I scrunch up my face and Carter laughs, closing the distance I so carefully put between us. He throws his arm around my shoulders and says, "See? This my girl, right here."

Eyes wide, I look at Olivia for her reaction. Her eyes are on his arm around my shoulders. "You two don't know good music." She rolls her eyes, *not* commenting on the fact that her boyfriend's arm is around my shoulders. "Fine. I'll get Marqueese to take me."

"That's what I told you to do, anyway," Carter says, releasing me, and handing me back my breath.

She whines, "But he'll think it's a date, and I don't want to use him like that."

"So go by yourself, Livvy."

I'm confused. Why wouldn't he go with his girlfriend to a music show? What kind of a boyfriend is he?

"You know I get freaked out about parking." She stamps her foot like a three-year-old. "Fine, I'll ask Marqueese." Then she turns away and says, "I hate you," getting in the back seat of my car, the engine still running, like she's done it a thousand times. Like Olivia Thomas being anywhere near my car is normal.

Carter doesn't respond. He's completely unconcerned. "You're encouraging your girlfriend to go out with another guy?"

He looks at me like I spit on him. "Girlfriend? You think Livvy's my—" He bends over, laughing. "*Hell* naw." Then he runs over to knock on Olivia's window.

She lets it down. "What?" She still sounds angry with him.

"Quinn thought we were dating."

Olivia sticks her head out the window, and looks directly in my eyes, hers full of disgust. "That's incest!"

"Practically," Carter says.

"I heard you on the phone yesterday," I say, confused.

He shifts his eyes. "She was keeping my baby sister while we were at Auden's. I was talking to my baby sister."

I blink away, my cheeks heating up. "Oh."

"Aww." He swaggers over to me and runs his hand along the stubble on his jawline. "Were you jealous?"

"Girrrrl, you can have him," Olivia shouts out the window, before rolling it back up.

"I wasn't jealous. I don't want you."

Then he smirks. "You sure about that?"

"I'm into Matt . . . remember?"

His smirk flattens. "Right. I almost forgot you were into white boys."

I wince. He says it like I'm strictly into white boys. Which is not the case, and I hate that he thinks that about me, but before I can argue, he walks to the passenger side of my car. "We're just waiting on Auden, then we can go." He closes himself inside my car.

I stand alone, gripping my backpack, gathering myself before we go on this two-hour drive. Two hours with Carter. Two hours with Olivia. Two hours of roller-coaster emotions. I prepare my mind, my stomach, and my heart for the ride.

Ironically, Auden, the only white one of us, is late. Once he arrives, apologizing nonstop, he jumps in the back seat beside Olivia. The car smells like a mixture of my Victoria's Secret perfume, Carter's shower soap, Auden's patchouli house, and Olivia, which I'm guessing is that lavender undertone. I adjust the AC, wishing someone would break the silence.

I guess Carter does too because he starts messing with my Apple Music.

"Absolutely not." I slap at his hand. I will not go two-plus hours listening to mumble rap.

He frowns. "You might be surprised by how much we have in common."

"What do we have in common?" I ask. "You don't know what kind of music I like."

"I knew that you didn't like Vontae."

"Yeah, and that's very suspicious. How *did* you know that?" I narrow my eyes at him.

He smiles, tilting his head. "Just trust me." Then he goes back to sifting through my touch screen. And it's hard to fight my curiosity, so I let him.

That's how I spend two hours listening to '90s R&B, my absolute favorite. Carter and Olivia sing loudly, while I sing under my breath. Auden stares out his window, silent.

An hour out of Austin, the morning sun is bright. We pass country home after empty pasture after run-down gas station.

"Oh my God!" Olivia gasps in the back seat. I look at her in my rearview. She's pressed up against the back window. "You have to turn around," she begs with pleading eyes.

"Why? What's wrong?"

"That gas station was so beautiful. I need pictures."

"We're kind of on a tight schedule."

Carter says, "Trust me, just do it. She's not gonna let it go."

Auden says, "How could you deny our head photographer a good photo op?"

I freeze.

I know he doesn't mean anything by it, but it feels like he's poking at my guilt. Like he emphasized a few words that didn't need emphasis. How could *you*, of all people, deny our *head photographer*—knowing how you helped destroy her reputation as such—a good *photo op*, considering how you let all her photos get destroyed?

She's an award-winning photographer. Our yearbook department is proud to have her. Our *school* is proud to have her. She was given the entire wall in C hall, to display her work. It was like her own little art gallery. She posted candids of students and photos that she'd taken around Austin, breathtaking photos.

Then over Christmas break, while most students were taking advantage of their vacation, a few were breaking into the building. All her photos were destroyed with red paint marker:

This just in: Head photographer gives amazing head.

Olivia Thomas is open for business.

Shooting heads and blowing them, too!

I look in my rearview. Olivia holds clasped hands beneath her chin. "I'll be quick, I promise."

My guilt crushes me. I U-turn so fast, Carter has to hold on to the side of his door.

As she's pulling out her camera, she turns to Auden. "You know how I told you I sell my photos online?"

He nods.

"If I give you a cut, will you edit my pictures?"

"Really?" His face lights up.

"Hell yeah! You're the best editor in yearbook, Audee."

Audee? And wait, they're in yearbook together?

He smiles ear to ear. "Of course, I'll do it, and you don't have to pay me."

"I'm definitely gonna pay you."

When I pull into the decrepit gas station, Olivia instructs me to pull my car to the edge of the street, so we don't get in her frame.

I inspect the walls covered in graffiti, the tin roof of the awning over what used to be the gas pumps, shedding to the ground, layer by layer. The windows of the tiny building are all boarded up, the door too. It even has a signpost, falling apart at the road.

Olivia jumps out, gushing, damn near crying. Auden gets out of the car and joins her, pointing at details on the walls. She takes close-ups from every angle of everything. Then she orders me to move my car to the other side of the street, because somehow, I'm still in the frame. I follow her orders without question.

Carter and I stay in the car with the music low—Tyrese. He sits back, spreading his long legs in the cramped space, and turns to me. He looks comfortable staring at me.

"What?" I ask, nervous.

His eyes are on my mouth. "Nothing."

My breath shallows, vanishes, abandons me. I turn to my

window, staring at the pasture outside, attempting to breathe as quietly as possible. "How You Gonna Act Like That," my favorite song by Tyrese, comes on. I lay my head back, closing my eyes, mouthing along to the words.

But then Carter turns up the music. He says, "This is my favorite song." When I look at him, he's smiling.

My eyes widen. "Mine too."

He throws his head back and suddenly starts belting the verse. When I jump in and sing the background part, he turns to me, surprised. Then we're singing all the words together—him loudly and very poorly, while I can hardly sing for laughing at his squawks.

During the bridge he holds out his hands like he's performing in a music video. Then he pulls me into his performance, running his finger along my jawline. "I was a player and made the choice to give my heart to you!" I nibble my bottom lip, afraid of how much I might be taking this to heart. Especially when he grabs my hand and starts swinging it to the beat. His hand is warmer than mine and much bigger.

I smile, hoping the song never ends, and at the same time, needing it to end immediately. You know that feeling you get when something amazing is happening, like if you try to keep it up for one more second, you might spontaneously combust and destroy everything?

I reach over and turn the music off, pulling my hand out of his.

"Hey," he protests. "What happened?"

I narrow my eyes at him. "How'd you know I like this kind of music?"

"Lucky guess?" He smiles.

"By that do you mean you read my journal and saw my list of favorite songs?"

His smile drops in quicksand. "*Jesus*, Quinn. By that I mean I remember in English our sophomore year, we had to make slideshows about a poignant moment in our lives, and you used a song by SWV."

"You remember that?" I hold my hand over my heart. I barely remember that. I made a slideshow about the time Hattie and I raised a baby rabbit, and how coyotes killed him. It was a much simpler time in my life when *that* was the most poignant thing I had ever experienced. It was the most pathetic slideshow of the class, which is why I'm so stunned Carter remembers.

"After the train of Taylor Swift, I expected you to play a song by Taylor too."

"Taylor's not so bad," I say.

He laughs, and I smile, glancing down to my hands in my lap. I can't believe he remembers that. "You played 'Strange Fruit' by Billie Holiday," I say. When I look up from my hands, he's just as surprised as I was. "It was a bold statement in a classroom full of white kids, but I don't think anyone knew that song."

"They didn't. Mrs. Dexter did, though. She looked so

haunted." I laugh, and he smiles. Then his lips settle, and he looks at me like he's seeing me for the first time. "I ain't know you were paying attention like that."

I shrug, glancing down at the console between us. "I didn't know you were either."

Then the back door opens, and we both jump, like we were caught doing something we shouldn't have been. It kind of feels like we were.

Olivia spills into the back seat. "Got a keeper!"

"You guys should have seen it," Auden says. "The back door was open. I bet teenagers go in there all the time—"

"Do drugs and shit," Olivia says.

Carter teases, "Is that what took y'all so long?"

Auden blushes.

Olivia says, "Well, what were *y'all* doing?"

Carter looks at me and I return his gaze, wondering the same thing. What *were* we doing? And why do I feel so dissonant about it?

Then he turns to his window without replying. So I turn the radio back up and jump on the highway, trying to forget about the fact that neither of us answered the question.

chapter 11

DAYS MY BLACKNESS
HAS BEEN ON TRIAL

HOUSTON LOOKS MORE LIKE A CITY THAN AUSTIN DOES.
The highways twist like spaghetti. People drive fast, jutting
off on left and right exits. I'm panicking, but Carter gives
me instructions on where to go. We arrive at the administration building as they're leaving for the tour. The people
in charge get us signed in and hand us bags of red-and-
white swag.

SEVEN TIMES CARTER GIVES ME DIRTY LOOKS
DURING THE TOUR

1. When I raise my hand and ask the tour guide
   how many students have gotten assaulted while
   attending school here.
2. When the tour guide asks how many of us have
   already been accepted to U of H, and I don't raise
   my hand.

3. When I start lagging, complaining that my feet hurt.
4. When I criticize the vegetarian choices in the dining halls.
5. When I ask him for a piggyback ride because I'm tired of walking.
6. When I scoff at a kid who brags about being accepted into the honors program.
7. When I step on his toe as Olivia tries taking our picture at the end of the tour.

He scolds me on the way to the car. "Why were you acting like you're too good to go here?"

"I'm *sorry*. I don't like the campus."

"That's not it," he says.

Olivia and Auden walk a few paces behind.

"You were dismissive, just like yesterday, like at some point you started believing you're Columbia material, when you're not."

"I know I'm not!"

"You have no reason to feel like you're too good for this campus, 'specially since you got a fifty-fifty chance of going here."

I don't respond.

Maybe he's right. Maybe I am bitter about the Columbia rejection. And maybe I haven't accepted that U of H might be my future. But I didn't come here to tour. I had no real desire to see this campus. I came here to appease my black-mailer. But I'm realizing now why I wrote it on the to-do list in the first place. I might actually end up here for the next four years. That's a huge decision to make ill-advised.

When we get to the car, no one says anything. I start the engine and stare at the cement wall ahead. "Where do I go now?"

"Livvy will give you directions."

Olivia instructs me without any outside dialogue. Just, "Left. Right. Stay straight. Keep going. Pull over."

I parallel park on a corner surrounded by dilapidated buildings, brown grass, and torn-up sidewalks. Carter says, "Livvy and Auden, stay here."

Olivia reaches over the seats as he's opening his door and slips him a wad of cash. "Get me some red beans and rice."

When he gets out, he comes around and opens my door. I don't want to go. This looks like *the* place to get your car stolen. I look at the run-down chicken restaurant behind him. "You know I'm a vegetarian, right?"

"We're getting food for the group, but you're still welcome to eat your rabbit food."

I scoff. "Why can't I stay in the car?"

"Why? Are you afraid of Black people, just like your dad is?"

I narrow my eyes. And there it is.

"I'm not scared," I say, getting out. Why should I be scared?

He leads me across the street, not using a crosswalk. Inside, Black people fill every table, either eating fried chicken and seasoned fries or waiting for their order to be ready. When the bell on the door chimes, fifty percent of their eyes fall on us. My skin crawls. I'm not used to being surrounded by people with my skin color. It makes me feel like they can see how *other* I am. But they can't, right? I could blend in if I tried. I could embrace the country in my accent. I could say *ain't* and *y'all* and the N-word and they wouldn't know a thing.

There's a serving counter on the left with Black ladies wearing hairnets running around like chickens with their heads chopped off (ironically enough). When we get to the end of the line, I stand close to Carter because, if I'm being honest, I am scared. It feels like they *can* see the other in me.

But I mean, I look just like them. I should feel safer here than in my neighborhood. White people used to lynch people who look like me, so why on earth would I feel safer around *them*? I take a deep breath and pull my head up.

When we get to the register, Carter has to shout to be heard. He orders and pays with the cash Olivia gave him. Once he gets his receipt, I follow him to a booth in the back. The tabletop is dirty, so I slide in with my hands as close to my chest as possible. It takes me a second to realize that he hasn't sat down. I look up at him, all my organs vibrating.

"I'll be right back. Restroom." Then he leaves me. Completely alone.

I make eye contact with no one. I will myself to disappear. But my invisibility cloak must not be working, because as soon as Carter is gone, an especially skinny Black boy stops beside me. "Aye."

Don't talk to strangers. Don't talk to strangers. Don't talk to strangers. But I do make eye contact. The stranger nudges his head to the side and asks, "Is that your brother?"

I shift my eyes and shake my head.

"Boyfriend?"

I shake my head again. And immediately realize my mistake.

His eyes drift over my face, down to my chest and back up. "Where you from?"

I don't know what to say. The truth sounds like a bad idea.

He smiles at my silence. "Aww, you shy. I like that." He reaches over, brushing my cheek, and I pull away, disgusted. Thankfully, Carter comes out of the restroom then.

"So what up? How long you gon' be here?" Then the boy reaches for my face again.

"Aye, man," Carter says, stopping behind the stranger. "Pretty sure she don't want you touching her."

Skinny turns around. "Oh. Is she yo' girl?" he asks, pointing his thumb at me.

Carter looks at me. "Yeah, that's my girl."

Oh. I drop my chin, heart racing. I know he doesn't mean it for real, but hearing him say it still stirs up my butterflies.

"Shit. Well, I ain't know, my nigga." Skinny glances at me.

"Whether or not she my girl don't really make a difference, though. You ain't got no right to put your hands on her." Then Carter steps closer, towering over the man/boy.

Skinny laughs, looking Carter up and down. "It ain't that serious. I ain't want her ugly ass anyway." Then he walks away, leaving me insulted, disgusted, and a little confused. So now I'm *ugly*?

Carter looks pissed. He looks like he wants to turn around and do something stupid, so I say, "It's fine."

"It's not fine at all." He sits down, his jaw clenched. "Like, what if I had said you weren't my girl? Would that have given him free rein to harass you?"

I'm surprised at his aggravation. I study the way he clasps his hands on the tabletop.

"I'm not cool with that." He shakes his head. "And what if you had come here alone? That asshole would have probably followed you to your car." Then he looks at me and pauses. "Why are you smiling?"

I laugh a little. "I didn't know you cared about me like that."

He drops his eyes. "It's not about you. It's about . . . women in general." Then he looks up, and his eyes soften. "But, yeah, of course I care that you're safe."

My skin tingles as I dodge eye contact, hiding my smile.

When we get our food and get outside, calm washes over me at the sight of my car. I run across the street and jump in the driver's seat, not considering what might have happened with Olivia and Auden while we were gone. I feel the charge in the air once my door is shut. Carter feels it too.

We both dare to peek in the back seat. Olivia's feet are in Auden's lap. She looks comfortable and bored. He looks tense, like he doesn't know where to rest his hands.

Carter looks at me with his eyebrows raised. Something definitely seems to be blooming between Auden and Olivia.

"Where to next, Livvy?" Carter asks.

"Oh! Let's go to my old park. Pull up to this stop sign and take a left."

We ride through a neighborhood with wire fences and houses with slabs falling off, cars rotting in the front yards, people sitting on stoops, holding babies wearing nothing but diapers.

My heart is racing. *Great idea, Quinn. Bring your brand-new Mercedes to one of the most crime-infested areas in Texas.* Someone is assaulted, if not murdered, every day in this city.

Olivia climbs over Auden to point at a run-down apartment complex. "My friend Holly used to live there. I wonder if she still lives around here."

"Did you live around here?" I ask.

"Not quite. A little farther south. But all my friends lived here." Then she points out the window again. "That's the Chevron that got shot up. Remember I told you about that, Carter?"

"Uh-huh," he says, gazing out the window.

"Were you there when it got shot up?" I ask, eyes wide. She nods.

"That's crazy," Auden says. "What happened?"

"Some idiots from the neighborhood tried to rob it. Two people died."

"But where were you?" I ask.

"Hiding in the back by the milk."

I don't even know what to say to that. This girl has not had an easy life. Now I feel even guiltier about making her life harder once she moved to Austin.

She directs me to a poor excuse for a park crowded with Black bodies day-drinking and *celebrating*? When I creep through the parking lot, I notice that my black-on-black Mercedes is the least interesting car here, the most interesting being a candy-coated red Impala parked diagonally across two spaces with the doors wide open and a group of people hanging around the grill. Hip-hop blasts from the speakers, and as I park across from it, I notice the pointed rims. I stare in my rearview mirror at how they extend the total width of the car by at least two feet.

"How do they get around with those pointy rims?"

Carter looks behind us with an excited smile. "Swanga rims."

"Swinger rims?" I ask, staring at the apparent owner of the car through my rearview mirror. He's a dark-skinned man with a blinding gold grill on his bottom row of teeth. He looks like he's on the set of a music video.

"No," Carter says, turning to me. "*Swanga* rims."

Olivia laughs. "One time I saw a guy with swangas try

to go through a narrow lane with cement barriers. It did not end well."

"Livvy, you've told that story a thousand times."

She falls over laughing. "But it's so funny!"

"Come on. Let's get out." Carter opens his door, but I'm still staring at the man in my rearview.

I'm scared to call attention to myself, to be noticed for what I am, or, I guess, for what I'm not. When we get out, though, no one even looks at us. Carter and I follow Olivia and Auden to an empty picnic table. They sit on one side, eating chicken and fries, while I sit across from them. Carter sits on the tabletop, facing me with his shoes on the bench by my thighs. He's taking bites, occasionally, with his old red spiral in his lap.

Olivia slings the back of her hand against Carter's back. "What's that you're writing?"

"Nothing," he grumbles, not lifting his head.

"What is it? Love letters?"

"No." He peeks his eyes at me, then back down to his notebook. It makes me uneasy.

I pull my eyes up from my cashew-butter-and-apple-slice sandwich into Olivia's unfaltering gaze. It stuns me still. She rips her teeth into a seasoned fry, gazing at me. "So, what's this shit about Columbia?"

My mouth dries, and my palms sweat. Auden peeks around Carter to look at me too.

"Um, well, I didn't get in."

"But you lied to everyone and said you did."

It sounds judgmental the way she says it. I correct her. "I lied to my parents. My parents told everyone."

"But why lie?" she asks, genuinely curious.

Carter lifts his eyes from his journal, wondering the same thing, I guess.

There are so many answers to that question, so many reasons. "My parents have been planning for me to go to Columbia since the day I was born. Unfortunately, they hadn't planned on me being stupid."

Olivia rolls her eyes. "You're not stupid."

"Have you seen my grades?"

"I've seen your writing. You're really talented."

I'm caught off guard. "When have you seen my writing?" English is undoubtedly my worst subject.

"You know last year when yearbook had that caption contest?" She glances at Auden. "Your captions were hilarious."

"Yeah, they were," Auden agrees.

"Pretty sure Gia Teller won that contest, though."

"Yeah, but—" Olivia sighs.

"There's a lot of politics in yearbook," Auden finishes for her.

She rolls her eyes. "Gia's dad bought, like"—she turns to Auden—"what was it? Two pages of ads for his family's stupid car dealership?"

"Yeah, I think so. Plus, he's a huge donor for the school."

"That's why you couldn't flip a page without seeing her stupid face."

I raise my eyebrows at her tone.

"God, I hate that bitch," she says.

I smirk, looking back down to my sandwich. "Me too."

When I look back up, she's smiling. She says, "You should have won. I always thought you should have been in yearbook. You'd make a great caption writer."

Wow, I never thought my captions were that great. And I never thought I'd hear that from *Olivia Thomas*.

"Thanks," I say.

Her smile lingers, and her eyes continue to watch me. "Hey, so, question."

I hesitate to meet her speculative gaze.

"How'd that pic get posted?"

My lips twitch. Wind picks up my hair. I push it behind my ear and look up to Carter. He says, "You should tell her. She'd prolly be a big help."

I hadn't planned on telling anyone else about my journal. I never planned on *Carter* knowing about my journal. But Olivia? I have secrets about her in that journal.

"Help with what?" She narrows her eyes.

I glance at Auden sitting next to her. His head is tilted curiously. He says, "Does this have anything to do with what you two were arguing about yesterday?"

I look at Carter again. He nudges his head.

"You can trust me," Olivia says out of the blue. I look in her eyes. That's not where my delay came from, but it's good to hear.

"Me too," Auden says.

I stand up, walk a few feet away from the table, my back to them. Having Carter know about my journal hasn't been all bad. Being able to talk about my lists has been great. And I know I wouldn't have gotten this far without him coming with me. Without *them*. Maybe they could be a big help too.

When I turn back around, Olivia sits on the tabletop beside Carter, leaning over her knees, her undivided attention on me. Auden sits on the tabletop behind them. I look at the three of them, waiting for me to open my mouth. It looks like story time, but sadly, the story I'm telling is about the worst day of my life.

chapter 12

HOW TO MAKE NEW FRIENDS

THE WIND IS HIGH TODAY, SO I PUT MY HAIR IN A PONY-tail, stalling. A baby's crying in the distance. Someone's laughing. Hip-hop's still playing in the parking lot.

"Dude," Olivia says impatiently.

"Okay, okay." I look at Olivia, but holding her gaze is difficult, so I look at Carter. "I have an entire journal of lists like the one that got posted. And it just so happens that yesterday that journal went missing."

Olivia's eyebrows flick up.

"Carter," I say. "Wanna take it from here?"

He sighs. "I grabbed her journal by mistake. Then I sorta kinda lost it."

"Carter!" Olivia whacks the back of her hand against his chest.

He frowns, rubbing his shirt. "It was an accident."

"So someone stole your journal and posted that list?" Olivia asks, turning back to me.

"Yeah, but it gets worse. After Carter told me he lost it, I got a DM from that anonymous profile that posted the list.

They're forcing me to complete one of my to-do lists or else they'll publicize my journal."

Olivia leans in. "They're blackmailing you?"

"Why would they want you to complete a to-do list?" Auden asks.

Carter nudges his head. "Show 'em the list."

I tighten my grip on my phone. My to-do list has been a secret for so long. Carter read it against my wishes, and the blackmailer did, too, but willingly exposing myself is a whole other thing.

"Hey," Carter says, pulling me out of my head. "It's okay. They're cool."

But I still don't know if *he's* cool. Either way, they already know about Columbia. The list doesn't really get much worse than that.

I open the DM chain between me and my blackmailer. "This is my 'To Do Before I Graduate' list. It's why we're here today." I hand Olivia my phone.

Auden reads over Olivia's shoulder. "Wait. What's the last thing on the list?" Olivia asks, one eyebrow cocked.

"She won't tell me," Carter says.

The last thing on the list is the *only* thing that's still a secret. Even the blackmailer doesn't know what it is. As long as that's the case, I can't be forced to do it.

"But look at this." Carter offers his spiral.

Olivia looks over his shoulder, as does Auden. I step closer, curious to see what he's been working on. It's a seating chart of Mrs. Yates's first period class. "This is where I sit." He points to his name in a square. "Look at everyone sitting close to me. Who hates you enough to do something like this?"

I frown. "I don't have haters like that."

"*Somebody* hates you enough to blackmail you." He points to all the squares around his desk. "Any of these people?" His finger lingers on the desk behind him: *Matt Rat.*

"Who is Matt Rat?"

He smirks. "Your li'l boyfriend."

I scrunch up my face. "His name is Matt Radd."

"Same thing. What matters is the fact that he sits right behind me."

"Yeah, but he'd never do something like this."

Carter leans forward a bit. "Are you sure?"

"Yes. We're friends. Why would he do this?"

"Well . . ." He sits back and raises his eyebrows at Olivia. "We've been hearing things about you and him and Destany."

I roll my eyes and take a few steps back. "None of it's true."

"Maybe he's bitter about the fact that you got in between him and Destany," Carter says.

"First of all"—I laugh, holding up a finger—"Matt and I already talked about this. He knows that he had nothing to do with what happened between Destany and me. Second, he's more committed to our friendship than anything with Destany."

Carter doesn't look convinced. "Way to delude yourself."

"Excuse me?"

"This is what I think: He was pissed that you got in between him and the girl he *actually* likes."

I wince.

"He found your journal, found an opportunity to expose your truth, so now he has a chance with Destany."

"That's stupid. He could just date her. Why does he need to blackmail me?"

"He has to sever all ties between you and Destany so that she'll agree to it. And there's his motive." Carter starts writing under Matt's name.

"Don't write that." I try to take the pencil out of his hand.

He looks at me like I'm crazy. "You need to be impartial."

"You need to be reasonable."

"Umm," Olivia says, cutting in. "How about we bring our attention to the fact that Destany is also in this class?"

"She sits kinda far away from me," Carter points out.

"Yeah, and she wouldn't do this either." I shake my head. They're really just grasping at straws here.

"How do you figure?" Olivia asks, stunned.

"Because we were best friends."

"*Were* being the operative word."

"Okay. So, what would be her motive?" I put my hands on my hips. "If she wants me to be her friend again, blackmailing me would be a little counterproductive."

"Who says she wants to be your friend again?"

"She did! She's been begging me all week."

Olivia shrugs. "I say we write that down."

Carter does, and I sigh deep. "Oh my God. You know who I think is really suspicious?" I point at Carter's square.

He glares at me. "Really, Quinn?"

"You were the last person to have my journal. While we're being 'impartial,' go ahead and write that down." I do the air quotes and everything.

"Write what down? What's my motive for blackmailing you?"

"To get revenge for how my dad treated you."

He licks his lips. "What your dad did was fucked up, but I'm over that shit."

"Are you?"

"I don't give a damn if your father hates the color of his own skin."

My face slacks. I look down at the dirt. So I'm *not* crazy for thinking my dad might hate being Black. Carter thinks so too.

He notices my sullen expression and dials back. "Look, fine, I'll write 'last known person to have journal' by my name. It's not a motive, but it's what we know for sure."

"Everyone's thinking in terms of who hates Quinn enough to do this," Auden says. "But the real question is, who could stand to gain something by making Quinn look bad?"

All our heads bend over the paper. Then I see it, sitting on the left of Carter: *Harvard-Kaide*. I point at his name.

"Showing everyone that I didn't get into Columbia would serve his racist agenda."

"Shit, you're right," Carter says. "Kaide is always on some racist shit. And he always assumes that I have to cheat in order to get a better grade than him."

"I've been *waiting* to beat his ass," Olivia says. "He hasn't been dumb enough to say racist shit around me, but I've heard so much about him." Olivia shakes her head, rubbing her right hand over her left fist. "I'm ready for his ass."

"Let's not get ahead of ourselves," Auden says. "We need proof first."

Carter nods, then he asks me, "Did you send our campus picture yet?"

"Oh!" I grab my phone off the picnic table, select the picture Olivia took of us on campus, and send it.

"Okay, so we have three suspects—"

"Four," I say, looking at Carter.

Olivia corrects herself. "Four major suspects, with one prevailing above the rest."

Then my phone dings in my hand. I look down and open the message. **Great. But this seems to be one campus? It says visit the TWO universities.**

My mouth drops open. "Oh my God."

"What happened?"

I hand Carter the phone. "This has all been a complete waste!"

"What's going on?" Olivia asks.

Carter hands her my phone. "How far is the other school from here?"

"I don't know." I shrug. "Like an hour or two. I don't have time for that. I'm supposed to be home right after school. What am I gonna do?"

Olivia looks up from my phone with a devilish grin. "I have an idea."

I raise my eyebrows, skeptical.

"One of the things on your to-do list says to experience downtown Austin."

Carter sighs. "No, Livvy."

"What is it?" I ask.

"Well . . . the Vontae show is on Sixth Street tonight."

I follow a silver Ford Super Duty across the countryside. They're going five over the speed limit, dodging slow goers. I go on autopilot and let them lead me. When I glance in my rearview, Olivia's slumped over, dead asleep with her mouth open. Auden's in his corner, staring out the window. I glance at Carter to see if he's awake. From this angle and the swiftness of my glimpse, I can't tell. His head is propped against the headrest, chin pointed to the sky outside his window, lashes low.

The Ford swoops around an old minivan. I do the same.

Once we get closer to Austin, we hit bumper-to-bumper traffic. The three o'clock sun blinds me, makes the white lines on the road disappear. I put my visor down, but it's useless.

"Your seat is too low."

I turn to Carter, surprised. I didn't know he was awake.

"That's why your visor isn't working. You need to lift the seat up," he says motioning to the side of his own seat.

I feel on the side and accidentally push my seat forward.

"No, it's the one farther back."

I haven't had this car long enough to really get familiar with all the buttons. I haven't exactly tried. This car still feels like borrowed time.

I lift a lever and the back of my seat falls like a lounge chair. "Oh my God," I say, pulling it back up.

"It's just—here." He moves the band of his seat belt, and with one hand on the head of my chair, reaches the other across my lap. I stop breathing as his arm brushes against my abdomen. My seat is rising, the visor shading the side of my face, and my eyes are falling to his lips right-fucking-there. In a low voice, he asks, "Better?" His arm is sorta kinda resting atop my thighs, and his eyes are sorta kinda taking me apart.

I nod, then a car honks behind us. When I look forward, there's a mile gap between my car and the car in front of us. Carter moves away, fixing his seat belt, and I speed forward, slamming on the brakes once I catch up to traffic.

Olivia's still sleeping in the back seat. Auden's still gazing out his window. When I dare to look at Carter, he's staring straight ahead, but then he feels my eyes on him, and he turns to meet my gaze.

I glance at the road, then back at him.

"I'm sorry for what I said about your dad."

"Oh." I shake my head. "It's fine."

I turn back to the road, move up an inch. He faces the windshield too. All is silent. I think about what Matt had to say about it last night. I ask, "Do you really think he hates the color of his skin?"

He looks at me like I bit off more than I can chew with that question. Instead of answering, he asks, "Do you?"

I sigh, relaxing in my seat. "I don't know. I think it's a little harsh to say he *hates* being Black. Maybe he's just . . ." I blink up to the roof of my car. "Like, I wasn't there. I don't know what he said to you."

Carter grinds the words between his teeth: "He didn't say, 'Hi, who might you be?' He said, 'Excuse me? What are you doing in my house?' Those were the first words out of his mouth."

My eyelids flutter as I turn back to the windshield. "All my life, he's taught me what challenges I'll have being Black—he's warned me about unfair grading and harsher punishments and stuff like that. But I never really experienced any of it. That kind of stuff isn't what I needed . . . preparation for."

Carter leans in. "Those were the challenges of their generation." He crosses his arms over the console. He looks excited to be talking about this with me. "And it's definitely still a threat for our generation, but not as much."

I nod, getting excited too. Finally, I have someone who wants to talk about this stuff. "My parents never warned me about the fact that the way I talk and the way I act might lead people to call me white."

"Yeah, I get that," Carter says. "My mom taught me about stereotypes, but she never taught me about the dangers of being the exception to stereotypes."

"Being the exception to Black stereotypes automatically means that you're not as Black."

He nods, blinking slowly. I look at him and all the stereotypes I thought he fit into. I never thought he had to deal with being the exception too. What with the way he talks and the way he carries himself and the fact that everyone at school considers him a "real" Black guy. I let all those assumptions color my view of him. I'm no better than the white kids. I'm no better than *my dad*.

"I gotta be honest with you, Quinn," Carter says. My brow furrows when I look at him. "I didn't think you minded being called an Oreo."

My eyes narrow. "I never used the word *Oreo*." I only used the word *Oreo* in my journal.

"You didn't have to," he says. "I've been called an Oreo before."

What, really? I'm sure my surprise shows on my face. He laughs and nods. "When I was much younger, back when I was still going to public school." He pauses, glancing out of his window. "I let it change my behavior, though. I changed the way I talked, the way I dressed, the way I acted, who I hung out with. Thankfully, I didn't let it change my grades. I was just more secretive about my schoolwork."

He turns to me and shakes his head. "Anyway, I'm just saying that what those kids did to me, I might have done to you. So I'm sorry."

I look in his heavy eyes, a weight on my chest lifting. How does he keep doing that? Making me feel more visible than I've ever felt, like all my dark parts are glowing golden.

My phone buzzes from its little cubby in my dash. I blink away from Carter's pensive stare and check the brake lights of the car stopped in front of me before opening the message.

Matt: Did you and Carter skip school together?

When I look at it, I can't concentrate enough to text back, or to even get excited about the fact that he definitely seems to be jealous. I put it back in its cubby and glance at Carter. He's still watching me in that thoughtful way. I say, "I'm sorry too."

It takes us thirty minutes to get through traffic back to the empty school parking lot. Auden shakes Olivia awake. She groans, yawns, and stretches. Then Auden opens his door. "Thanks for the ride, Quinn."

"Auden, get to my house at eight," Carter says.

"Okay."

Olivia throws a hand over the back of my seat, landing on my shoulder. "You too—get to my house by eight. We need to get you a fake ID."

"What?" I spin around.

"If we're doing this, we're doing it right." Then she gets out of my car, leaving me alone with Carter.

I look at him. "Fake IDs? No one said anything about fake IDs."

"Quinn, it'll be fine. Just think about how to get out of the house tonight. We're gonna be out *all* night."

Then he leaves too.

Going downtown is one thing, but fake IDs? I'm eighteen. I could go to prison.

I look at the clock on my dash. It's going up to four o'clock. *Shit.* My parents are expecting me home. I pull out of the parking lot as Carter gets in the driver's seat of Olivia's old Honda. He watches me pull away. I watch him, too, my heart thundering in my chest.

chapter 13

WHAT I KNOW ABOUT MY FATHER

WHAT I KNOW ABOUT MY FATHER

1. He never cries.
2. He hates being outdoors.
3. He loves reading about the history of technology.
4. He's either cheating on Mom or he doesn't require much sex.
5. He went to Columbia to get away from here.
6. His father disowned him for leaving.
7. He came back after his father died.
8. He hates his father for giving up.
9. He became a surgeon to save people.
10. He visits Hattie every Saturday (without me).
11. He blames himself for not being around when his dad died.
12. And yet stays away while our family dies.

We take Mom's Land Rover; Dad drives. They're listening to Tyrese low. They only put him on when things are good. I guess that's why he's my favorite.

Dad holds Mom's hand on the console. His fingers trickle up her arm. I watch, bracing myself for the second Mom realizes that Dad never apologized, and for Dad to realize that Mom never sympathized. I don't want to be waiting for the end. I want to revel in this moment. I want to sing along to Tyrese, but I can't stop thinking about how it's only a matter of time.

"I love driving your Land Rover," Dad says, looking at Mom, then back to the windshield. "It's so smooth."

"Get one."

"Yeah? We can be a Land Rover family. We'll trade Quinn's Mercedes in too." He looks at me in the rearview. "How about that, Quinn?"

I shrug.

"When you graduate, we'll get you a Land Rover. It'll be a lot more space for when you drive to New York."

"You want her to drive to New York?" Mom asks. "I didn't think she'd take a car. It's not like she'll use it in the city."

Boyz II Men comes on.

"Somebody has to drive those boxes up there."

"What does she need to bring besides a couple of outfits? She doesn't have to move her entire life, Desmond."

Uh-oh.

"Wendy, she's getting an apartment. She'll want to bring a lot more than a few outfits."

"That's totally unnecessary. She's going to be a freshman, for God's sake. Get her a dorm. Let her get established as a student before getting her an apartment."

"A lot can happen in a dorm with all those people sharing one space. I would feel a lot better knowing my little girl is in an apartment."

"I stayed in a dorm my first two years at Columbia. Nothing happened to me. I think it'll be good for Quinn to start out in a dorm. It'll teach her a little gratitude."

"Are you saying she's not grateful?"

They're talking about me like I'm not right here.

"You bought her a Mercedes at *eighteen*. Do you know what I was driving when I was eighteen?"

"Wendy, please don't start."

They don't say any more about it. They're still holding hands, but their hands look rigid. The music is still playing, but it sounds less purposeful.

When we get to Olive Garden, Dad runs around to get Mom's door. But they don't hold hands on the way inside. It's more disappointing than I expected.

The host seats us in a booth against the wall. Mom and Dad sit on one side, the space between their arms ginormous. The dining room is full of parties of two and four, light chatter rising above the background acoustic music, interspersed with the clinking of silverware against plates. We're surrounded by white people, as usual in this part of town.

I wait a few minutes, looking around the dining room, then back to the space between my parents. "Can I sleep over at a friend's house tonight?"

They both look up from their menus.

Dad asks, "Destany? Of course, sweetie. Will that other girl be there? What's her name?"

"Gia," Mom answers, not looking away from her menu.

"Never much liked that girl," he says.

"Her dad's a big donor for Hayworth," Mom says. "She hasn't seen many consequences for her actions, and it shows."

"She always calls us by our first names," Dad says. "'Hey, Wendy. Hey, Desmond.' It's . . ." He goes back to his menu, shaking his head. "At least Destany was always respectful."

"Yeah, but Destany tends to follow Gia." Mom looks at me. *And I tended to follow Destany, so . . .*

"It's not Destany," I say, crossing my arms on the table.

They're both surprised.

"Her name's Olivia Thomas."

Dad asks, "Where does she live?"

I pause. I don't want to lie. I've done enough lying to them for a lifetime. "East Austin."

They both frown. "And she goes to Hayworth?" he asks.

"She's on scholarship."

Mom gives a qualifying nod. "She must be pretty smart."

"She really is." I smile. "She's the yearbook head photographer. She's really talented."

They both pull their menus back up. Mom says, "That's fine."

Dad flips over his menu, as if he's not going to order the same thing he always orders (steak, well done, with fettuccine alfredo), then he asks me, "Did you look at those apartments I sent you?"

That's what he does: he emails me links to different apartments in New York. I used to look at them, study them, imagine living in them, but, after a while, it hurt too much. "I liked the first three," I say.

He raises his eyes. "I only sent you two."

My mouth drops open. I say, "Yeah, that's what I meant. I liked both."

"Quinn Jackson."

Here we go.

10 QUESTIONS DAD ASKS ABOUT COLUMBIA BEFORE OUR FOOD ARRIVES

1. You didn't even open the email, did you?
2. Do you plan to be homeless?
3. Do you understand that rates increase the longer you wait?
4. Do you know how expensive New York is?
5. Have you thought about your major?
6. Do you plan to be homeless after you graduate?
7. What type of job can you see yourself doing for the rest of your life?
8. Do you want to be homeless?
9. Did you call your advisor?
10. You can't depend on us forever, so do you plan on being homeless?

When I printed out that fake acceptance letter, I thought that maybe later I'd tell them New York was too far, and I'd rather stay in Austin to go to UT. But then UT wait-listed me, and *everything* became impossible. I didn't even get into my safety school.

"Dad, the reason I haven't been looking for a place to live in New York is because . . ."

This is it. This is when I tell them.

"Because what?" he prompts, not as patiently as I would like.

So I chicken out. "Because I'm scared."

"I know it's scary leaving the nest, but—"

"No, Dad, I'm scared that when I move out, you're moving out too."

Suddenly, he looks deflated. Mom glances at him, her eyes fearful.

"It feels like the only thing you guys have in common is your interest in me. What happens to this family when I leave?"

"Nothing is going to happen, sweetie." But he looks away when he says it.

When the server brings our food, he can feel the tension. It's tangible, emanating in waves. And I don't even feel like eating. I just want to leave, go to Olivia's house, so they can get back to fighting.

chapter 14

REASONS I WISH WE'D BEEN
FRIENDS SOONER

AS SOON AS THE DOOR OF OLIVIA'S APARTMENT OPENS, she shoves a fake ID in my hands. "You're twenty-two. Memorize the birthday."

I'm standing on the landing, looking down at a familiar picture of myself.

"I used your yearbook picture from last year."

My eyes look clear and carefree. I was so carefree back then. I read the birthday over and over. December 14, 1998. My fingers tremble. "This is highly illegal."

She opens the door wider. "Come in. You're letting the cool air out."

The inside of her apartment is dark. It smells like incense and candles and cigarette smoke. A white lady sits on the couch, her blond hair in a messy bun. She's making what looks like a necklace out of green leather while watching a crime show. She glances up at us, squinting to see us in the dark.

"Momma, this is Quinn."

I lift my hand. "Hello."

"Hey, baby." Her voice sounds raspy and tired.

Olivia leads me past the couch into a dark kitchen, where she grabs a six-pack of Dos Equis from the fridge. I'm stunned still at her gall to drink in her mother's home, *while* her mother is home.

"You can go ahead to my room. It's on the right." She searches the countertops. "I gotta find that damn bottle opener."

"Language, Livvy," her mom says from the couch, as though that's really the concerning factor in this situation.

I head down the dark hallway. Her room's the only room with a light on. As soon as I'm inside, I'm captivated by white Christmas lights arching across the ceiling and her photography tacked to the walls and hanging from strings.

A lot of her photos are of the city. There's one of Carter laughing, sitting on the stairs outside. I stare at it, staring holes into the dimples in his cheeks. He has dimples? I guess I've never seen him smile that big around me. Good thing, too, because I'd have lost myself, like I'm losing myself now, swimming in the adorable trenches in his face.

When I move to the photo next to his, my heart stops. It's a photo of Kristina Lowry sitting in the cafeteria next to her friends. She's looking directly at the camera, stoically, like the photo was snapped the second before she realized that her picture was being taken. It's gorgeous, all except the red paint marker circled around her face in the shape of the letter D.

I look at the photos to the right of Kristina. The entire line is pieced together just as it was when the photos were first vandalized, spelling out: *This just in: Head photographer gives amazing head.*

She kept the vandalized photos? Not only kept them. She's displaying them in her bedroom. Why would she want to remember this? I stare in horror, sweat prickling on my forehead.

Then she walks in behind me with the six-pack of beer in one hand, and the beer opener in the other. I turn, throwing my hand on the back of my neck. She looks at me curiously, then at the row of vandalized pictures. A knowing look crosses her face.

"Oh, that." She shuts the door with her foot, then goes over and sets the beer on her desk. "I always thought the red paint really added to the art. You know?" She turns, leaning against her desk, waiting for my response.

I'm speechless.

"Like, I must really be making a statement if someone felt moved enough to destroy my work." She smirks, then shrugs. "I don't know. They make me feel like a real artist amid a sexual revolution or something."

I look down, hiding my shame.

"Get one of these," she says, pointing to the beer.

"Oh, I—that's okay," I stammer. "I don't really drink."

"You don't go downtown, either," she says with a smile. "Have you ever drank before?"

"I've had a few sips here and there." Usually unwillingly.

Destany and Gia loved drinking, and I was never really a fan, but when I would protest, they'd question my loyalty. Gia would say, "You're going to tell on us, aren't you?"

I would assure them that I wasn't going to snitch, but then Destany would say, "Just have a few sips so we *know* you won't tell." And from there, they'd pressure me to have more. I started avoiding their houses when I knew their parents wouldn't be home.

"Here," Olivia says, handing me an open bottle. "Smoothest lager out there."

I look at the rim for a while.

"You don't have to if you don't want to," she says, putting her hands up. "I mean, more for me, right?" She laughs, grabbing one and opening it for herself.

I take a bitter sip, curious about the hype and grateful for the lack of pressure. Then another, less bitter sip.

"It's good, right?" she asks.

"Sure." It's not *disgusting*.

She opens her laptop and presses play on a playlist entitled *Get Ready Bitch*, full of popular hip-hop songs and a shit ton of Vontae. I try not to cringe. Tonight is going to be . . . challenging.

"Now." She turns and looks at me, tapping her lips. Nervous, I take another sip of the Dos Equis. "Have you ever straightened your hair?"

"Umm." I take an inadvertent step back. "No. And I really don't want to."

"Dude, I get it." She laughs. "My mom wishes I didn't keep my hair braided up all the time, but I mean, she doesn't know the first thing about combing Black hair. It's just easier this way."

"Do you do it yourself?"

She smiles, running a hand through her microbraids. "Carter's mom." Then she walks over to me, reaches up and picks her tiny fingers through my hair. I flinch, bracing myself for her reaction. "Your hair is so thick. It's beautiful." She glances at my face, then back to my hair. "All right, stay here."

I watch her go, my heart slowly restarting.

I don't let people pick through my hair. Not anymore. I've always worn my hair naturally. My mom showed me how to wash, deep condition, detangle, and moisturize it every week. She's never brought up the idea of straightening my hair—chemically or otherwise. And I've never felt the desire. I love my fluffy hair.

But I don't know. Destany and Gia only ever wanted to straighten it. Whenever we'd get ready to go out, they'd beg to straighten my hair. And I broke one time. Gia was straightening Destany's hair, and I said, "Can you do mine too?" It was one of the most ignorant things I've ever done.

They both paused and looked at my hair. Gia said, "Um, well, this is a brand-new straightener." And I didn't understand what she meant, so she clarified, "I don't want to get it dirty."

My throat clogged. I felt embarrassed and sick to my stomach. Destany walked over, and she ran her fingers through my hair. "It is pretty greasy, Quinn. Maybe if you washed it first."

Olivia comes back, her arms full of hair products, some that I recognize, and a makeup bag, setting it all on the desk. Then she motions for me to sit down. I take a gulp of beer, anxious. She does too.

She pulls her fingers through my hair without pause. She's not afraid of getting oil on her fingers. I relax as she reaches for the same detangling spray that I use at home.

"So you've got this middle part going on," she says. "What we're gonna do is take your part *all* the way to the left."

She sounds like she's on a cooking show, narrating her every move. She takes a comb and makes a part on the far-left side of my head.

"Good. Now we'll take this portion and pin it back." She takes a gulp, then opens a jar of hair gel, slapping some on the side of my head, vaguely dancing to the song playing low over her speakers. "Brush it back," she says for all her viewers.

She's just about done with her first bottle. I grab mine and attempt to catch up. Clearly, I need to get on her level.

Before pinning the left side of my hair back, she combs out my baby hairs. "We gon' get this shit laid, momma. Get you lookin' fine as hell."

I laugh, taking another gulp of beer. It tastes like apple juice, minus the apple? It tastes like it looks—bronze. And it makes me feel like I'm wading through wet cement. I finish my first one while Olivia is working on her second.

As she lays my baby hairs, I look at the wall before me. It takes several seconds for my brain to catch up. The entirety of this wall is covered by a tapestry. Splotches of ink bleed into the fabric. I take it in, drop by drop, until I can grasp the whole image. It's a photograph of a woman smoking a cigarette in a patch of dead grass.

"Oh my God," I say. "This tapestry is amazing."

Her hands pause on my head. "Thanks," she says. "That's my mom."

"Really?" I look at it harder, the blond bun, the smoke protruding from her lips, the cigarette between her fingers. "She's so beautiful." I look at the whole of the portrait. "Jesus, you're good."

"You think so?" She puts down the comb and the brush and takes another sip. "Honestly, I would love to be commissioned to do one of those generic calendars. You know the ones at the dollar store, with the beautiful scenery and shit?"

"Yeah," I say. "But you could do better than that. This tapestry belongs in museums."

"It's crazy 'cause I took this picture on the side of the road. I'm always looking for beautiful places to shoot, like that old gas station today. Can't wait to upload that picture. Me and Auden gon' make so much *money*."

I never knew they were such good friends. I would have never pegged it.

I finish off my second beer; she hands me a third and then starts on my makeup. She's leaning over my face, her beer breath bumping against my skin. "Close your eyes." After applying primer, she brushes shadow over my eye. "About this journal thing," she says out of nowhere. "You know how I *know* it's not Carter?"

"How?" Then I catch myself. "Wait, did he tell you to say this?"

She laughs. "Damn, Quinn. I'm not some mindless pawn."

"Well, I don't know. I don't know who to trust."

Then she steps back. I can't feel her breath on my cheek anymore. I open my eyes, and she's twisting her mouth in thought.

"What?" I ask.

"I know today's, like, the first time we've ever actually talked, and I know you were best friends with Destany."

I stiffen.

"I'm sure you know about the bad blood between us. You've probably heard the rumors that Holden and I had a thing while he was still dating her—"

"I never believed the rumors."

"You had to," she says, nodding. "You two were friends."

"It made her feel better to blame you after he broke up with her. But I never believed the rumors." I want to apologize for not trying harder to change Destany's mind, but I can't get myself to say the words. I'd basically be admitting my involvement in the vandalism.

"Well, for the record," she says, stepping closer, eyeshadow brush in hand, "I never believed the rumors about you dumping her because of Matt Rat."

"Radd," I say.

"What?"

"His name is Matt *Radd*."

She smirks. "Close your eyes." She gets back to my eyeshadow. "The only reason I brought up Carter was because I know for a fact he's not the one doing this to you."

"How do you know?"

"Because that idiot's had a crush on you since he started going to school at Hayworth."

I open my eyes, and she nearly pokes my eye out with the eyeshadow brush. "Impossible. He hates me."

"If he hated you, he wouldn't care about clearing his name. Not enough to help you this much. He can't stand that you think he would do something like this to you."

I think back to the way he treated me the first time he came to my house. "Why is he so mean to me, then?"

"Carter's not the most tactful bulb in the toolbox."

I ponder the multiple idioms she just screwed up with that sentence.

She laughs at my face. "He's trying to figure you out. Pushing you to make you mad."

"Why?" I ask, bewildered.

"Because you're hot when you're mad?" She shrugs. "I

don't know. He's stupid." She picks up a tube of mascara. "Don't blink."

"Why would you think he has a crush on me?"

She sighs, running the wand through my eyelashes. "Because." She sighs again, her breath blowing against my forehead. "For one, he calls that boy Matt Rat because he hates how much you like him. Two, he's going to a Vontae show for you. Do you know how much I would have had to pay Carter to go to a Vontae show?"

"That doesn't prove anything."

"Maybe not to you, but it's all the proof I need."

She takes another thirty minutes to finish my makeup. All the while I'm rethinking every moment I've had with Carter since we got grouped together in Mr. Green's class. He was so hateful toward me. I can't imagine that came out of *love*.

But then I think about our moments today. The way he remembered my English project from two years ago, how he sang along to that Tyrese song, holding my hand and staring into my eyes, the way he stood up to that skinny guy for me in the restaurant, the way he apologized for his assumptions about me. I don't know. I don't know what to think.

I feel my face tightening as Olivia pokes at my mouth. "My lips feel like they're going numb. What kind of lipstick is this?"

"That's not the lipstick. That's the beer."

"Beer makes your face numb?" I ask, appalled.

She laughs. "When you drink enough of it. *And* when

you're a lightweight." Then she pulls me up from the chair. "Go look."

I hobble to the bathroom and stare at myself like I'm someone else. My kinky hair shades one side of my face. My thick lips are stained dark-purplish brown, and the way she did my mascara, my eyes look even bigger. I love it.

Olivia takes much less time to do her own makeup and hair, and then she's pushing a red dress into my hands—one with cutouts and mysterious straps—and a pair of black stilettos.

"I can't wear this," I say, looking down at it.

She gripes, "At least try it on."

"No, I mean, I've never worn heels like this. I've only ever worn wedges."

She thinks. "Okay, wait." She runs out of the room and comes back with a pair of black wedge-heel booties. "They're my mom's. It won't look as great, but they'll do." As she's closing me in her tiny bathroom, she says, "Make sure you step in. Don't pull it over your head and screw up all my hard work."

It takes me a while to figure out that the strap at the top is a built-in choker. Once I get it on, I check myself out in the mirror. I can't stop looking at my body, cleavage popping, curves running, melanin radiant and exposed through the cutouts and the extra-high slit. I've never seen myself look like this.

When I finally step out, Olivia's eyes start watering. "Oh

my God, Quinn. You look so gorgeous."

My eyes light up. "Really?"

"So, *so* gorgeous."

Olivia turns me around. "Look at that ass! Girl, you have to model for me someday."

"No!" I laugh.

"Yes! You're fucking gorgeous."

I shake my head, but I'm mentally agreeing with her. For once I feel like I can compete with the best: Destany, Gia, even Olivia. But Olivia doesn't make me feel like I *have* to compete.

REASONS I WISH WE'D BEEN FRIENDS SOONER

1. Maybe then I would feel more welcome in Black spaces. Hanging with Olivia makes me feel okay to show the parts of me that are rooted in my Blackness. Like, for once, I'm not trying to come out of my skin. Like an entire hemisphere of Quinn Jackson comes alive, and I never even knew that side of me existed.

2. Maybe then I wouldn't be so judgmental toward people of my own race, namely Carter. Because Olivia has this way of embracing and defying stereotypes all at the same time. And she doesn't care what it says about her or what people think.

3. Maybe then I wouldn't have let anyone call me an Oreo or say the N-word in my presence. Because

Olivia is Black and white, all mixed up, but she still feels enough obligation to beat up racist white boys on the fly.

4. Maybe then I would have never lied about Columbia, because I've never had friends as true to themselves as Olivia. Someone so fearless.

5. Maybe then I would be more fearless.

chapter 15

TAKING TEQUILA SHOTS IS EASY
WHEN YOU'RE ALREADY DRUNK

EVEN WITH STREETLIGHTS, THE PARKING LOT IS TOO DARK for comfort. In large part because of the guy at the bottom of the stairs, watching our every move. He licks his lips as we reach the landing. "Livvy. Who's your friend?"

Olivia keeps walking. "Ignore him," she whispers to me.

But it's hard to not look back when he's following us through the parking lot. I'm breathing heavy, and my eyes tear up.

"It's okay." Olivia grabs my hand and squeezes my fingers. "I'll protect you."

I look at her tiny build, then at the muscular man behind us, and somehow, I believe her. I've seen her fight, on multiple occasions, multiple guys. This girl could take down a football team, if she needed to. I relax, squeezing her hand back.

We head toward her car in the back of the parking lot. Both Carter and Auden are already there, leaning against the side, but my eyes get stuck to Carter. He's wearing a short-sleeve floral print button-down, tucked into belted black slacks with clean white sneakers. I miss a step and wobble in the boots. Olivia catches my arm, laughing. "Are you okay?"

My cheeks warm as I nod, brushing my hair out of my face. Carter is facing us now, lips parted, eyebrows pushed back in astonishment as his eyes take me in inch by inch. The warmth spreads from my cheeks down to my neck.

We approach in our heels and our dresses, Olivia's arm hooked in mine.

"Everything all right?" He glances at Olivia, but then his eyes fall right back to me.

"We're just a little tipsy," Olivia says, laughing.

Then Auden steps off the car. He's wearing fitted black slacks with a white button-down and black shoes. His curly hair is shaved on the sides, his glasses gone, green eyes unexpectedly captivating. He owns contacts, and he hasn't been wearing them?

When he sees Olivia in her short, strapless black leather dress, and stilettos, his pupils dilate.

Hers must dilate, too, because she says, breathless, "Auden, wow. You clean up nice."

He blushes, then laughs, ducking his head. "Thanks. So do you."

"We both got fresh cuts today," Carter says, rubbing his hand over his trimmed beard. He says it while looking at me, like he's awaiting my stamp of approval.

I scan the gold chain hanging from his neck, the sparkling studs in his ears, his fresh lineup. My breath escapes me. He's already so beautiful, but this is too much. I take a step back, stumbling in the boots again.

He reacts quickly, grabbing my arm.

"Damn, Quinn!" Olivia laughs. "You're such a light-weight."

I smile. It's not the alcohol. I'm simply weak in the knees.

Carter drives Olivia's car, while Olivia sits in the passenger seat. I sit in the back with Auden, trying to get a grip. December 14, 1998. Wait, fourteenth? Or was it fifteenth?

"What if they find out my ID is fake?"

"They're not even gonna look at it." Olivia turns in the passenger seat. "You're hot. You're good to go."

"Listen to Livvy. She's been through this a million times," Carter says, glancing at me in the rearview.

I take a deep breath.

"But if they catch you," she says. I give her my frantic eyes. "Just act dumb. They'll let you go. I've done it before."

"You've gotten caught?"

"They asked for my address, and I was so drunk that I messed up the street name. But I was like, 'Oh, what does it matter? It's not like I'm going home tonight anyway.' Then I batted my lashes at the bouncer, and he let me go." She shrugs.

"I can't do that!" I don't know how to flirt, and I have zero sex appeal. In a sea of girls, I'm not the one guys typically pick. So I never learned how to command their attention. I can barely stand up when Carter looks at me. How can I be bold enough to flirt with a bouncer?

As we're exiting I-35, I get a glimpse at the city lights. Downtown Austin is a lot different at night. Any time I've driven past, the lights have always caught my eye. They're so beautiful and inviting, but when it's where you're headed, it feels different. I'm throbbing and so are the other three, throbbing to the same beat of anticipation.

Carter parks in a garage on Fifth Street, and then we're walking. Olivia and I hold hands, keeping each other steady in our heels, but once we're on Sixth Street, Carter and Olivia take the lead, while Auden and I follow behind.

The sidewalk is crowded with people older than us, all walking in the same direction. Heels click against cement. Laughter fills the air. Girls strut in dresses more revealing than mine or Olivia's, while guys huddle in sweaty tank tops and shorts. It's hot and humid as hell. I can hear my hair frizzing.

The closer I get to people, the more clouds of perfume, cigarette smoke, and beer breath I pass through. The farther we go into the chaos, the louder the music gets, and the harder my heart beats. It's absolutely nerve-racking.

The sidewalk gets more crowded, like we're building up to something. Then we reach a blockade of police cars and policemen in the middle of the street. My heart races at the sight of them, like they must know I'm not old enough to be here. Carter and Olivia aren't fazed, pointing at bars as we pass. Auden is right behind them, but I'm lagging, stunned by everything, looking up at the string lights arching over-head.

On one side of the blockade is a swarm of parked cars with their flashers blinking, Lyft stickers in their windshields, alongside a train of pedicabs. On the other side is chaos. People swarm the street, like a festival, like South by Southwest, but it's just a regular Saturday night.

Then we come upon a line of people that stretches all the way around the corner. Olivia turns to the three of us, bouncing. "This is it!" None of us are as excited as she is.

We stand against the brick wall, Olivia, then Carter, me, and Auden. People pass us on the sidewalk, staring curiously. The more stray glances I collect, the more I bounce between feeling sexy and feeling self-conscious in this revealing scar-let dress.

I drop my eyes. Suddenly I feel like I have no right to bring this much attention to myself.

I notice groups of girls in extra-sexy dresses and extra-high heels, with shapelier bodies, straighter hair, and perfectly made-up faces. Looking at them, I feel like I made a mess playing dress-up in my mom's closet. Compared to them, I'm just a high school girl with unruly hair, way too much body, and not enough makeup.

"I don't belong here."

Carter gives me a bewildered expression. "Why not?"

I don't even know where to begin with answering that question.

REASONS I DON'T BELONG HERE

1. I don't look like the girls who come here.
2. And I don't have their confidence.
3. I've never had fun at parties.
4. If I get caught with my fake ID, I don't have what it takes to flirt my way out of prison.
5. I'm not comfortable dancing in public.
6. And I'm not comfortable standing on the wall, either.
7. I'm not comfortable talking to strangers.
8. I'm not comfortable with this many people staring at me.
9. I'm not comfortable with this many people judging me all at once, because I'm pretty sure I don't measure up.

I say, in summary, "I'm not the type of person who's comfortable doing this kind of thing."

He steps away from the wall and stands in front of me. "I don't think you should explain your discomfort by ascribing it to the type of person you are. Seems . . . limiting."

I look up, stunned by his logic.

He continues, "Because maybe one day you won't feel uncomfortable." He looks over his right shoulder at a group of high-heeled girls and loud college boys surging toward us. "If you ascribe your discomfort to who you are as a person—"

The group stampedes past, and he steps closer to me, *really* close. We're nearly chest to chest. He places one hand on the brick beside my arm. I'm swathed in the smell of his shower soap, staring up at his kissable neck. Then he looks down into my eyes. He says, "I forgot what I was saying."

My eyes roam over his lips, back to his neck and the gold chain there. "Me too." I forgot what he was saying, what I was saying, what I was feeling before this aching desire to get closer to his breath, and why I ever thought that I hated him.

The raucous group passes us by. Carter takes a step back, clearing his throat. "After you." He motions for me to proceed, looking at me like he forgot his reason for hating me too.

I hadn't realized the line had moved up. There's a huge gap between us and Olivia, who's looking over her shoulder at me with an *I told you so* smirk. I push off the wall and hurry to catch up to her, feeling Carter's eyes on my back like hot rocks. She grabs my hand and pulls my ear down to her lips. "What did I tell you?"

I smile. "That proves nothing." I look behind us, and Carter's talking to Auden, both of their eyes on us. I bite my lip, turning back around.

"Yeah, whatever," she says, unconvinced. "You're gorgeous, and he can't keep his eyes off you. Even you can't deny that."

I look over my shoulder again. He's still watching me. When he catches my eye, he smiles and turns away. I turn too, smiling giddily.

The line takes us around the corner. When we get in front of the venue, Olivia pulls Carter by the arm. "Take a pic of us for Kaide."

He takes my phone. "We don't know for sure that he's the blackmailer." Then he goes out to the edge of the sidewalk. People pass in front of us, but as soon as there's a clearing, Olivia and I press our cheeks together, making ridiculous duck faces.

After he snaps the picture, he brings back my phone, looking down at the screen. As he's handing it over, I ask, "Did it come out okay?"

Carter strokes his chin, smiling at me. "It's perfect."

I blink away, hiding my smile behind my hand. Olivia gives me a knowing look. She's such an instigator.

When I look down at the picture of me and Olivia's faces smushed together, somehow I don't look out of place beside her, or in front of the bar. I look like I'm having the time of my life.

I think, *There's no reason I can't.*

I send the picture to my blackmailer and decide that I'm not only here to appease them. I'm here because I've always wanted to experience this, so damn it, I'm taking advantage of this moment.

I'm grinning ear to ear when I look up from my phone at the concert officials, and suddenly I remember that this is the point where I have to lie. I'm twenty-two and my birthday is December . . . something. I can't even check my ID because

Olivia has it stashed somewhere.

The bass from inside thumps through my chest, pushing my anxiety up my throat. I swallow it down again and again. I'll take advantage if I don't get thrown in jail first.

"How old are you?" the official asks Olivia.

She smiles, hugging her chest against my arm. "We're both twenty-two."

"ID and ticket?"

Audacious, she cups her left boob and pulls both our IDs and paper tickets out of her bosom.

The official, a young Hispanic guy, not too much older than us, smirks at Olivia's brazenness, scans our tickets, and only glances at our IDs before handing them back to us.

He shakes his head with a laugh. "Hold out your wrist like this." He shows us his arm covered in tattoos.

She does, and he fastens a green wristband around it. Then she waits for me to get mine. When he nudges his head for us to go in, Olivia smiles and pulls me along. *Well, that was easy.* Maybe I am the type of girl who can do this.

Inside, I take a deep breath, letting the air dry my sweat. My eyes take everything in. It looks like an arcade, but with darker lights, much louder music and without all the game machines. The floor in front of the stage is overcrowded with eager teens and twentysomethings. The DJ is playing a mashup of popular hip-hop songs. People everywhere are finding their place either at the bar or at the back of the crowd.

Once Carter and Auden walk through the doors, Olivia bounces in excitement. "Drinks!" We follow her to the bar against the far wall, squeezing through bodies and bumping hips. Olivia and I find a space at the serving counter, Auden and Carter behind us.

"What do you want?" Olivia asks.

"Beer?"

She smiles. "How about shots?"

"I don't know." I widen my eyes, feeding off her excitement.

"Less liquid, more power," she says, raising her brows. "Shots'll have you dancing around here, screaming, getting naked."

"What?"

She laughs. "I'm just kidding . . . *sorta*." I laugh, too, glancing at the bartender. He's making his way over to us.

"Let's do it," I say, meeting her eye.

"Yeah?"

I nod, and she squeals. When the bartender gets to us, Olivia orders four shots of tequila. She throws a stack of tens on the counter, takes one of the shot glasses, and downs it. I look at her like she's superhuman.

"Go!" she shouts. "Auden! Come on!"

He and Carter step up to the bar, both of them grabbing shot glasses. I grab mine too. It's a clear liquid in a tiny glass. No big deal. I'm just curious to see how much "power" it has. I try doing like Olivia and throwing it back all at once, but I'm no pro. I swallow it in three gulps, leaving the alcohol in my mouth for too long. It burns, and *oh God*, it's nasty.

Olivia rubs my back as I cough. "You did it! I'm so proud of you."

I smile, feeling the liquor warm my stomach and pulsate outward. Auden's shot glass is empty, too, but Carter's still holding his. He's trying to convince Auden to take it for him. "Does Carter not take shots?" I ask in Olivia's ear.

"He's our DD. He's being responsible," she says, smiling big. "You should go offer to take it for him." She raises her eyebrows, mischievously.

I roll my eyes.

"It would be so hot," she says.

"I don't like Carter like that."

She freezes. After a few seconds of staring at me, stupefied, she bursts into laughter. "Bullshit." She pulls on my arms and pushes me toward Carter.

Then I'm standing in front of him, my mouth slightly open, my body slightly swaying. And he's looking down at me curiously, midconversation with Auden.

"If you don't want your shot, like, I'd be willing to take it off your hands."

That was definitely not hot. I think Olivia forgot who I was when she got this idea.

But, still, he laughs. "A'ight." He hands it over, checking me out. "Go for it."

I take the shot from him, attempting to woo him with my steady eye contact, because, for once tonight, I feel confident enough to hold eye contact. He watches me, amused. I lick my lips, then slowly pour the liquor into my mouth. My cheeks fill with the disgusting poison, and my eyes water. I swallow it down, then scowl at the lingering taste.

"That was so graceful," he says, laughing.

"Shut up." I turn away, smiling, laughing, blushing.

Olivia shakes her head at me. "Girl." She pulls me back to the bar. The boys hang out on the other side of her, while she whispers to me, "What is your play?"

"My play for what?"

"Getting Carter," she says, like it's obvious. She flips her braids over her shoulder and pulls up the top of her strapless dress.

"Getting him in what way?"

She rolls her eyes. "Getting him in bed, duh."

I pull my lips back in panic. "I don't—what? Are you serious?"

"Oh. Are you a virgin?"

I press my lips tight and nod.

"So start slow. How are you gonna get Carter all up on your mouth?"

I scowl. "I hardly know him."

She sighs, turning back to the bar. "I'm getting another drink. Want one?"

I shake my head. I think that second shot is kicking in. The warmth intensifies in my middle and all throughout my body.

As she's leaning over the bar, ordering another shot, my

eyes flow across the counter to Carter. He and Auden are leaning over the bar, with their arms crossed on the counter, talking animatedly. Of course, I've imagined a thousand different ways to kiss Carter, but I've probably imagined ten ways to kiss every attractive guy here.

It has nothing to do with liking Carter. The way he looks at me makes me feel awake. Feminine. Attracted. It's strictly how I'm wired—biology and chemistry, pheromones and hormones. So tragically hetero that any boy, *any* boy could make me feel like this. It's not just Carter.

But then he lifts his chin and meets my eye.

I swallow my tongue, bite my lip, and hold on to everything I am. Because everything I am is trying to rush out to get to him.

He doesn't smile. He studies me, continuing his conversation with Auden, like he's not outright staring at me.

Olivia gets her drink, shouts, "Let's go!" then shoots it back. She turns to me, her expression showing exactly how drunk she is—the same look that's probably on my face right now.

Suddenly, the house lights go out, as does the music. The crowd screams. Olivia turns to the stage and screams too. Then an upbeat hip-hop track bangs over the speakers, somehow louder than before. A skinny Black guy comes on stage, shirtless with a blue jean vest, white pants, and gold chains plunging from his neck.

That's not Vontae.

Damn it, I forgot there'd be an opener, and there's no telling how long this guy will perform. He raps/shouts into the microphone and the crowd bobs their heads along. Most of them don't know him either.

Olivia sneaks her way closer, pulling Auden with her. They stand at the back of the crowd, Olivia dancing fearlessly and Auden watching awkwardly.

I laugh out loud. Then Carter turns and looks at me, catching the latter half of my laugh. My stomach plummets as he steps closer to me. "I remember what I was saying outside."

I raise my eyebrows in response.

"If you say that you're not the type of person to feel comfortable in this situation, you're telling yourself how to feel the next time."

"I'm not telling myself how to feel. I'm inferring from how I naturally feel."

"It's not fair to infer from your first time downtown. Of course you're uncomfortable. It's a new experience." I look at him with a tilted head and pursed lips. He leans away, motioning around us. "Come back to this club two or three more times, then see how you feel."

I look around at the dark corners, the open floor filled with bodies, the stage, the flashing lights. Then I look back at him, blue and green lights shining in his eyes, dancing across his cheeks. A smile finds its way to my lips. I try pushing it down, but the alcohol makes it hard to control my muscles. So I hide my smile with my fist.

The opener ends his set, and the crowd cheers. I check my phone: nine thirty p.m. If he's on time, Vontae will probably start at ten. But there's no telling when he'll end. Eleven? Twelve?

Auden and Olivia come back, Olivia out of breath and Auden red-faced. Carter pulls Auden to his side. They're talking in hushed tones, but I catch a few words here and there. "Take her closer," and Auden's protest, "So many people."

There's a mirror behind the bar that I somehow didn't notice until now. I look at myself. My lips are parted. They still feel numb. I close my mouth and study Carter as he encourages Auden—his eyes, his lips.

But then I hear Auden say, "Look, I just need another shot."

The bartender is on the opposite end of the bar.

"You can't wait for shots. You can't wait all night, man."

Auden rolls his eyes, but he should have listened to Carter. None of us realizes how much he should have listened to Carter until the sexiest man alive walks up and says, "Livvy?"

She turns around in her tight leather dress.

The mystery guy is light skinned with heavy amber eyes and long sandy-brown locks. Oozing confidence, knowing he can have any girl he wants, he reaches for Olivia's hand. "Long time, no see."

"Yeah, there was a reason for that," Carter mumbles beside me.

"What are you doing back here? I know you love Vontae. You should be up front," the guy says.

She frowns. "How? Look at all those people."

"So?" He laughs. His laugh sounds like the laugh of an angel. "I'll get us through. Come on." And I can't believe it, but Olivia follows him to the edge of the crowd without one word. I mean, I would, too, but I expect more fight from her.

"Damn it!" Carter shouts in frustration. "That guy is Livvy's kryptonite. She's no doubt going home with him tonight."

"Who is he?" I ask.

"Her ex, Kendrick."

Auden watches Olivia disappear into the crowd with Kendrick. I can feel the waves of dread wafting off him.

Finally, the bartender makes it over to us. Carter leans forward. "Two shots of tequila."

"Make that four shots!" Auden shouts, pulling out his wallet. He throws money on the counter as the bartender pours four shots for us.

"Are you insane?" I shout.

Auden ignores me, throwing back one shot and then another. I pour one into my mouth with my eyes closed. The answer is yes. Yes, he is insane.

Taking tequila shots is easy when you're already drunk. I need to add that to my list of life lessons. Honestly, though, everything is easy when I'm drunk, except standing, walking, using the restroom, and talking coherently. I'm three beers and four shots in. I've gone to the restroom twice. I'm swerving when I'm supposed to be standing straight. Auden is talking so much, too much. Carter's trying to keep us in line, but we're too much for him.

Because then a song by Toni Braxton comes on. Carter can see in my face how much I love this song. I sing along, bobbing my head. He smiles, watching with caution. Then the hook comes on, and I can't help it: I sway my hips. Carter can tell it's a mistake before I do. It happens so quickly. My ankle twists, the wedge heel completely forsaking me, and I go down.

But Carter's there in a flash, one hand wrapped around my back, the other pulling me up by my arm. "Oh my God, Quinn."

"You're fast," I slur.

"Are you okay?" he asks, helping me to my feet.

I get lost in his eyelashes and his eyebrows and the trim of his beard. My hand comes up to trace the straight line along his jaw. I check his eyes. He looks surprised and unprepared. I giggle. "I like your haircut, by the way."

"*Wow*, you're really drunk."

He releases me and takes a step back.

"I'm not that drunk. I'm not as drunk as Auden." We both look at Auden leaning his back against the bar, bobbing his head to the music with his eyes closed.

Carter snorts a laugh. "True, but you're right behind him." He pulls my hand off the side of his face and my other hand off his chest. "Sober Quinn wouldn't be all over me like this."

I frown. "Sober Quinn's too afraid of her feelings."

He raises his brows. "What does that mean?"

"That's what the journal's all about: getting all my feelings out so I never have to talk about them." I tsk-tsk at myself. "It's a pretty nasty habit."

He's looking at me, contemplative. "Well, maybe you should stop."

"My journal's gone, so." I wobble past him, back to the bar. "Auden, do you even know this song?"

"Yes! I love this song."

I don't know this song, myself—some modern hip-hop song. Definitely not my taste.

Then it's finally time. Vontae starts his set with a haunting instrumental fit for an opera singer. The crowd goes wild. Auden's on the tips of his toes, looking for Olivia and Kendrick. Carter's leaning against the bar behind me, his attention on the stage.

It isn't until the crowd sings along that I realize how much of a minority Carter and I are here. How most of the crowd is white, and how they have no problem rapping every word, even the N-word.

I know that it's just the lyrics. I know they're not calling me the N-word, but every time I hear it chorused, I recoil.

And I can't do anything about it. I'm not supposed to be, or even *allowed* to be, offended by it.

My blood boils because I am offended by it. My skin slicks with sweat because I'm also scared.

Two girls at the back of the crowd are dancing like no one's watching. One of them has blond hair and a lime-green baseball cap. The other has brown curls with blond highlights. They look like Destany and Gia. It's probably not them, though. They wouldn't dance like that. But it's enough to hurt me all over again. I know the N-word is slipping between their lips too, just like everyone else.

Carter leans into my ear. "Are you okay?"

I almost forgot he was standing behind me. I'm grasping my own hands, rubbing my left thumb over my right. I turn around to face him. When he sees my expression, his face falls. "It's okay," he assures me.

"I'm scared," I whisper. There's no way he heard me. I think maybe he read my lips.

"Don't be scared. You're okay."

"What's going on?" Auden asks from behind us.

"Let's go sit!" Carter shouts. He starts walking toward the couches in the back of the club and grabs my hand without looking, as if his hand always knew where to find mine. He sits me on a low, firm, purple couch. This area is deserted. I guess no one's crazy enough to buy tickets to this and then not watch.

Carter sits on one side, Auden on my other. "What

happened?" Auden shouts.

Carter says over my head, "You see how those people look more like you than they look like us?"

I squeeze my eyes shut at how good it feels to hear him say *us*. It makes me feel better, like I'm not alone, which just makes me want to cry, because if only I hadn't been alone at that party last weekend, maybe things would be different now.

"Did you hear the lyrics and the fact that they were all singing along?"

Finally, Auden says, "Oh."

Carter nods. His jaw is clenched as he focuses on the stage. "This is why I didn't want to come to this. It's not just because of the trash music."

His eyes drop to mine, and then his face softens. "You're okay," he assures me. "I'll go get you some water."

"Not water. Beer. Dos Equis."

He fights a smile, but the smile wins.

"I second that," Auden slurs behind me.

"Y'all are crazy if you think I'm getting you more alcohol. I will get you water."

"Party pooper!" Auden shouts after him, then he turns to me. "You know, Quinn, I'll never understand why white people fight tooth and nail to be able to say that word. I just don't see the appeal." He's staring toward the wall across from us, the empty couches and the dim lights.

"Me either."

"I know from experience that there are places where that word is still used hatefully."

I scrunch my eyebrows. "What do you mean you know from experience?"

"My parents are from a tiny town in East Texas. The backwoods." He looks down to his hands in his lap. "When we visit, I have to sit through my family's racism." He looks back up. "It was particularly bad when Obama was president."

I flick my eyebrows up. "I bet."

"I don't think white people should say the 'friendly' version of that word, knowing that somewhere, someone is still using it as hate speech. Doesn't seem fair to Black people that every time they hear it, they have to figure out whether or not they're being insulted."

I look at Auden and nearly cry. "Wow, Auden."

"What?" He turns to me, confused.

"Thank you." I've never felt this *seen* by a white friend. I feel like buying him a gift. I feel like hugging him. Hell, I feel like running to the stage, snatching Olivia away from Kendrick, and screaming in her face how good of a guy Auden is. She'd be lucky to date him.

Carter comes back with two Dos Equis. The sight of him stirs me up even more. "Thank you, thank you, thank you!" Auden and I cheer, snatching our beers from him.

"Y'all are gonna be so messed up tomorrow," he says, watching us drink. "Remember, we're supposed to watch our second JFK movie tomorrow."

I turn to him. "Oh, yeah."

"We are *not* going back to my house," Auden says, pointing his beer at us. "Carter, it's your turn."

He suddenly looks uncomfortable. "I actually . . . I don't have anything that plays DVDs."

"Oh, right. You told me that," Auden says. "Guess we're going back to Quinn's."

"That's probably fine," I slur, guzzling more beer. The chorus of rap lyrics are starting to muddle together now. Everything is.

I'm staring at the empty couch across from us, my head filling up with something heavy, until Carter says, "You sure we can't go back to your house, Auden? I thought your mom was really sweet."

"Is something wrong with my house?" I ask, snapping my head in his direction.

His lips tighten. "I mean, your dad thinks I'm a criminal."

My jaw hinges shut. I can't argue with him, not after he just comforted me. I can't deny him his feelings. "You're welcome at my house," I say, looking away. "My parents fought about it all day after you left. I know my dad's ashamed for how he reacted."

"I don't know that. Fear is dangerous. Fear kills Black men."

"You think my dad would kill you?" I ask, meeting his gaze.

"If your dad had a gun on him that day, I think I might be dead right now."

It hurts that he would fear for his life at my house. That a boy with skin as dark as mine doesn't feel safe around my father. "Honestly, I doubt my dad will be home tomorrow. He rarely is on Saturdays."

Carter looks at me, skeptical.

"And I'll keep you safe. I promise."

He smiles, his eyes twinkling, then he laughs. "You'll keep me safe?"

I nod. "I'll be like your bodyguard. If you need to go to the bathroom, I'll stand outside the door and escort you everywhere."

He laughs, throwing his head back. Then he meets my gaze. I sink into the dimples in his cheeks. "All right. Deal."

He holds his hand out, reminding me of the first time we made a deal in Mr. Green's class, just yesterday. I thought he was the bad guy, but now, I think I believe him. He couldn't possibly be my blackmailer. He has too many soft spots . . .

Like the center of his palm.

I put my hand in his, and he shakes it once. He's smiling, and I'm thinking back to what Olivia said about finding a way to get him "all up on my mouth." Then I'm leaning in. And I think he might be leaning away from me. I can't be sure, because then Auden's head slams into my lap, his empty beer bottle clattering to the floor, rolling under the couch.

Carter jumps back, and so do I.

"We need to go," Carter says, staring at Auden's head in my lap.

"But what about Olivia?"

"She texted a while ago. She's going home with Kendrick." Carter stands, looking down at me. "Do you think you can stay here and not get stolen?"

I look at him through wide open eyes.

"I need to pull Olivia's car up. Just watch Auden. Don't let him throw up on you."

My face is even more horrified.

"You'll be okay. I'll be right back, I swear." Then he disappears.

I look at Auden's red cheeks and open mouth. He groans and squeezes his eyes. I grab his sweaty hand. "It's okay. We're almost outta here."

"Quinn, why did Olivia leave me for that other guy?" he slurs, opening his eyes and turning to me.

"She has history with that other guy. Sometimes that's all it takes."

"Do you think it's because I'm white? Maybe she doesn't like white guys."

"She's half white."

"That doesn't mean she likes white guys."

"She likes you, Auden."

"How can you tell?"

"Before Kendrick walked up, she was all over you."

He wags his head. "She totally was." He lays his head back and closes his eyes again. I hold his hand until Carter comes back.

"Car's outside," he says, his voice breathy. He grabs my hand and pulls me up from the couch.

"What about Auden?"

"I'll come back for him. He's not going anywhere."

When we get outside, the night air slaps me in the face. Chills break out all over my exposed skin. "Carter, I don't feel good." I close my eyes.

He grabs my waist and pulls me along. "I know. We're gonna get you some water."

"I don't want water. I just wanna lie down."

"You can lie down in a minute. Let's get to the car first."

"I don't know if I can make it."

"It's right here, Quinn."

"But my feet hurt."

He sighs.

"I hate these boots. How do girls do this in stilettos?" I lean my head against his arm.

"I don't know," he mumbles, trying to keep my body upright.

"Do you think I look slutty in this dress?"

He looks down at me with a flicker of amusement. "No."

"Do you think I look sexy?"

We get to the car, and he opens the passenger door, not answering me.

"Carter," I whine, dragging the last syllable out. Then I stop him in the middle of the sidewalk and look into his eyes with a pout.

"What, Quinn?"

I slip my arms around his neck, standing on the tips of my toes to get really close to his mouth. "Do you think I'm sexy?"

Carter looks down at me. He holds my hips with the tips of his fingers, like he's not comfortable being this close to me, but doesn't want to push me away. "Quinn, you've always been beautiful. You know that."

I bite my bottom lip and tilt my head. Has he always thought that? Is Olivia right about his crush? Just as I'm about to ask, the world starts spinning. My head feels like it's made of air. My eyes squeeze shut, and I can feel bile rushing up my esophagus.

Carter must know what's happening because he jumps out of the way right in time. Vomit splashes on the cement, splashing on the boots Olivia lent me.

"I'm sorry, Olivia's mom," I whimper.

Carter pulls my hair back, but I'm empty. I think he gets me in the car, but I don't remember sitting or putting on my seat belt or riding. The darkness feels good, so I let it swallow me whole.

REASONS I BELONG EXACTLY WHERE I AM

1. I think I wouldn't be here if a part of me didn't want to be here. Wherever "here" may be.
2. And if being "here" is a mistake, I think I'll probably learn something from it—something that I need to learn.
3. There are enough closed doors and glass ceilings in the world. My comfort zone shouldn't be one of them.

chapter 16

THE WORST THINGS ABOUT
BEING HUMAN

BEFORE I'M ALLOWED TO OPEN MY EYES, I HAVE TO FEEL.
Everything. My head is pounding, throat dry, stomach
churning. I don't know if I *can* open my eyes.

Last night pours back to me, each fracture of time more
horrifying than the last: me falling in the middle of a nightclub, me all over Carter, him prying me off, me almost
throwing up on him. Was that all real?

When I finally open my eyes, I jump out of my skin. A
little girl with pigtail braids kneels beside the bed, staring me
dead in the mouth. "You're pretty," she says.

It's the *last* thing I'm expecting to see, so a screech, short
and quick, jumps right out of me. I slam my hand over my
mouth, and she lurches back.

The door swings open. Light floods in from the hallway.
"Imani," Carter calls. The little girl stands at attention, her
hands behind her back. "I told you not to come in here."

"I just wanted to see—"

He opens the door wider. "Go eat."

She frowns, running out of the bedroom.

I'm speechless under his comforter, in his twin-size bed, and I don't remember how I got here. He looks at me, drying his hands on a towel. He's shirtless with black basketball shorts. Back to his usual. "That goes for you too. Come eat." The door swings shut behind him.

When I sit up, I look down. I'm still wearing my dress from last night. My hand flies up to my matted hair. Damn it, I didn't wrap it last night. I can't even imagine how my face looks.

I swing my legs over the side of the bed and stand up too fast. My head spins, and my stomach convulses. I hold on to the mattress until everything settles. Everything except my stomach.

When I get to the door, I squint against the light pouring down the hallway, listening to silverware clink against the murmurs of a children's TV show. Then I shuffle into the kitchen to find Carter stirring a pot of oatmeal on an old-fashioned gas stove.

"Get a bowl," he says, nudging his head to an open cabinet of blue plastic dishware.

"I can't even think about eating," I croak.

"It'll make you feel better."

I look around, wearily. "Are your, uh, parents home?"

He doesn't look away from the pot. "Nah."

"What time is it?"

"It's like eight, I think." Carter pulls his phone out of his pocket. "Eight thirty."

"I need to get my stuff from Olivia's. Where is she?"

Carter puts the spoon down and turns to face me. "I already got it." He points to the living room.

I shuffle through the doorway. My backpack's on the floor in front of a ratty brown couch, my phone sitting on top, but I pause when I spot Auden passed out across the cushions with a trash can by his head. Carter's little sister is sitting in front of a tiny box TV in the corner, watching an unrecognizable Nickelodeon cartoon with a bowl of oatmeal, as if this is all so normal.

When I get back to the kitchen with my stuff, somehow my stomach feels worse. I hold myself against the doorway, closing my eyes.

"You okay?"

"I need to go. My parents—" I swallow hard.

"We still doing the movie at your house?"

My eyes pop open, then I groan. "I forgot about that."

"I told you and Auden. Y'all went so hard."

"Way too hard."

Carter shrugs. "If you want, I can drive."

"Drive? As in, *you* drive *my* car? No way. Are you kidding?" I laugh a little, shaking my head too fast.

He can see it on my face. "Trash can's right there!"

I hurl, holding on to the sides of the can with my eyes

squeezed shut. Vomiting is on my *Worst Things about Being Human* list, and now I need to add being hungover. Everything burns, my nostrils, my throat, my eyes, as I spit into the trash can.

"Like I was saying"—Carter laughs—"you want me to drive?"

I look over my shaky shoulder. "Yes, please."

Carter shows me to the bathroom, where I change out of my dress, attempt to tie up my hair, and brush my teeth. Mascara crumbles in the base of my eyes. I look awful. I feel worse.

When I emerge, Carter is shuffling through his dresser. "Give me a sec. I gotta find a shirt."

I look at the muscles in his back, the definition of his spine like a ditch I want to dive into, and think to myself, *No you don't.*

"Can you get Auden up?" he asks, looking over his shoulder, catching me staring at him.

Eyes wide, I spin on my heel. "Yep."

Imani is still occupied by the TV when I sit on the couch by Auden's feet. I tap his ankle, calling his name. He doesn't move. I squeeze his ankles and shake him. Still nothing.

Then I get distracted by the pictures of Carter on the end tables. God, those eyes. I stare at a picture of him as a preteen, holding his baby sister. She was looking up at him in wonder, but he was looking at the camera, midlaugh.

During a commercial break, Imani comes up to me with

eager eyes, resting her hands on my knees. She's got lashes as long as her brother's. "What's your name?"

"Quinn," I say.

"You're Carter's girlfriend?"

I shake my head with a smile.

"But Carter only lets his girlfriends sleep in his room."

"Imani, what are you telling her?" Carter walks in, black T-shirt in hand. I try not to watch him put it on.

"Oh." She's surprised that he was listening. "I was telling her how only girlfriends sleep in your room. Like, Livvy never does."

"How many girlfriends?" I ask.

Imani grins. "A lot, like seven hundred. But you're the prettiest."

I wonder if she tells all the girls that.

"Imani," Carter says, widening his eyes. "That was supposed to be between us."

She turns to him with puppy dog eyes. "No, 'cause you said to not tell Mommy when girls sleep over, and I'm not telling Mommy. I'm telling . . ." She looks at me with a twisted mouth. "What's your name again?"

"Quinn."

She turns to Carter. "Queen."

I open my mouth to correct her but decide that her mistake was definitely an upgrade. *Queen Jackson.*

Carter looks at my complacency and snorts. Then he nods at Imani. "You're right. I did say that. But how about we not talk about it to *anyone*? Okay?"

She shrugs, suddenly uninterested in the conversation when her show comes back on.

"Good move, Carter. Make your little sister keep your seven hundred girlfriends a secret," I say, standing up with my backpack. "Good to know I was sleeping in a pool of who knows what."

"Show some gratitude. I could have made you sleep on the couch." He grabs his keys off the table by the door, dropping them in his pocket. "Speaking of, I thought you were gonna get Auden up." He goes over to the couch and rips the blanket off Auden's body, shakes his shoulder and slaps his face, a notch above gentle. Auden opens his eyes and sits up.

Carter must be really good at spotting the *I'm about to vomit* face, because he shoves the trash can into Auden's hands, and Auden immediately spills his guts into it.

"Gross," I say, turning away.

Carter scoffs. "You're one to talk." He takes the trash can once Auden finishes, and somehow, he's not squeamish. I, on the other hand, feel like I'm going to vomit again.

While Carter gathers the trash in the kitchen, Auden sits on the edge of the couch, holding his head in his hands. "Can I stay here all day?"

"We gotta go do the movie at Quinn's," Carter calls from the kitchen.

"It'll be okay," I say. "We'll watch it in my den. I have a really soft couch and a popcorn maker." I'm standing at the door—as far away from the vomit as possible.

Carter comes out of the kitchen with a big black garbage bag in his hand. I grimace, trying to hold my breath. I don't care if half of that is my vomit. I can't stand the smell.

"Imani, let's go. You're going to Momma Sandy's."

She gasps, jumping up with her fists by her side. "No, please! I want to come with you."

"We're gonna be doing homework the whole time." She frowns as he puts his shoes on. "Might as well stay here."

Imani grumbles, turning the television off, and follows her brother to the door. He helps her put on a pair of light-up sneakers, and I try to control my attraction to him. Why is that so freaking adorable? Then he kneels and lets her ride his back.

I follow them out of the apartment, squinting against the morning sun, Auden shuffling behind me. When we get to the bottom of the cement stairs, Carter tells us to wait, then he takes off running with Imani squealing/laughing/bouncing on his back. I smile. I can't help it.

He chucks the trash in the dumpster on the other side of the parking lot, then comes running back to us. By the end of it, he's breathing hard, and so is Imani, laying her head against his shoulder.

"Do it again," she says.

He smiles. "In a minute."

Then we're walking down the sidewalk toward Olivia's apartment complex, traffic zooming past. I look at the point of Carter's elbow as he holds on to Imani's legs. I'm reminded of how close I got to kissing him last night, how much I still really want to. I must still be drunk.

When we get to Olivia's apartment, we head toward the stairs, but Auden hangs back. "Hey, can I wait in the car?"

"Livvy's not here, man," Carter says.

"Still." He drops his head. "I just really want to lie down."

I pull my keys out of my pocket and unlock the doors to my Mercedes, sitting safe in the back of the parking lot. "Don't throw up in my back seat." Auden heads to my car, and I follow Carter up the stairs. "He's avoiding Olivia?" I ask.

"Wouldn't you? Kendrick practically pried her from Auden's arms." He knocks on the door, Imani resting her head on his shoulder.

Olivia's mom opens the door. "Hey, Carter." She grins with a sleepy smile. "Imani." Then she looks at me. "And I forgot your name, baby."

"Quinn."

"Quinn," she repeats, her voice breathy.

"Good morning, Momma. Do you mind watching Imani for a little while? We have to work on a school project."

Olivia's mom looks at me then at Carter with a tilt of her head. "A school project, huh?"

"Yes, ma'am."

"Boy, you ain't gotta lie to me. Come on, Imani."

"I swear I ain't lying. We have a project for history."

"Whatever," she says. "I wasn't born yesterday."

I look at Carter, and he shakes his head with a roll of his

eyes. He swings Imani off his back and onto her feet. She pouts, looking up at him.

"I'll be right back," he says, rubbing her head.

She twists her mouth to the side and stomps inside the apartment, her shoes lighting up all the way.

"Thanks, Momma."

Olivia's mom nods and waves us away.

"I like her," I say, following Carter down the stairs to the parking lot.

"Momma Sandy? Yeah, she's great."

"No, I meant Imani."

He turns to me with a bright smile. "Oh, yeah. Me too."

When we get in my car, Auden's curled up in the back seat with his eyes closed. Carter starts the engine, grinning ear to ear, sliding his hands over the steering wheel.

"Be super careful, okay?"

"I've seen how you drive this thing. I'll do a hell of a lot better. I promise."

I roll my eyes closed and lay my head back.

As Carter drives, with my eyes closed and my head pounding, I relive last night, and how Carter looked at me. He couldn't keep his eyes off me, like Olivia said. I relive how he closed me in against the brick wall when that crowd passed us by. How he forgot what he was saying. How we both forgot.

"Do you remember last night at all?" Carter asks, reading my thoughts.

"I don't remember anything after I threw up."

"You were so dead. It took me twenty minutes to get you up the stairs to my apartment."

My eyes pop open. "Wait. What was I doing?"

He glances at me with a smile. "You were wild. You kept begging me to sleep with you."

My jaw drops. "Noooo." Oh, the horror.

He laughs, throwing his head back. "I'm just kidding, Jackson."

"Don't do that." I frown, pointing my finger at him. "That's not funny." Because that seriously sounds like something I would have done.

"You were wild last night, though. You were all over me, talking 'bout, 'Do you think I'm sexy, Carter?' Trying to kiss me and—"

"Yeah, let's not talk about it."

He falls silent, but I can hear the smirk cracking across his lips. "I had no idea you wanted me like that."

"Hush." I scowl at him. "I was drunk."

He tilts his head with an infuriating little grin.

"All that matters is that I kept the blackmailer at bay." I pull out my phone and check to make sure that I don't have any messages. Nope, nothing.

"No, what matters is if you had fun." He looks at me, eyebrows raised.

I nod, turning back to the windshield. "I did have fun." Then I close my eyes and lay my head back. "But you know what the worst part of this hangover is?"

"What?"

I turn to look at him. "I'm craving fried chicken."

"Yes! Can we stop at Popeyes?" Auden asks, sitting up. I look back, surprised. I could have sworn he was asleep.

Carter laughs. "I'm pretty sure there ain't a Popeyes anywhere near Quinn's house."

"There's not. But how about Jason's Deli? I could go for some soup."

Auden groans, lying back down. "I guess."

THE WORST THINGS ABOUT BEING HUMAN

1. Having to watch each other die.
2. Diarrhea.
3. Constipation.
4. Vomiting.
5. Psyches built for prejudice.
6. We don't come with a switchboard for our emotions.
7. We are at the mercy of our DNA and our heritage.
8. Hangovers.
9. We can't choose who we fall for.

When we get to my house, my dad's car is in the driveway. I reassure Carter that I'll protect him, but he doesn't laugh. He looks nervous.

We get out of the car and walk to the door—me, then Auden, then Carter. I step out of my sneakers. The boys do the same. Then, quietly, we walk through the foyer in our socks. I glance into the living room and turn into the kitchen. "All clear," I say.

I lead them upstairs to the den and get them settled on the couch. "Water?" I ask.

"Yes, please," Auden says. Carter nods.

As I'm going back downstairs, I spot Dad in the kitchen, tucking his polo shirt into his khaki slacks. My already upset stomach sinks in on itself.

He hears me and turns. "Oh, good, you're here. You and I are going to see Hattie today."

I stare at him, speechless. He doesn't say it like it's a choice. He doesn't say it with an ounce of patience.

"No, I need to work on my project today."

"Quinn." He stops in front of me, furious. "How can you just sit here while your grandmother is unwell?"

"I can't see her like that." My eyes well up. I'm not ready to talk about this right now. I need a few more hours of sleep. I need food. I need time.

"You're going to regret every second you don't spend with her." He grabs my wrist. "I'm not going to let you do that to yourself, or to her. Come on."

He turns me around.

"Dad."

He pulls me toward the foyer.

"Dad."

I refuse to go to that awful nursing home to see the Hattie

who can't walk without help, the Hattie who probably doesn't even remember my name, much less my face—the impostor.

"Dad, stop! I can't go!" I'm spitting tears out of my mouth, pulling back. If he gets me in the car, I swear I'll jump out the first chance I get.

"Desmond, you can't make her go if she's not ready!" my mom shouts from the top of the stairs.

He stops pulling me, but he doesn't let go of my arm. "That's your problem, Quinn." He turns on me, his eyes watery, but not wet enough to put out the fire. "You sit here, waiting until you're ready. You will never be ready for anything! You can't pick a place to live. You can't pick a major. You can't get off your ass and go see your dying grandmother. She's dying, Quinn! And you sit here like she'll live forever."

He throws my wrist away. "Don't come crying to me when she's gone and you didn't get to see her."

He rushes into the foyer, and my mom rushes after him.

I shake like an earthquake, staring into the empty living room until it blurs into an array of muddled colors.

Carter catches me in the kitchen before I double over. I don't know when he came downstairs, or how much of that he heard, but I fall into him, grateful that he's here.

My breath rushes from between my lips. I'm gasping against his black shirt. I'm not crying. I'm *ugly* crying. I've never ugly cried in front of anyone. I doubt he'll be able to see me as "beautiful" after this.

Mom catches Dad at the front door. "I swear, Desmond, I

don't care what it's about. You cannot talk to her like that!"

"She will regret this for the rest of her life. And for what? Because she's scared to see Hattie change?"

Mom says, "Hattie has always been strong. Quinn doesn't know how to wrap her head around her being anything else."

"That's no excuse. I can't just stand by and let her throw away time!" His voice cracks on *time*. Then the front door slams shut.

All is silent, except for my gasps and hiccups. Carter pulls my face away from his shirt. He wipes my cheeks. I can barely see through my tears, but I can make out the pinch of his brow and the rounding of his eyes.

My mom comes up behind us. Carter meets her gaze and takes a few steps back, so she can replace him in front of me. "Carter," she says, not breaking eye contact with me, "go on up to the den. Quinn will be there in a minute."

I watch Carter over her shoulder, wiping my eyes, clearing my vision. He's walking backward, but he's looking at me like he doesn't want to leave. I don't want him to leave either. I look at my mom. She wants to talk about what just happened, but I just want to go upstairs, eat my cheddar-broccoli soup, and watch a boring movie with my friends.

"Mom, I'm okay," I say, meeting her gaze. I wipe my hands over my face.

"Quinn." She furrows her brow. "Your father was totally out of line—"

"Can we talk later? Right now, I just want to . . ." I point to the stairs behind her. "We have a project to do."

She contemplates, searching my eyes, then nods. "Okay, sweetie. We'll talk later."

I walk past and follow Carter up the stairs.

The air is tense, but the farther we get upstairs, the more my shoulders relax, and the less I feel like I need to apologize for what he just witnessed.

I guess there's no perfect place for us to watch this movie. Carter's house doesn't have much in it, no parents (that I ever saw), not even a DVD player to play the movie. Auden's house has a mother who can't leave us alone long enough to get through the movie. My house has parents who fight and a daughter who breaks down, so much so that we can't even start the movie.

But we all know that none of our homes are perfect. And there's an understanding between us. I can see it in the way Auden lies on my couch, right in the bend of the L, putting his feet in the cushions like he's been here before. I can see it in the way Carter sets our food on the table and hands out our orders, like none of what just happened is new or surprising or *weird*. Which is shocking, especially after he just saw me at my absolute ugliest. I can't believe he didn't run away screaming after seeing me like that.

"You ready, Jackson?" he asks, looking up at me.

Dear God, his shirt is probably still damp.

"I'm gonna go get cleaned up." I tear down the hall to my bathroom, change into my most comfortable pajamas, wash my face, then moisturize my hair and tie it up.

I look better. Not great, but better.

When I get back to the den, they're both nearly done with their food. I sit against the arm of the couch, putting my feet up on the cushion, and start the movie.

It's boring, as expected, and after the night we had last night, and the sheer amount of Jason's Deli we scarf down, all three of us fall asleep not even thirty minutes in.

When I wake up, the movie is over. I don't think any of us got a full page of notes. The DVD is sitting on the menu screen, haunting presidential music loudly drowning out Auden's snores.

I lift my head. Auden's stretched out on the other half of the couch, head back, mouth wide open. Carter's sitting next to me with his head laid back, tilted in my direction, eyes closed.

My legs are curled up in his lap. I drop my head back on the couch cushion and stare at the television screen, reveling in his warmth and being this close to him.

Then I get greedy. I flip over onto my other hip to face him, my knees curling into his abdomen. One of his hands lands on my thigh, the other on my shin, but his eyes are still closed. I stare at the shape of his thick lips, the bridge of his wide nose, the spot where his dimples would be.

Then his eyes open. They hold my gaze, calmly, word-lessly. There's a knowing admission within our stare. His hands grow heavy on my skin. And I grow hot. Sweaty. These pajama pants are thick, and his body heat is blazing.

I'm thinking of all the ways to kiss him again, but before I can talk myself into it, he says in a deep, groggy (sexy) voice,

"You snore in your sleep."

My face draws up. "I think you're mistaking me for Auden."

"I know what I heard." He smiles, squeezing my calf.

My cheeks catch fire. I swing my legs out of his lap, sitting up. "I don't snore."

"How would you know?"

I stretch my arms above my head, yawning. When I turn to him, he's looking over my body, shamelessly.

"I just know." I stand up, pulling my shirt down. Then I look over my shoulder, as I make my way around the couch. He's still watching me.

When I head down the stairs, I hear him following behind.

chapter 17

THINGS I WOULD'VE NEVER DONE
IF I STILL HAD MY JOURNAL

THE PATIO DOOR CLOSES BEHIND HIM. "WANNA TALK about earlier?"

I assume he's referring to my parents fighting and my ugly crying and Hattie. "No."

He glances at the patio furniture behind me, then back into my eyes. He's squinting, even though the sun isn't so bright anymore. Clouds soak up the light, casting a gray ambience over everything. It looks like rain.

"But thank you for comforting me. You didn't have to do that."

I feel small looking up at him. Him, with his hands casually in the pockets of his shorts. He looks down at the cement between us.

When I go to Hattie's porch swing, he follows, sitting close beside me. "You know, even though she's different now, she's still your grandma. Don't punish her for being sick."

"I'm not punishing her." I turn, knocking his elbow with mine.

"But you can't accept that she's different now," he says calmly.

I search his eyes and steal a little of his calm. Then I face the yard, the cloudy sky, the green grass, the sidewalk leading to our in-ground pool. After a while I say, "It's just hard watching a person you love deteriorate before your eyes." He turns to me, eyes somber. I pat the seat of the swing. "You know, this is hers."

"Oh." Alarmed, he stands up. "Should I—"

"No, you can sit." I grab his hand without thinking, then immediately let go, returning my hands back to my lap. "This is where she would tell me all her stories."

Warily, he sits down again. "Tell me one."

"Okay." I smile, excited, turning toward him. "When Hattie was a kid, she had to walk to school. And it was, like, *miles*. I don't know how many, but it was a lot. One of the neighbor boys would try to fight Hattie and her brother when they were walking to school."

"Why?" Carter asks, baffled.

"I have no idea! People fought back then because they were bored."

Carter laughs. "Why wasn't that boy in school?"

He searches my eyes, then my smile fades. His question makes me realize how much I don't remember this story. Why *wasn't* he in school? Maybe there was a deeper reason for why he fought them. I can't remember if he was Black or white. Maybe he was a racist neighbor who wanted to stop Black kids from going to school . . .

"I don't remember. I never wrote it down."

"It's okay," he says. But it's not okay, because Hattie probably doesn't remember either, so that memory is lost forever.

"Hey, look at me," Carter says, cutting through my rampant thoughts. My eyes focus on him. "What do you remember?" he asks.

"Umm." I look away, swallowing. "I just remember that he'd chase them every day. He never caught Hattie, but he'd always catch Sonny, her baby brother." I look at Carter's face. "So Hattie would trick the bully, run circles around him and make him chase her, so Sonny could get away."

Carter smiles. "That's some cartoon shit."

"It is." I laugh, resting my back against the swing, setting both my feet on the ground. I think of all the stories about how fast Hattie was. I wish I could have seen her run. But I can imagine it, her back straight, her muscular legs pounding into the dirt. She was so strong. She's always been so strong.

We swing, looking out at the yard, not talking. It feels good to just sit outside again. To sit still like a tree and let the wind filter through my leaves.

Then all at once, the sky drains, rain falling in sheets over my house. I stop swinging and take a deep breath, letting the smell breeze through my nostrils. "God, I love when it rains."

I climb out of the swing, step to the edge of the patio, and allow the droplets to pour over my hand. It's cooling and calming. I look over my shoulder. Carter's watching me from the swing, just as content. He smiles when he meets my eye, unsuspecting. I smile, too, then I rush over and flick rainwater in his face.

His smile turns to disbelief. "That's how you wanna play?" He stands up.

I laugh, backing away from him. "Don't. These pajamas are silk. You cannot get these wet."

He shrugs, heading to the edge of the awning. "You should have thought about that." He puts his hand in the rain, and I take off running to the other side of the patio, but he's faster than me. He grabs my waist. "Now I have to throw you in the rain," he says, pulling me back.

I squeal, laughing. "No, don't!" I squirm out of his arms and turn to face him with crazy eyes. I push on his chest with all my might, attempting to push him into the rain. He doesn't budge. He just laughs at my puny attempt.

But then I press my hands into his abs and dig into the ground with my bare toes, using all my strength to drive him back. He moves a couple of feet with a devious smile on his lips. Then he grabs my forearms. "If I go in the rain, you're coming with me."

"Good luck with that." I continue to push him until his back hits a pillar at the edge of the patio. Rain splashes in the grass inches from our toes, some of it misting onto the cement, some of it spraying onto our feet.

When I look up into his eyes, a playful smile still bright on my lips, I notice that his is gone. He looks like he's deep in thought. His back is flat against the pillar, but my legs are still lunged, my hands flat against his abs. Without a word, he pulls me up by my arms, my toes landing on the toes of his black socks, our chests and our breaths inches apart.

My smile fades, too, my eyes falling to the chain around his neck, over the hair on his chin, up to his lips. "Please, don't throw me in the rain," I say quietly, nervously, breathlessly.

His fingers crawl around my lower back. "I'm not." He says it the same way.

The rain fades into distant white noise as he cranes his neck down. I crane my neck up, anticipating his breath and the warmth of his lips.

Then the patio door opens behind us.

I gasp, spinning out of Carter's arms.

"Carter!" Out runs Imani, unfazed by what she interrupted, jumping into his arms.

And right behind her steps Olivia, smirking at me.

"Livvy taught me how to make necklaces," Imani squeals, hanging from around his neck.

I walk over to Olivia, who can't *wait* to say *I told you so.*

"If only I knew I was interrupting a make-out fest, I would have waited a few minutes."

"Hush. Nothing happened." I lead her back inside. Carter and Imani follow slowly.

"Nothing happened *yet*," she whispers in my ear. Then she stops me at the bottom of the stairs, facing me with apprehension. "Is Auden here?"

"Oh." I glance at Carter approaching. "Um, yeah, he's upstairs."

"Really?" Her eyes get wide and nervous.

"You should give him space, Livvy."

She looks at Carter pointedly. "I really need to explain about Kendrick. It was a huge mistake leaving with him last night."

"Of course it was," Carter says unapologetically.

Then Imani cuts in. "Hey, Queen! Is this your house?" I smile, loving her new name for me. Then I nod. She wiggles out of Carter's arms and runs straight to me. "Can I see your room?" She grabs my hand with her tiny, soft palm. Then I'm leading her, Olivia, and Carter up the stairs.

Auden looks over the sofa as we cross the landing. "Thanks for abandoning me," he says. "You could have woke—" He pauses when he sees Olivia behind me.

"Hey, Audee," she says sheepishly. "Can we talk?"

The air is extra tense.

"So, my room is this way," I say, leading Imani and Carter down the dark hallway, leaving Olivia and Auden alone in their awkward tension.

When I turn on the light, Imani lets go of my hand. I stand in the doorway, looking around my room like it's my first time seeing it too.

Empty pink walls, dresser top full of beauty products,

desktop full of scattered papers and coconut oil and records for my record player.

Imani squeals, running and jumping on my bed, looking at the pink-and-yellow flower print on my comforter. "This is a big bed," she says. "It's as big as Mommy's bed. Right, Carter?"

"It sure is." His voice is right by my ear, making me shiver. He makes his way past me and sits on the edge of my mattress, looking around.

"I didn't get to choose my wall paint. It's been pink ever since I was born."

Carter leans forward, resting his arms on his thighs. I stare at the image of him on my bed, committing it to memory. "What color would you paint it? Baby blue?"

My breath catches, surprised. "Yeah, actually. How'd you know?"

"It's obvious." He shrugs with a smirk. "And I'm observant."

I smirk. That reply is familiar.

"Your nails always match your phone case," he clarifies.

"I like blue too!" Imani shouts, jumping off my bed and running over to my desk.

He joins her, and they start flipping through my records. I sit on my bed, watching his reactions to my Mary J. Blige album and my Lauryn Hill album. "You know, it's kinda crazy. I thought you'd have lists all over your walls." He turns, leaning against the desk as Imani finds my box of nail polish.

"Lists belong in my journal."

He nods. "Because why post your feelings all over the wall? You have no intentions of ever sharing them with anyone. Right?"

"You make it sound unhealthy or something." I pick at a thread on my pajamas.

"You yourself said it was a nasty habit."

I smirk, looking up.

He's walking toward me, hands in his pockets. "So, what have you been doing now that you don't have your journal?"

I chuckle, ripping off the thread and rolling it between my pointer finger and thumb. "I've been bursting."

"Bursting?" he asks, stopping in front of me.

"Saying and doing *way* too much."

His eyes look like they remember we almost kissed a few minutes ago. I drop my gaze, because I don't have the courage that I had back there, when it was raining and it felt like we were on our own little island.

Imani runs over to me with my baby blue nail polish. "Can you paint my nails this color?"

"Maybe next time, Imani," Carter says.

She turns to him, pouting.

"Most definitely next time," I assure her.

She smiles and runs to put my polish back.

"Go find Livvy. Tell her we're leaving."

She jumps to it, running out my door, calling, "Livvy!"

Then it's just us. He says, "For the record, I think all that you've said and done has been perfect," and walks past me to the doorway. "Wouldn't hurt if you said and did a little more."

"In regard to what?" I ask, tilting my head.

"In regard to your feelings." He crosses the threshold, shooting me one last breathtaking glance before disappearing down the hall.

THINGS I WOULD'VE NEVER DONE IF I STILL HAD MY JOURNAL

1. Talk to Olivia Thomas and become friends with her.
2. Go to Houston and face my judgments about my own race.
3. Talk to Carter Bennett about my dad and stereotypes and Oreos.
4. Talk to Carter Bennett about my lists and my feelings.
5. Go downtown and see a completely different side to straitlaced Auden Reynolds.
6. Get wasted in a nightclub and wake up in Carter Bennett's bed.
7. Nearly kiss Carter Bennett again and again.

chapter 18

REASONS I DON'T SLEEP
THAT NIGHT

THE BLACKMAILER FINALLY TEXTS ME THAT NIGHT: **You have until midnight tomorrow to do something else.**

I text Carter a screenshot.

Carter asks, **So . . . what's it gonna be? Hattie? Columbia? Destany?** Then in a separate text: **Matt?** Like he had to force himself to mention that item as a possibility.

But, in all actuality, I had almost forgotten about that item—*Admit my love for Matthew Radd.* Suddenly, *love* seems like too strong a word.

I don't want to do any of that.

When are you gonna tell me what happened with you and Destany?

He acts as if I promised that I would, like he's entitled to that information. But after he comforted me last night at the Vontae show, maybe it wouldn't be so bad telling him.

Tomorrow? You guys are coming over to watch our last movie, right?

Yeah. Or, I could call you, and you could tell me right now.

My pulse quickens. Call? As in talk with our voices? With pauses and awkward silences and breathing and *voices*? My skin crawls with anticipation. I turn over on my mattress, onto my stomach. **Okay.**

He calls, and I stare at his name displayed on my screen. *Carter Bennett.*

I answer. "Hey."

"Hey." He adds a couple of *y*'s to his. "Are you in bed?"

"Yeah. Are you?"

"Yeah," he says.

I imagine it: his head where my head lay last night, his body under that blue comforter, wearing only boxer-briefs. Well, I guess . . . I don't really know what he'd wear to bed.

Then, reading my mind, he asks, "What are you wearing?"

A surprised smile pops up on my lips. "Carter, that is so inappropriate."

"What?" He laughs. "Like you weren't thinkin' it."

I totally was.

"Don't play with me," he says.

"Why do you want to know? What are *you* wearing?"

"Nothing," he says.

I open my mouth, but nothing comes out. Nothing, like what he's wearing.

He laughs. "I'm kidding, Jackson."

I choke out a nervous laugh.

"Nah, I'm wearing underwear and socks. Honestly, I don't know how people wear entire outfits to bed. That's too much fabric for me."

"I agree."

Complete silence. I wonder how his face looks right now.

"You agree? So, what does that mean? What are you wearing, Jackson?"

"The same thing you are, minus the socks."

"Whoaaa," he howls. "Shit."

I bite my bottom lip. "But anyway! That's not what this is about."

"It wasn't at first, but now it is. When you say the same thing, does that include something on top?"

"Carter!"

"What? That's crucial information."

"Do you want to hear about Destany or not?"

"I honestly don't know if I can concentrate on that now."

I cover my smile as if he can see it. "Then I'm hanging up."

"Wait, no!" He takes a deep, calming breath. "Okay, okay. I'll be good."

I laugh. "Are you sure?"

"Yes. Go ahead with the story." When I don't say anything, he adds, "Please," his low voice tickling my spine.

"Okay." I take a deep breath, too. "You know that party at Chase's house last weekend?"

"I heard about it, yeah."

"I was there with Destany and Gia. We were outside, and Gia was venting to a whole group of people about a Black lady who had accused her of stealing at the Gap, which she *had* been." I roll my eyes. "But while she was venting, she kept calling the Black lady the N-word." I whisper it, feeling ashamed all over again. "And I just sat there and let her say it."

He doesn't speak. I thought he might rail on me about being a coward, but no.

"When Gia realized that I was standing there"—my voice gets cloudy—"she was like, 'Oh my God, Quinn is right here.' Then everyone looked at me."

"That's awful."

"That's not the worst part. After they realized I was there, Destany, my *best friend*, said to them, 'Don't worry about Quinn. She's practically white anyway.'"

I close my eyes, listening to him breathe. It still stings, reliving that moment, because just when I thought Destany would stand up for me, she dismissed me and my feelings. I wasn't allowed to be offended. She assumed I wasn't.

"I think I walked away without explaining because I was ashamed of myself. I mean, that wasn't the first time they'd said racist shit, but that was the first time I realized they could be talking about *me*. You know what I mean?"

"I know exactly what you mean." He takes his time choosing his words. "I believe there comes a time when you have to learn what it means to have our skin. It's like an awakening."

"When did you have your awakening?" I ask.

"Remember when I was telling you about when I used to go to public school?"

I nod as if he can see it.

"About how my white friends would think of me as an exception to their stereotypes?"

"Yeah."

"I was about nine or ten, and my best friend, Derrick, was throwing a pool party."

"Uh-oh."

"Yep." He laughs. "You already know where this is going. He said that everyone was invited, but I noticed I was the only Black person on the guest list. I asked him why, and guess what he said."

"Tell me."

"He said, 'I figured none of them would come.' He was like, 'Because Black people can't swim, and doesn't it mess up y'all's hair or something?'"

"Wow. I figured it'd be one of those things, not *both*. What'd you do after he said that?"

"Nothing. I just stopped hanging out with him, like how you ghosted Destany."

"Really?" That makes me wonder. "So, if you had a list of seven things *you're* too afraid to do, what would be on it?"

He doesn't answer me right away. I listen to him shuffle in his bed and let him take his time. After a while, he says, "I could think of a lot."

"Like what?"

He pauses. "Well, if I tell you, I'll feel pressured to actually do them. Like, I give you mad props, Quinn. You're brave as hell. Do you know that?"

My eyes open, lips parting. I've never thought of myself as brave. It's really good to hear, especially coming from Carter. "I haven't done that much."

"But you've done *some*."

"And I had you guys to help me."

He pauses and then hums.

"Maybe if you had us to help you, it'd be easy for you too," I say.

He sings, "Maybe."

I go quiet, phone pressed between my ear and the pillow. He's quiet, too, I imagine, in the same position. Neither of us says anything for a few seconds, a few tens of seconds. Then, "Quinn," he says in a breath, like an afterthought, like my name had been sitting on his tongue, and he didn't even realize he'd let it roll off.

"Carter." I say it the same way.

It's past midnight. I'm tired, especially considering last night, but I'm not ready to hang up with him. His voice, his words, his presence comforts me. I can admit that. He comforts me.

"So," he says, "panties and bra, or just panties?"

I take that back. I am no longer comfortable.

"Carter, I feel like you shouldn't be asking me that."

"Why not?"

"Because it's dirty, and you and I, we're not like that."

"We're not dirty?"

"We're not *together*."

"So? That's not what this is about."

"What's it about, then? What will you get out of it?"

He exhales, dramatically. "Closure."

"It's none of your business, Carter." I pull my covers up to my chin.

"All right, you're right, Jackson," he says, giving up.

I turn on my side, facing the wall. Why do I feel so disappointed that he gave up?

He says, "I should probably go, though. It's getting late."

"Yeah, okay."

"Good night, Quinn."

Those three words alone stir up my butterflies. I feel like I'm floating above my body, like Carter Bennett couldn't possibly be telling *me* good night.

"Good night, Carter."

When I hang up, I place my phone facedown on my mattress and close my eyes. I'm more awake now than I have been all day. I should *not* feel this giddy. I should *not* already miss him. I should *not* pick up my phone and text him: **Only panties.**

But I do.

REASONS I DON'T SLEEP THAT NIGHT

1. Carter texts back: Holy shit. What have you done to me?

2. I try and figure out what he means. Have I done something to him?

3. I imagine him in his bed, thinking about me in my underwear.

4. Which requires reciprocal thinking about him in his underwear.

5. I'm pretty sure we both know what we're both thinking about right now and I'm not sure I'm comfortable with that understanding.

6. I don't know how I should act around him tomorrow. I keep imagining every possible scenario.

7. And I keep imagining what would have happened with us had Olivia and Imani waited five more minutes before coming outside.

8. I realize I never texted Matt back yesterday. And that I don't care to.

9. So now I don't know what that means for my to-do list, because if I should tell anyone about my feelings, it's Carter.

10. I think I just might do that. Tomorrow.

chapter 19

HOW IT FEELS TO KISS CARTER

CARTER TEXTED ME EARLY THIS MORNING: **Things didn't go well with Olivia and Auden. He's not coming over today. It's just me.**

So I'm freaking out. I don't know what to wear. Nothing I own is as sexy as that red dress.

My dad comes to my door, surprised to find me wrapped in my towel. "What's going on?" He steps over my mess of clothes.

"Dad, I have no clothes. Like *nothing* but bags and"—I pull out a white shirt with frills and lace—"whatever this is."

Dad sits on my bed. "Is this because of that boy? Carter, right?"

I'm surprised he remembers his name. But then I realize he's sitting on my bed, and the only time he ever comes into my room is when he wants to talk.

When he sees me looking at him, he pats the bed. "Come sit with me."

I join him on my bed cautiously. *Please don't let this be about Columbia.*

He looks at his hands in his lap. "I want to apologize for how I talked to you about Hattie yesterday."

Oh. That is not what I expected, especially because Dad never apologizes. I don't respond, because what are you supposed to say when someone apologizes to you? Thank you? I forgive you? It's okay? None of that sounds right. None of it feels true.

He looks up at me. "When I lost my dad, I felt so angry at him for dying. It felt like he died just so I would regret going to Columbia. He never wanted me to go that far away."

I nod. I know that about Granddad.

"I came back from New York to bury him and to spend every second I could with Hattie. And so *you* can too."

"Dad, the Hattie she is now isn't the Hattie I know. I'm scared of who she is now. I'm scared that she doesn't remember me."

He looks at me, wounded. "Of course she remembers you, Quinn. She asks about you every time I visit her."

My eyes bulge, and my lips tremble. "She does?"

"Yes, baby." He holds me by the chin. "Of course she does."

I haven't seen Hattie in over a year. And through all that time, through her worsening Alzheimer's, she still asks about me.

Dad stands up. "Get dressed," he says.

I watch him go, his words echoing in my mind. *She asks about you every time I visit her.* My Hattie asks about me. Maybe that's the real her, and not just the shell of who she used to be. Maybe she's still in there.

"Wait, Dad," I call after him.

He turns in my doorway.

"I need to talk to you about something else."

"What is it?" He crosses into the middle of my room but doesn't sit down. It's intimidating, but I can't keep avoiding this. I haven't been able to look at him the same since that first day Carter and Auden came over. I just need him to tell me he's exactly who I think he is, that Carter misinterpreted the situation.

"Dad, what happened with Carter that day you found him in the house?"

He looks at me with narrowed eyes, like he's about to point his finger and yell at me for bringing that up again, but then he drops his shoulders and sighs. "Quinn, sweetie, why are we still talking about this?"

"We never talked about it," I say. "And I can't stop thinking about it because, Dad, my skin is the exact same color as Carter's, and I don't know what that means." I bite my lip to keep myself contained, but I can feel everything I've been holding down coming up for air, coming out to be heard and seen and finally acknowledged. "I don't know what that means for how you see *me*."

His eyes turn down, as he comes to join me on the bed again. "I see an amazing, smart, talented, beautiful Black girl."

"And when you look at other girls who look like me, is that what you see?"

He frowns. "Of course, Quinn."

"Okay, so please explain what happened with Carter." I lean into him with pleading eyes.

"I made a mistake." He shrugs, eyes unsettled. "I hadn't slept in a while, and I honestly don't think I've ever seen a boy who looks like Carter step foot in my house. *Ever.*"

"So you thought he was trying to rob us?"

He looks down at his hands in his lap. "I don't know what I thought. But, yeah, maybe." He looks up and meets my gaze. "But please don't question my love for you and just how much I value you. I made a mistake with Carter, and honestly, it was a wake-up call. I need more Black friends."

"Have you ever had Black friends?" I can't imagine him with Black friends, not in high school, and definitely not in college.

"All I had were Black friends at Columbia. I was a member of the BSO. I've talked about this before." He shakes his head. "You always tune me out when I talk about Columbia."

"Well, anyway," I say, rolling my eyes. *Let's not turn this around on me.*

"Anyway, I need more Black people in my life. I didn't realize, until now, how important that is. There's something about having Black friends that makes you feel . . . *whole.*"

I close my mouth, *whole* ringing in my ears. I know exactly what he means. Having Olivia and Carter in my life, even for such a short period of time, has been life changing. I've had conversations and experiences with them that I could have never had with Matt, and especially not Destany.

"So . . ." I say, "I was thinking, since you're in the apologizing spirit, Carter's coming over today."

And with that, he stands up. I watch in anticipation as he heads to my door. Then he stops and turns in the hall. "Okay, yeah. Maybe I'll do that."

Carter shows up around noon. My father opens the front door as I'm running downstairs.

When I reach the foyer, Carter's taking off his shoes. He's wearing black gym shorts low on his hips, a white T-shirt, and those sparkling studs. His eyes meet my gaze, and then he glances at my legs exposed in these extra-short shorts, and my cleavage in this low-cut tank top.

Dad turns and looks at my outfit with a frown. "Carter, you can have a seat at the bar. Quinn, let's talk upstairs." He walks past me to the kitchen, his eyes blazing.

But then, for a second, I'm alone with Carter. "Hey," he says, swaggering forward.

"Hey." An embarrassed smile tempts my lips, remembering our conversation from last night.

"Quinn!" my dad shouts from the kitchen.

I startle, rushing through the doorway after my father. I look over my shoulder as Carter walks into the kitchen behind me. He's smiling, watching me.

My insides are shredding into paper cranes, fluttering

along the lining of my torso. I'm breathless by the time I get upstairs, where my father waits with his hands on his hips. "Change. Now."

I walk past him with a roll of my eyes. "Which part?"

"All of it!"

I take off the shorts and the tank top and settle for a longer pair of black Nike shorts with a white T-shirt. When I get back downstairs, my dad's leaning over the counter across the bar from Carter. "I haven't had a single Black person, outside of my family, in this house in *years*." Carter nods, staring down at the counter. I sit at the bar beside him, hoping to make him more comfortable.

"On this side of town, it's hard to come by Black families. And this one," Dad says, looking at me, "has only had white friends. That's no excuse, of course. That's probably my fault, too, when it comes down to it. Fighting off prejudices is a conscious effort, even for Black people, and I realize I haven't been fighting for a long time." Dad points at Carter. "Do me a favor and stick around. I love that Quinn has you as a friend."

Carter looks at me, and he smiles. "If she'll have me."

I shrink in my chair, incapable of handling him and his charm today. I turn away, biting down on my smile, thinking about all those different scenarios I cooked up last night.

"What type of engineering are you thinking?" my dad asks, snapping me out of my trance.

"Civil," Carter answers.

"Wait. You're majoring in engineering?" How did I not know that?

"At UT on a full-ride scholarship," my dad says to me, his arms crossed over his chest.

How did I not know that?

"You're going to UT? On a full ride?" This nonparticipant, perpetual sleeper-in-class got a full-ride scholarship while they wait-listed me? My surprise is probably a little more than insulting, but Carter just shrugs.

"Quinn has no idea what she wants to do once she gets to Columbia." Dad looks at me with tight lips and disapproving eyes.

And there's my cue to leave. Before he can start griping at me, I say, "We'll be upstairs, Dad," and stand, nudging my head at Carter.

"Keep the door open, please," he calls after us.

Carter sits on the couch in the den, while I set up the movie on the big screen. "UT, huh?" I ask, glancing over my shoulder.

He has both his arms spread atop the cushions, chest wide open. "Yep."

"When'd you plan on telling me that?" I ask, like he had any responsibility at all to tell me about his future.

I glance over my shoulder again, and he shrugs. "It just never came up."

"Whatever." I open the DVD case and pop out the disc. "Congratulations, though. That's amazing." I smile, turning and walking over to him.

"Thank you." He smiles back, flirting with his eyes. I think that's what it's called, the way his gaze runs the entire length of my body up to my face.

I sit on the couch beside him, both my feet flat on the floor, his arm emanating warmth against the back of my neck. As I'm grabbing the remote from the coffee table, I notice the three sheets of paper laid out. He says, "We have to take notes for Auden, too."

"What happened between him and Olivia?" I ask.

"Livvy can be an idiot sometimes. Let's not even talk about it."

I sit back, pressing play on the movie. I'm curious as to what he means, though. "But she said that Kendrick was a mistake."

Carter turns to me with a tired smile. "Let her tell you about it. Okay?"

"Okay." I shrug. "Fine."

"I know that if I tell you, I won't do her side any justice."

Whatever that means.

First, we fill up our own pages, then we jointly work on Auden's. But our hands keep bumping into each other as we try to write the same notes at the same time. After a while, we decide to alternate.

Once we finish Auden's notes, we relax. His arms find the back of the sofa again, and I scoot closer to him, just a teensy bit. The rest of the movie plays, but I don't watch it. I can only concentrate on him and how every five minutes, it feels like he scoots closer to me, too.

Then my dad comes stomping up the stairs. Carter's arm burns behind my head. I tense as Dad walks around the couch, glances at the two of us without a word, and grabs his iPad off the ottoman at the other end of the room. Then he crosses back in front of us, eyeing the nonspace between our thighs. Still, not a word. But I feel like I'm on fire from the heat of his inquisitive stare.

And then, I swear, not even three minutes later, my mom comes in. She asks, "Quinn, have you seen my sunglasses? You know, the ones with the blue frames?" She looks at me and Carter sitting close together, finger over her lips, hiding a smile.

I press my lips tight and shake my head. "Nope."

"Darn." She puts her hands on her hips and looks around the den, as if they would ever be up here. I know for a fact they're somewhere in the kitchen, just by knowing her habits.

I raise my brows and look over at Carter. He's smiling, like he knows what I'm thinking. "We've got our notes. Do you wanna just . . . ?"

"Yeah. Sure." He pulls his arms down from the back of the couch, as I turn off the movie.

"Oh, the movie's over already?" Mom asks.

I stand up, exasperated. "We'll be in my room."

Carter follows me down the hall.

"Oh, okay," she calls after us. "Keep the door open."

I roll my eyes, flicking on the light in my room. "Sorry about that."

"No, that's cool." As I sit at my desk, he sits on my bed. The image gives me pause. I watch as he sifts through his backpack and pulls out his old journal.

"Should we talk strategy?" He looks up and meets my stare, smiling, knowing that this is about the tenth time he's caught me staring at him since that day in my backyard.

"Strategy for what?" I spurt.

"For what you're doing from your to-do list today."

I stare at my hands. "Oh. That."

He flips to a blank page in his spiral. "What options do you have left?"

I sigh and grab my phone off my desk, unplugging it from its charger. I pull up the blackmailer's thread, then scroll up to the to-do list. "Today's Sunday, so I can't go to the second campus until tomorrow."

"Right," Carter says, writing.

"I could tell Matt about my feelings." I immediately grimace. "Tell my parents about Columbia, visit Hattie, talk to Destany."

"Matt, your parents, Hattie, Destany, and the unknown last item," he says, slowly writing them all down.

"My parents and Hattie are not options. Neither is the last item."

"What is the last item?" he asks, looking up. I purse my lips at him like he's crazy. He smiles, looking back down.

"Thought I'd give it a shot. Okay, so that leaves Matt or Destany. The Destany thing shouldn't be too hard, right? You told me what happened last night. So just tell her, right now."

I widen my eyes. "It is *not* that easy."

"Why not?"

"I've let them get away with so much worse in the past, and now all of a sudden I have a problem with Gia's racism?"

"That doesn't matter."

"But it does. You know it does."

"No matter how long it took you to realize that it's wrong, that doesn't change how wrong it is or how much it hurt you."

"Yeah, well." I look down. "It's hard."

"Okay, so confessing to Matt would be easier?" When I meet his gaze, he looks conflicted. I'm conflicted too. I don't even know if I have those feelings anymore. I haven't been able to think about anyone besides Carter since Friday.

"If you don't do something, Quinn, what's gonna be posted tomorrow? Which list?"

"I don't know," I whine, standing up to join him on my bed. I leave a galaxy of space between us.

Carter looks down at his sheet of paper, falters, then looks back up. He studies me for a second, then asks, "What exactly are your feelings for Matt?" The question catches me off guard. I cross my legs on the bed, facing him, but not looking at him. Then he crosses his legs, too. He says, "You're in love with him?"

I shake my head, running my hair behind my ear.

"But you like him?"

"I don't know, Carter." I play with the star-shaped stud in my ear. "I wrote that item on my list months ago."

"So your feelings have changed?"

I shrug, holding his eye.

"What do you feel for him now?"

I look down in my lap and try to imagine that I'm on Matt's trampoline. I try to summon the peace and the attraction I felt for him, but when I look up, it all flies out the window. Because here Carter is, sitting right in front of me, and all I can think about is *him*.

His eyes are centered on me. He's waiting. All the words that come to mind are about him. And then suddenly those words pour out. "I can't think about Matt. Not when you're here."

Carter's eyes widen.

My desire for him is bursting again. I should cover my mouth. Because maybe all his sexy looks and all his heartfelt words mean nothing more than friendship. Maybe he doesn't feel the same way I do. But looking at him right now, I can't stop myself. There are too many reasons for why I'd rather be here than with Matt. And they all come flooding out of me.

"I can't focus when you're here. Because being around you is so . . . When we talk, I feel like you see parts of me that I never knew existed. And I haven't even thought about Matt since we went to Houston together. And you were right. He's definitely been jealous after seeing me with you, but I can't seem to care about that because . . . of you."

When I look up, his face is devastatingly blank for a long time, until his lips slowly crack a smile. "Did you just confess your feelings for me, Quinn Jackson?"

I blink down to my lap, stunned at myself. "I think maybe I did."

"Wow." That's all he says. And I can't meet his eye. I can't look away from the blue polish on my fingernails. *Please say something.* Anything. For God's sake, I can't take this anticipation.

He scoots closer to me. I watch the space between our knees shrink. My body temperature shoots up ten degrees. "I think I feel the same way."

My stomach somersaults. I look up, searching his eyes. "You do?"

He scoots close enough that our knees are touching, nodding.

"So, what does that mean?"

"I don't know. This is *your* confession. What do you want it to mean?"

"Um." I smile, embarrassed, rubbing my clammy hands together. I filter through all the imaginary scenarios that kept me up last night. Every single one of them ended with us kissing. But the transition into that was always smoother than this. I leaned in, and he leaned in, and just like that, we were kissing. But in reality, I have no idea how to get there.

Carter looks in my eyes. "You look terrified."

"I *am*."

He laughs. "Relax. It's just me."

He says that like he's not clearly the problem. I look at him in his simple white shirt and black shorts, those studs in his ears. Damn, he's fine.

"What do you want, Quinn?"

"I want to kiss you."

My eyes bulge. Did I just say that out loud? God, this bursting is getting out of control.

But he doesn't question it. He doesn't hesitate. He says, "Okay," and leans in, grabbing my chin. My heart stops. "So do it."

Then I make the mistake of looking at Carter's lips. His lips are all I've wanted for the past twenty-four hours. Forty-eight hours. Hell, seventy-two hours. I find myself leaning in too. His breath shakes out from between his lips, beating in light waves against mine. I lean closer, closing my eyes, brushing the tip of his nose with mine.

I wait a second, for an inevitable interruption—for my mom to come asking where her sunglasses are again—anything to keep me from actually kissing Carter. But all is silent. All except our breathing and the clinking of dishes downstairs.

"I'm scared," I whisper.

"Just do it."

And without giving it a second thought, I press my lips against his.

HOW IT FEELS TO KISS CARTER

1. Like everything in me is rushing to my lips to get a taste of him, too.
2. Like swimming in the ocean, when all the water's trying to get inside of you, and you're afraid that it just might succeed.
3. *Wanting* it to succeed.
4. Better than brushing fingertips and squeezing palms, bumping elbows, and pushing abdomens. Better than all of that combined.
5. Like it doesn't matter if this is all a game, because I must be winning if I get to kiss him.
6. Like I really hope that this isn't just a game to him, because kissing him doesn't feel like a game at all.
7. Like *finally*.

His lips caress mine, softer than I thought possible. Then I press harder against his mouth, and he reciprocates. I feel breathless and weightless, tingles spreading all the way down, taking over my body. I push against him until he's lying on my bed and I'm falling on top of him.

His fingers slide up my back, lifting my T-shirt so he can press his hands against my bare skin. I shiver, opening my mouth against his lips. His tongue slips inside.

I've never been kissed like this. My list of boys I've ever kissed is extremely short and all occasions happened in elementary school, but Carter doesn't know that. And I hope he doesn't suspect by the way I kiss him back. I go with his flow, let him lead, dissolve into a bunch of sensory receptors and natural urges.

Until my dad starts clapping his hands in my open doorway. "Hey!"

We jump apart, nearly falling off the bed.

"Olivia is here," Dad says, frowning at us. She's standing behind him in my doorway, waving at us with a ridiculous smile. "Please make sure that doesn't happen again," he says to her before walking away.

"No problem." She walks into the room, shaking her head at us, that devilish grin growing wider. Then she starts slow clapping. "That was awesome."

"Shut up, Livvy," Carter says, pulling his shirt down.

She looks at me. "You should have seen your dad when he walked in. He was *flabbergasted*." She laughs, forcing her way between me and Carter on the bed. Then she throws her arms around our shoulders. "I'm so glad y'all are finally doing it."

I pull from under her arm, standing up. "We only kissed."

She gives me a look. "I've seen kissing. That was more than kissing."

"I thought you were gonna call before you came," Carter says, changing the subject.

She lies back on my bed, looking up at the ceiling. "I was hoping Auden would be here."

"Haven't you hurt him enough?"

"Don't say that," she whines, turning her head to Carter. "I really like him."

"So what happened?" I ask, too curious for my own good.

She sits up to look at me. "I apologized for leaving with Kendrick. But then I told him that I'm not ready to date right now." I cringe. *Ouch.* "It's not fair to him. He'd just be my rebound, and he doesn't deserve that."

I lean against my dresser. "I get that."

"What'd you want to see him for?" Carter asks.

"I didn't get to explain. He left after I told him that I couldn't go out with him."

Poor Auden. I can't even imagine his drive home after that.

Carter stands up abruptly. "Wait, where's Imani?"

"She's with my mom," Olivia says.

Carter releases his breath, but he doesn't sit back down. "I guess we better get going."

Olivia stands, then she slaps hands with me and says, "Don't start making out until I leave the room," and walks out.

Carter follows her, and I watch him, my heart aching. But then he pauses in the doorway and looks back at me. He says, "So, do you feel ready to talk to Matt?"

I laugh. "Are you kidding?"

"Kind of." He smiles, taking a few steps back inside. "But what are you gonna do? You only got till midnight."

"The list says to tell Matt that I love him, but I don't have those feelings anymore." I look down, then glance at Carter. He's looking at me from under his brow, smirking. "I think I'll try to explain that to the blackmailer."

He raises his brow, taking a few steps closer. "You think they'll listen?"

"It's my to-do list, and that item no longer applies. As far as I'm concerned, I just crossed it off my list by confessing to you."

He closes the distance between us, checking my eyes, my lips, then my eyes again. My heart is slamming against my chest. I can't speak. I can barely breathe. But I can nod.

He kisses me, and just like that, I'm putty in his hands.

I got number two done, except not with Matt. I don't feel that way about Matt anymore, so unfortunately that item no longer applies. Instead, I confessed my feelings toward Carter.

I attach a photo that Carter snapped of us kissing. Then I press send.

chapter 20

HOW TO LEAD A
SMEAR CAMPAIGN

1. Delude yourself into believing the target purposely destroyed a healthy relationship.
2. Spread rumor that she is a homewrecker.
3. Destroy her reputation; remove all girlfriends from her life.
4. Spread rumor that she only hangs with boys because she doesn't want competition for the dick.
5. Take anything exemplary about the target, such as the fact that she is head photographer of the yearbook, then destroy her merit as such:
   a. During Christmas break, gain access to the school.
   b. Make sure to have a getaway driver parked behind the building.
   c. Make sure to have a lookout planted at the front.

d. Deface her life's work with red paint markers.

e. Remove all footage from hall cams before you leave.

I wrote this how-to on the day of the vandalism. The guilt was so immense, I had to confess what I'd done, if only to my journal. No one was ever supposed to see it.

But when I wake up, the whole school is tagged in this how-to, including Olivia.

Everyone will think I started the smear campaign against her. I didn't start it, but I was involved. There's no getting around that. I was there, parked behind the building, when her photos got vandalized.

And here I was, thinking we might become friends. Not only that. Carter will never talk to me again after seeing this list. Same with Auden.

Then I get a message from my blackmailer: **The list says to tell Matt about your feelings. Not "any rando who'll like me back for sure." You've got until midnight.**

I throw my comforter on the floor. This is too far. This, in and of itself, is a smear campaign against me. All my new friends ripped away in one instant.

I think of our four suspects: Matt, Destany, Kaide, or Carter. There's no way this could be Carter. I take him off the suspect list. Matt, Destany, or Kaide. Whoever it is, they're dead.

But when I get to school, my adrenaline abandons me, leaving me cold and scared. I'm not ready to face Olivia. I'm not ready to lose her and Carter and Auden. So I sit in my car in the parking lot, engine still running, reading through the comments under the post:

Jealousy will lead you to do some crazy things.

I always thought it was her who did that to Olivia. She just has that desperate energy.

Then there's a tap on my window. I jump out of my skin and fall into Carter's concerned eyes. Astonished, I roll my window down.

"Are you okay?" he asks.

My heart soars. I am *now*. I didn't expect him to ever talk to me again. I don't know what to say. I'm so grateful and relieved that he's here. With watery eyes, I show him the message from the blackmailer. While he's reading, I watch him, my breath stabilizing.

He hands my phone back and says, "It's gonna be okay. We'll figure this out."

I nod, trying to grasp a little bit of his confidence.

"We're still visiting your second college today, right?"

I nod again.

"I need to go see Mr. Green real quick, but I'll be right back. Okay?" He lowers himself, resting his arms on my window. The sun shines in his face, brightening the brown on his cheeks, the brown in his eyes, and the pink on his lips. He leans down, and like a magnet, his lips pull me in. He pecks me once, twice, three times. Then he pulls away. "Stay here. I'll be right back." He turns and jogs across the parking lot.

I watch him go, taking my heart with him. I'm stunned.

How can he kiss me after seeing the list that got posted today? I don't want to question it. I just want more. I want to thank him and hug him and cherish that he's still here for me.

I turn off my engine, not bothering to let my window up, and jog after Carter. He's long gone, though, and I can only stand jogging for about twenty seconds. By the time I get down the hallway to Mr. Green's room, Carter's sitting in a desk up front and Mr. Green is standing over him. "You missed Friday. You can't miss today, too."

Oh, damn, this is about us skipping. I step against the wall before Mr. Green can admonish me too.

"We're taking college days, Mr. Green. It's legit."

"You already know you're going to UT. Auden's going to Texas State, and Quinn's going to Columbia."

Carter says nothing. I sweat, leaning against the wall.

"Look, I know you hate this school."

"I don't hate it," Carter says.

"You resent that your father is paying your tuition."

I scrunch up my face. His dad can afford the tuition here?

"Well, I got a full ride to UT, so that won't be a problem next year." He sounds angry.

"That's true, but you haven't graduated yet. And you won't if you keep skipping class."

"I'm not skipping," Carter insists. "We're allowed to take college days."

"Not when you already know what college you're going to."

"Mr. Green—"

"It's because of me. Okay?" I step in the classroom, my fists balled in my pockets.

They both turn, surprised.

"I didn't get into Columbia, so we've been visiting the colleges I got accepted to."

"What do you mean you didn't get into Columbia? Your parents were telling everyone you had."

"Yeah." I nod, looking at my white tennis shoes against the red tile. "Because I lied to them about getting in."

"Do they know?" Mr. Green asks, befuddled.

"I haven't told them yet."

Mr. Green places his hands on his head, his eyes stressed. That reaction is not helping. At all. "Quinn . . ."

"So we have to go. Okay?" I wave Carter over. "Our tour starts at eleven, and we have a long drive ahead of us."

"When are you going to tell them?" Mr. Green asks, breathless.

"Soon," I say. Carter follows me to the door. "Please don't jump the gun, Mr. Green. I need to be the one to tell them."

We hurry down the hallway before he can come after us.

"You didn't have to do that. I had it under control," Carter says.

"Well, now he knows the truth." I press my lips together, hoping Mr. Green won't rat me out. He has more allegiance to my parents than to me.

Carter stops me. "Maybe we shouldn't go on the tour today. This blackmailer is out of control."

"All the more reason to go and cross this off the list," I say.

"All the more reason to stay and find out who the hell is doing this."

"Or not to stay . . . and not face Olivia today." I peek into his eyes. "I can't. I don't think I can look at her."

"You can't keep—" He spits the word and stops.

Keep hurting her? Does he believe I'm the one who started those rumors?

"Keep what?" I ask, quietly.

"Running away from your problems." He relaxes his shoulders, his eyes somber. "Auden's coming on the tour with us today, by the way. He's avoiding Olivia too."

Huntsville is farther north than Houston. The drive there reminds me that we live in Texas. Austin kind of shields me from that—the conservative, country, rural side of Texas.

We drive past a sign showing support for Donald Trump. "Wow," Carter croaks, staring at the trailer house and the wooden fence, also holding an infamous "Come and Take It" flag, printed with a black rifle and a single black star at the top.

"I'd love to live next door to them," Auden says sarcastically in the back seat.

"Bad first impression," I say, glancing at Carter.

"We're not there yet, Quinn. Give it a chance."

Carter and I jam to '90s R&B for most of the way. Auden sits quietly in the back. We've been careful to not talk about Olivia around him. I mean, Auden and I are both here to avoid her . . . but I'm sure he's seen the how-to by now. I'm curious as to what he thinks.

Once we get to campus, Carter tries to figure out where to park. It takes us twenty minutes to find the *one* garage on campus, and then we're rushing to get to the visitor center.

"Bad first impression," I say again, running behind him and Auden.

"No," Carter shouts back at me, slowing down to grab my hand.

The tour begins with a presentation about student life and financial aid at Sam Houston. A lady with a tight blond bun and stilettos paces up front and rests one hand under the other like she's holding something captive in her palms—I'm not sure what, but it definitely isn't our attention.

We're all three sitting in the back, empty chairs on either side of us, and we're all three staring down at our phones. So many comments popping up on the post, but nothing from Olivia.

First Columbia and now this? Your entire existence keeps getting worse.

Funny, she doesn't show up to school today.

"Hey."

I look up from my phone. People are filing out of the room. Auden's already heading out to join the group. Carter's standing over me, offering his hand. I put my phone away and take it.

As we're joining the group, he lowers his lips to my ear. "Reading all those comments isn't helping. It's just a distraction." I look up, a bit irritated. He waffles our fingers. "Be here with me," he says. Then he smiles and kisses my temple.

How can I say no to that?

And he's right. I can't squander this campus visit like I did Houston. After all, I could end up here for the next four years.

There's nothing special about the campus. Students walk the sidewalks with earbuds in their ears, eyes on the screens of their phones. And that's not a bad thing. A big campus like Columbia with its ancient architecture and its pretentious student body would only overwhelm me. Sam Houston knows what it is. A stepping stone. An opportunity.

At the end, we get bags of information pamphlets and swag. Carter grabs his orange-and-white baseball cap out of his swag bag and places it on his head, putting it on backward. Auden wears his front-facing. I don't wear mine.

On the way back to the car, I'm trying to remember how to get to the garage while Carter and Auden flip through a pamphlet about things to do in Huntsville.

"Ooooh, they have a museum about Sam Houston. It has a duck pond," Carter says like that's the selling point.

"And we should go see the statue," Auden chimes in.

"Wait, guys. I think we're lost."

Carter looks up from the pamphlet. We're standing in

the middle of a random parking lot. "Quinn, where the hell are we?"

"You two weren't helping me!"

He puts away the pamphlet and pulls out his phone. Then he grabs my hand and leads me and Auden in the opposite direction.

When we get to the garage, Carter takes me to the passenger side of my car. "Let me drive. There's some places around here that you need to see."

"We can't stay too long, or my parents will wonder where I am."

"Yeah, same," Auden says.

"Say you're studying at a friend's." Then he lets go of my hand and starts walking to the driver's side of my car. "Realistically, how could you choose to go here without seeing the city you'd be living in?"

He's got a point. So, for the second time in my life, I slide into the passenger seat of my car, Auden slides in back, and Carter takes the wheel.

TEN THINGS TO DO IN HUNTSVILLE, TEXAS

1. Study at Sam Houston State University if you're lucky enough to find parking.
2. Find out right away why the locals call it Prison City. There's literally an alarm on campus for when an inmate escapes.
3. Go to the movies for really cheap.
4. Get excited about the prospects of there being

a mall right down the street, only to be disappointed. I've never seen a shopping center so empty in my entire life. I wonder how they have the audacity to call it a mall.

5. Get pricked by a pine needle and pummeled by a pinecone, because there's nothing but trees around here.

6. Get lost somewhere between Avenue N and Avenue S and wonder why they couldn't have given the streets real names.

7. Watch Carter pretend to know where he's going.

8. Stop on the side of the freeway and visit the world's largest statue of an American hero. Take pictures.

9. Stop on the side of the freeway and take pictures in a field of bluebonnets—look up whether it's actually illegal to pick them (it's not).

10. Pretend to be irritated with Carter when he does something really cute like miss the turn.

We get back to Hayworth just as class is letting out for the day. I'm sliding down in my seat, hoping no one spots my car, for fear that they might throw eggs. As Auden's getting out, Carter calls him back. "Livvy wants to talk to you. You should listen."

I don't watch Auden's reaction, but I can feel the tension. He shuts the door without a word.

As Carter's pulling out of the parking lot, I ask, "Do you think Auden hates me?"

"What?" He laughs, confused. "Why would he hate you?"

I'm staring straight ahead. "I was there when Olivia's photos got vandalized. I was involved." I turn to him. "Don't you hate me?"

He stares straight ahead too. "No."

"Why not?" It's like I'm begging him to hate me. I deserve to be hated.

"Because." He sighs. "Things are different now. *You're* different now. And Livvy really likes having you as a friend. She's not gonna play the blackmailer's game and abandon you. She knows all too well how that feels."

But don't I deserve to be abandoned? I was pissed at the blackmailer this morning for posting that how-to, but if they hadn't, would I have ever said anything to Olivia about it? It's not like apologizing to her was on my to-do list. I'm realizing now that it should have been.

I've been avoiding this conversation for months. But I have no right to accept her friendship if I can't look her in the eye and apologize for the part I played in her smear campaign.

My dad used to hold my mom's hand on the console. Looking from the back seat, I didn't think much of it, until he stopped.

I started lying to myself when he stopped.

So when Carter entwines our fingers on the console, as he drives us to his side of town, my stomach flips, because something about it feels finite.

We're sitting in the parking lot of Olivia's apartment complex, just looking at each other. The sun is setting, as is our time together.

"How'd you like Sam compared to U of H?"

"It was like a completely different universe. I'm so used to the city. Houston would probably be easier to get used to." Then I drop my eyes to our hands on the console. "Good thing you got that full ride to UT. Now your dad doesn't have to pay your tuition."

He tenses. "You heard that?"

I nod.

He pulls his hand away. Now it feels like he's worlds away. I know so little about him. He's always been worlds away.

"Carter—"

"I really don't wanna talk about it."

"Okay." I back off, literally backing away from him. But it's not okay, because he knows so much about me, while I know almost nothing about him.

Then he looks at me and the distance between us. "Hey, come here." He beckons me closer. "Please." I lean into the console. He says, "Don't worry about me. Everything's good."

"I'm not worried. I just want to know you."

"You do know me."

"I don't, though," I say. "Like, at all."

He sighs, resting his elbow on the console. "Okay. So, I'm a Virgo. My favorite color is red. Sometimes yellow. My favorite food is probably hot wings with blue cheese. Umm—"

"Although I didn't know *any* of that, that's not what I meant by wanting to know you."

He looks at me and smiles. "Okay." He digs deeper. "I've never had a girlfriend before you."

I jut my head back, surprised. The way he kisses, he's had to have had practice. "Um. What about the seven hundred girls your sister was talking about?"

He laughs. "First of all, that is a gross exaggeration on Imani's part. Second, those girls were just *girls*."

"What does that mean?"

"They weren't serious."

"You used them for sex?"

He narrows his eyes. "It was always a mutual relationship."

"So they used you for sex too?"

"You make it sound really clinical." He turns away, looking out the windshield. "I guess I never *wanted* to get serious with them. I never wanted to make a girl feel like she had to compete for my time."

"Compete against what?"

"My sister," he says, turning to me, his face serious. "We ain't got a dad, but as far as I'm concerned, she'll never be that girl with 'daddy problems.'"

"What about your mom?" I ask.

"She works all the time to keep the lights on, so I babysit. Olivia helps out, but I try not to bog her down. I don't have time to take a girl on dates every weekend. Or the money." He avoids my gaze. "I'm sorry. I probably should have told you that before . . ."

I smile. "I just have one question."

"What?" He looks up, bracing himself.

"If that's true, then why are you taking a chance with me?"

He glances out the windshield at the stairs leading to Olivia's apartment. "Imani likes you," he says. "And that one morning, you told me you liked her too. I was hoping maybe you wouldn't mind hanging out with both of us from time to time."

I stare at the reluctance on his face. My heart swells, and my eyes well. "See? That's what I meant by wanting to know you."

He rolls his eyes. "Don't start crying."

"I'm *not*."

"I can see it in your eyes. Come here."

I lean in. "I would love to spend time with both of you."

He kisses me slow and deep, running his hands up the sides of my neck into the back of my hair, getting his fingers tangled in my coils, and it doesn't even bother me. I'm sure he's no stranger to Black-girl hair. I let him tip my head back as Brandy whispers through my speakers, singing beneath the sounds of our lips parting and rejoining.

"You should probably go. Huh?" Carter asks after a while.

I nod, closing my mouth against his again, closing my eyes. He kisses me back for a minute, because it truly is the best thing in the world, and it's so hard to stop. But we do, eventually, because Olivia's home, and it's time for me to finally face her.

chapter 21

HOW TO TRAP A BULLY

HER MOM ANSWERS THE DOOR. "I'M SORRY, SWEETIE. I forgot your name again."

I'm too flustered to be offended. "Quinn."

"Right." She smiles. "Come on in. Livvy's in her room."

My heart thuds like a bass drum.

I walk past the sofa and the sitcom on the TV, into the kitchen, the linoleum clicking against my shoes. When I get to Olivia's room, I see her light seeping from under the door. I hear Vontae on her speakers.

I'm standing in the hallway, trying to build my courage, when her mom comes up behind me. "You gotta knock loud." She bangs on Olivia's door. "Always got her music too loud. Livvy, turn that shit down! You got a visitor!"

The music lowers. "Who is it?"

Her mom opens the door, and there I am, standing with my mouth open.

Olivia looks away from her laptop, hostile, until she sees me. "Oh, it's just Quinn." She gets up from her desk, pulls me inside the room, and slams the door behind us. "I hate when she does that shit. If I ask who it is, answer the question. You know?" She walks back to her desk. "Come look at this."

I pace over to her desk, vibrating with apprehension. She's flipping through the pictures from our road trip to Houston—the ones at that run-down gas station.

"I gotta edit them myself now . . ." She trails off, leaving out Auden's name.

I say, "They're amazing shots."

She looks back at me, smiling. "Thanks, Quinn." She keeps smiling, and my heart keeps beating faster. I expected her to hate me. For some reason, I think I could have handled that better than this.

"Olivia." Then I take a deep breath. Carter and I practiced this in my car. *Just come out with it*, he said. So I do. "I know you've seen the newest list."

Her smile fades.

"I'm sorry I didn't do anything to stop the smear campaign. I was a coward. But, I swear, it wasn't me spreading lies."

She rolls her eyes. "I know it wasn't."

"You do?"

"I've always known, Quinn." She hugs her thigh to her chest, resting her chin on her knee. "It was Destany."

I start to shake my head, but she continues, "Holden had just broken up with her over Christmas break. He started flirting with me. Rumors spread about us having sex while they were still together." She smiles. "Obviously, it was Destany. That's why I think, if it's not Kaide, she's the one who has your journal. This kind of thing has her name written all over it."

"It wasn't Destany, though," I say.

Olivia looks at me, confused.

"I mean, Destany was there, but she wasn't the one who planned the whole thing." My mouth drops open. "Oh my God."

"What?"

"You're right about something. The same person who started your smear campaign started mine."

Destany doesn't do this kind of thing. She's not this conniving.

"I gotta go." I head to her door.

"Quinn!" Olivia shouts, standing up from her desk chair. "Who is it?"

I turn, unsure, because Olivia seems like a loose cannon, and I don't know what she'll do if I tell her.

She walks toward me like I'm a baby deer. "Whoever did this ruined my reputation. I deserve to know."

She's right. I watched her reputation get ruined, and I did nothing to stop it. The least I can do is tell her who was behind it. "I drove the getaway car," I admit. "Destany stood guard, but Gia did the vandalism and spread all the rumors."

Olivia tilts her head curiously, then goes back to her

laptop and closes the lid. The soft breath of Vontae cuts off. "Let's go."

"Wait. What are we about to do?"

"We're about to go *Bring It On* on her ass."

I scrunch my eyebrows. "We're about to bring it . . . on her ass?" I ask, trying to clarify.

Olivia looks at me like I'm from another planet. "No. *Bring It On*—the movie."

"Oh." I grin. "I love that movie."

"We're the Clovers. And they're the—" She snaps her fingers. "What were those white chicks? The red dragons, or some shit?"

"It was something red. I don't think they were dragons, though."

"Know what I appreciate about that movie?" She brushes past me and hurries out her bedroom door. I follow. "They bring attention to appropriation. And in the end, the appropriators lose. That movie was so ahead of its time!"

She turns to her mom sitting on the couch, beading a necklace. "I'll be back later, Mom. Don't wait up."

"'Kay. Be safe. Love you."

"Love you too!" She steps out the front door.

"Bye, Quinn," her mom calls after me.

"Bye." I wave, happy that she finally remembered my name, then step outside after Olivia.

She's already ten steps down the stairs. "You're Gabrielle Union! I'm the feisty girl who wants to fight and says"—when she gets to the bottom of the stairs, she turns and faces me—"'You been touched by an angel, girl.'" She smiles when I reach the bottom. "Do you remember that part?"

"Totally."

"That's me," she says, grabbing my hand. "This shit is about to be on."

When I pull into Gia's driveway, we don't have a plan. We tried thinking of one on the drive over, but it's hard to think when you're this angry. And Olivia did a hell of a job of getting me angry.

"How could that bitch come for you? I thought she was your friend."

But Gia was never my friend. Gia is manipulative. Gia is condescending. Gia has always done whatever she could to put herself between me and Destany. Now she's finally done it.

"But how did she get my journal? She's not in Mrs. Yates's class," I say, staring up at Gia's brick house.

Olivia turns to me, shaking her head. "Quinn, it was Destany."

My stomach falls. "No. She couldn't have known. She wouldn't let Gia . . ." Destany has always followed Gia, but to this extent? So far that she'd willingly tear me down? Me—her best friend of ten years? "But that would mean that Destany stole my journal."

Olivia nods. "How else would Gia have gotten it?"

"Maybe she's working with Kaide," I say, hopeful. "He's racist. She's racist. They're perfect for each other."

Olivia twists her mouth and turns back to the windshield, unconvinced.

There's no way Destany could have known about this. Gia would have tried to fill her head with nonsense about me, but she wouldn't have listened.

I look up at the brick house and around the open green pasture. Then I finally notice the emptiness of the driveway. "Wait. She's not even here." I look at Olivia.

She looks at the fact that mine is the only car in the driveway. "Shit. Should we wait?"

I shrug. Then I think. The whole reason she did this was to get Destany to herself. I throw the car in reverse. "I know where she is."

Ten minutes later, we pull up to the familiar white farmhouse. Everything looks the same. The flower garden in the side yard, the rustic lawn furniture at the edge of the wraparound porch, where Destany and I used to paint our nails, the American flag hanging from the awning.

I'm parked behind Gia's white Tahoe.

Olivia turns to me. "You ready?"

I'm about to face the biggest bully at Hayworth. I look at Olivia, the septum piercing in her nose like a crown above her lips, her chocolate-brown eyes caked in black liner, long and skinny braids in a high ponytail. But I'm with the biggest badass at Hayworth, the girl who's actually beaten boys' asses. I nod. I'm ready.

"Our first priority is getting your journal back." Her eyes are on fire.

I can't believe she's here for me, despite how I wasn't there for her before.

When she opens her door, I say, "Wait, Olivia." She pauses, one foot in the car, one foot in the driveway. "I'm so sorry I didn't stand up for you back then."

She relaxes in her seat. "Quinn, I know you are. What matters is that you're here now." She turns to me, brows raised. "And you can call me Livvy. Okay?"

I nod, grateful, grinning ear to ear.

"Let's go," she says.

We walk around Gia's truck and Destany's Mustang. There aren't any other vehicles in the driveway. Her parents must be gone.

My heart is pounding. We walk up the porch steps, the tap of our feet reverberating around the property. My hand trembles as I raise it to the edge of the screen door. I knock too quietly, so Livvy follows it up with a bang.

I turn to her. "I'm scared."

"No, Quinn. You're fearless, and you're here to get what's yours. You're Gabrielle Union. Right?" Neither of us remembers her character's name in the movie.

I nod, turning back to the screen door. "I'm Gabrielle Union. I'm here to get what's mine." But I'm scared to find out if Olivia is right about Destany.

Then the front door opens. Destany stands before us, her eyes surprised to see me, but even more surprised to see Olivia. "Quinn, what are you doing here?"

I look into her gray eyes, feeling my emotions rupture in the pit of my stomach, feeling the words form in my esophagus. I swallow them down and watch her, because I can tell by the way she can't hold eye contact that she knows exactly what I'm doing here. There's guilt in her eyes. She knows.

My world crumbles at the realization. Surely, I'm jumping to conclusions. There's no way she'd let this happen to me. She's always been so loyal. I remember the Friday before Chase's party. Matt waited until the very last minute of school to ask Destany out. He said, "Hey, how are you getting to Chase's tomorrow?"

And she said, "I don't know. Probably with Gia and Quinn."

"Oh, well, you should let me take you. We can go together."

She squealed, "Like a date?" She was caught off guard, especially with the fact that I'd always given her the rundown of our little trampoline moments. She and I both thought that Matt was into *me*.

"Yeah. Like a date." He smiled.

And Matt's a hottie. He's not used to being rejected. But she flat out said, "Absolutely not," and practically ran away.

She stopped me in the parking lot and told me the whole thing.

It broke my heart to know that he had feelings for her and

not me. But she pleaded, "I would never go out with him, Quinn. Not knowing how you feel about him."

"I mean, if you like him—"

"I like *you*," she said.

And I almost cried from how much I appreciated that. I jumped on her and we hugged for about five minutes straight, laughing at how stupid she probably looked when she ran away from him. I loved her so much. I thought she would protect my feelings at all costs. I thought she would never, ever do anything to hurt me.

So it's a lot to process and a lot that I don't know how to process. Ten years of friendship, and it only took one week for her to desert me.

I finally open my mouth. "Is Gia here?"

Destany shifts her eyes between me and Olivia. "Why?"

"Go get her," Livvy growls.

Destany doesn't hesitate. She turns, leaving the front door open, but keeping the screen door closed. I can see the canvases of wild horses and paintings of crucifixes in the hallway.

Livvy turns to me while we wait. "What do you think?"

I nod. "They have it." My whole body heats up, including the back of my eyes. I push away the tears. They don't deserve my tears.

It's not difficult to cling to my anger once I see Gia's smug face. Destany stands a hair behind her, both of them behind the screen door.

"How can I help you?" Gia sings.

"I would like my journal back now," I say, trying to keep calm.

"I'm sorry?" Gia tilts her head with mock confusion. "What journal?"

"Bitch." Livvy spits the word. The sound is so rich, it sounds like a slap, like palm colliding with cheek. They both recoil.

"You know exactly what journal I'm talking about," I say. Gia looks at me, the smile wiped off her face. "Go get it."

Neither of them moves.

"Now!" Livvy opens the screen door. Now there's nothing separating her from them.

"Go get it," Destany says.

Gia breathes a furious laugh, then stalks off, leaving Olivia and Destany facing off.

But I hadn't realized it would hurt this much to get confirmation of my suspicions. I bend over, feeling like I got the wind knocked out of me. When I look at Destany, I shake my head. "Wow. It only took you two seconds to throw me away, to run my name through the mud, to fucking spit on ten years of friendship."

Olivia takes a step back, giving me room to get at Destany.

"Quinn, you threw me away first."

"I *walked* away! You took my personal property and spread it around the whole school. I would never do anything like that to you, because friends don't do that!"

She's scrambling. "We weren't friends. You walked away

from me because of a guy. Ten years of friendship and you let a *guy* get between us. And I didn't even date him! Nothing happened between me and Matt, but you got jealous that he was showing me attention."

"I didn't walk away because of Matt. Do you even know me, Destany? How could you think that's the reason I walked away?"

"Well, why'd you do it?"

Gia walks up then, holding my journal. I look at Destany, lowering my voice. "Because I'm 'practically white anyway.'"

She furrows her brow, then her eyes light up. "Are you serious? Because of *that*? That was just a joke, Quinn. I mean, obviously you're not white."

"Obviously," Gia says, sneering at my dark skin.

I take a step back. "A *joke*? You think Gia degrading that Gap employee's humanity by repeatedly referring to her as 'that fucking N-word' is a joke? And the second I thought you might tell her to stop, you denied my right to be offended, you dismissed my identity as a Black girl, and completely erased my voice in the conversation, all with just four little words. That was a *joke* to you?"

"Quinn, you always blow this race stuff out of proportion," Destany says.

"Like I said, Dessie, she does it for attention. She's not hurt. She just wants someone to feel sorry for her—"

"Say something else, I swear!" Livvy steps nose to nose with Gia. "When it comes down to it, I don't need an excuse to whoop your ass. We already *got* beef. But my patience wears thin when bitches get racist. Ask your friend Hailey. Ask your friend Paul. Ask your friend Sean."

"Livvy, Livvy." I grab her arm and pull her back. "She's not worth it." I look at Destany. "Neither of them is. They're both cowards."

Livvy walks away to pace the porch, hands on her hips, but I continue. "Cowards will do anything to feel safe, to feel in control. I used to be a coward, too, but the first brave thing I ever did was to stop being your friend." I hold my palm out. "Journal."

Gia untucks my journal, but she doesn't release it when I grab hold. She says, "If anyone hears about this, I'll send a message to your father about Columbia—"

Livvy hustles back over. "If you send a message to her father, I'll send a message to hell letting them know you're on your way there." Gia lets go of the journal, and I block Livvy from getting close.

"We won't tell. But I want all the pictures of my journal deleted."

"Done." Gia smiles.

Livvy scoffs. As I step back, pushing her out of the doorway, she points her finger over my shoulder into Gia's face. "You been touched by an angel, girl." Then she turns and we walk away, letting the screen door close behind us.

As we climb down the steps, Livvy hisses, "I said it! Just like in the movie."

I smile. "That was perfect."

Then she flicks her hand across my arm. "But what's up? We're letting them get away with this?"

I smile, pulling my phone out of my back pocket. "Nah." I say it, understanding immediately why Carter says it so much. It just rolls off the tongue. "I'm not playing by their rules anymore. I just recorded that whole conversation."

Livvy grabs my phone as we head to my car. "You sneaky little bitch. I love you."

"Oh, and Quinn!" Gia calls after us. She's on the porch, Destany behind her. "I'm glad you were able to forgive Carter after he lost your journal."

I roll my eyes. "He lost it by accident."

"Yeah, well, I'm sure he stopped being careful after he read that list you wrote about him. You know, the one about him being a pretentious bastard and an arrogant asshole. You remember that list?" Gia's smirking.

Livvy stops and turns. "Quinn, let's go. They're trying to start some mess."

"He didn't read past the first page of my journal."

"That's not what"—Gia turns to Destany—"that's not what Destany saw."

Destany nods. "He was flipping through it before I took it."

My breath picks up. No, that's not possible. He specifically told me he only read the first page. If he lied . . . then he knows *everything*. This whole time he's known every grody detail about me.

Livvy asks, "Why should she believe a word you say?"

"Believe what you want," Gia says, turning away.

Destany follows, saying, "It's true, Quinn."

The screen door slams behind them and then the front door. I'm frozen in place, trying to tell myself that they're lying. Livvy grabs my arm. "They're just trying to get in your head. You can't believe them."

I look in her eyes, letting her words sink in. "Yeah, you're right." I follow her to my car and get in, holding my journal against my lap. It smells like the inside of Destany's house. I hate that. I toss it in my back seat and back out of Destany's driveway.

"You were so badass," Livvy says to me.

"Not as badass as you."

She shakes her head. "Even more."

But I don't feel badass. I feel spent, like I could sleep for days. My clothes are drenched in sweat. And I'm still so worried.

That day at Carter's locker, when I asked him if he read my journal, he looked at me like he was trying to figure out the best answer for the circumstances—not the true answer.

After driving in silence for ten minutes, I finally ask her, "But what if he did read it?" I glance at her with trembling lips.

"Let's just ask him."

I shrink at the thought of asking him and hearing what I don't want to hear. I think about the way he kissed me today, how he confessed why he doesn't have girlfriends, and why he decided to take a chance on me. In that moment, I dove in. I fell. I committed to the idea of being with him. And now, this. What if he's been lying to me the whole time?

"I don't think I have the energy for another confrontation."

"Okay," Livvy says. "We'll ask him tomorrow. Okay?"

"Okay." I take a deep breath. For tonight, I'll believe what I want. He didn't read it. Everything is fine. Everything is perfect. "Do you wanna come over?" I ask her. "I'm not looking forward to being alone tonight."

Because everything is not perfect. I used to be good at lying to myself, but not anymore.

"Oh," Livvy says, surprised.

"You don't have to," I say fast. "It's cool if you don't want to." Maybe she still hasn't forgiven me for being involved in her smear campaign. I can't blame her, and I don't want to rush her.

"No!" she says, excited. "I would love to come over, Quinn."

My eyes light up. "Really?"

"Of course! Just let me call my mom." She pulls out her phone and calls. "Momma, I'm staying over at Quinn's tonight."

I head toward my house with a smile blooming on my face, full of something indescribable. Just full. I feel *full* for the first time in months.

chapter 22

IF CARTER READ MY JOURNAL

BOTH MY PARENTS' CARS ARE PARKED IN THE DRIVEWAY. When I get out, I glance up at the half-moon. It's light out, but the sun is down in most of the sky. Dusk.

"I'm hungry," Livvy says, shutting her door.

"Yeah, me too."

The lights are off when we get inside. We walk into the kitchen and hear murmurs from the television in the den.

"Quinn?" Dad calls before I've reached the top of the stairs.

The light from the television bounces off the walls, spraying me with colors. He's lounging against the arm of the couch, my mom's head low on his chest, her body wedged between his legs. It's so intimate and almost foreign seeing them wrapped up like this.

"Hey, sweetie," Mom says. She's drunk. I can see it in the easiness of her smile. Then Livvy steps beside me, and she sits up halfway. "It's nice to see you again, Olivia."

"Yes, ma'am. You too."

"Baby," my dad says, reaching toward me half-heartedly. Yep, he's drunk too. "Your mom and I—"

"We found a couples' therapist," she blurts out.

"Oh." My eyes widen. "I didn't know you were looking for one."

They nod. That's good, right? That's trying. They're still trying.

"We start tomorrow," Dad adds.

They're both smiling nervously.

"That's great. Congratulations." I smile at them reassuringly. I grip the straps of my backpack, glancing at the movie on the screen—some movie they've never seen before because they refuse to watch movies twice. "Is it okay if Livvy stays over tonight?"

They look at her again, like they forgot what she looks like. Then they look at each other, communicating through their eyebrows. "That's fine," my dad says, lying back against the arm of the couch, Mom settling between his legs.

"Can we order pizza?"

"Oh!" Mom says, sitting back up. "I want some wings, Quinn." Then she looks at my dad. "What kind of pizza do you want, Dez?"

"You know what I want."

She smirks flirtatiously. I sigh and Livvy grins. "Mom, since you apparently know what Dad wants, can you order it for us?" I turn to Livvy. "What kind of pizza do you want?"

"Anything."

Mom says, "Sure, sweetie." Then she waves us away.

We walk down the dark hallway to my room.

"Your parents are cute," Livvy says, setting her backpack against my wall.

"They aren't always." I sit down in my desk chair, thinking back to the shouting and the silence, and then to them just now on the couch, cuddled up. "But, yeah, they are cute."

My phone rings. When I look at it, his name surges through me. My body remembers him, misses him, but my head can't get around what Destany and Gia put between us. I stare at the screen until it stops ringing.

Livvy's sitting on the edge of my bed, expression conflicted. "Carter?"

I nod. Then he texts me: **How'd it go with Livvy?**

I silence my phone and put it on my dresser—out of sight, out of mind. Because I want to text him back that it went great. When Livvy and I were walking away with my journal, everything was perfect. I had proof that Destany and Gia were my blackmailers. I had my journal. I had Livvy and Carter, and everything was on the way up.

But then I turned around.

"I have homework. Cool if I do it right now?" Livvy asks.

"Of course."

She grabs her books from her backpack and lounges on my bed. I sit at my desk and open my long-lost journal. It's almost hard to look at, knowing that Destany and Gia have had it all this time.

I flip to the first page: the sinister to-do list. If only I had never written it. I cross off the items I've done, replacing Matt's name with Carter's on number two, ending with telling Destany the real reason I ghosted her. A tiny smile plays on my lips as I look at everything I've accomplished.

But looking at Columbia and Hattie sitting uncrossed on the list swiftly extinguishes it.

Then I flip past my to-do lists, my how-tos, and once I get to my favorites, I imagine that I'm Carter—that I'm learning all these raw facts about Quinn.

1. Her favorite color is baby blue.
2. Her favorite tree is the one that bends over Hattie's swimming hole.
3. Her favorite place in the world is Hattie's swimming hole.
4. Her favorite song is "How You Gonna Act Like That" by Tyrese.

Wait, he said that was his favorite song too. Was that even true?

If Carter read my journal, he had impossible insights into me. And his insight is a big reason we connected in the first place. He made me feel like he could see parts of me that weren't visible to anyone else, that he could understand me on a level that no one else could. But was that only because he'd read my journal? I shiver with disgust.

Then Livvy's phone rings. When I turn, she's looking at me, undecided.

"Don't," I say.

"If I don't answer, he'll know something's up." She sighs and answers. "Yo."

The phone is loud enough that I can hear him all the way across the room. "Aye, you seen Quinn?" Hearing his voice makes me want to pick up my phone and call him myself. I want him in my ear.

"Um." She looks at me, her eyes wide. "Yeah, she came by a little while ago."

I join her on my bed. He says, "Then where'd she go?"

"I don't know. Home, I guess."

"Oh." Then he's quiet for a while. He says, "So where you at?"

She looks at me, panicked. I shake my head.

"Out."

"Out where?"

"Why do you need to know? Shit. You ain't my daddy."

I smile, holding in my laughter.

"Look, Livvy, I know you're at Quinn's house. I just talked to Momma Sandy."

Both our jaws drop.

"I don't know why you're lying to me, and I don't know why she's avoiding me, but I would love it if somebody told me something."

Livvy looks at me, not responding, her eyes blinking fast.

"Olivia." He uses her full name.

"Just give her the night. She'll talk to you tomorrow."

He's silent for a second. "Okay, but do you know what I did?"

"Just give her the night. Okay?"

We both wait for his answer. "A'ight."

Then they hang up. I go back to my desk. Livvy gets back to her homework. We don't talk about it. I'm glad we don't, because the farther I get through my journal, the nastier it gets. And I can't imagine he got this far. If he flipped through it, as Destany said, surely, he didn't flip this far. Surely, he didn't get all the way to "Miscellaneous."

When the pizza arrives, Livvy puts up her textbook. She gets three slices of pepperoni, and I take the entire box of veggie pizza. We eat and watch *Bring It On*. I shower, and then she showers. She wears one of my T-shirts to bed. It fits her like a mini dress. She takes the side of the bed that's against the wall. I lie on my side and face the door.

My phone lights up on my desk. After a few seconds, it goes black again. I turn over on my other side, facing Livvy.

"Get some sleep, Quinn. It does you no good to worry about tomorrow."

I close my eyes. "I know."

"Celebrate your victories. And maybe tomorrow we'll find out those bitches were lying the whole time. You and Carter can live happily ever after."

I've been hoping for that exact scenario. But a large part of me believes that Destany is telling the truth.

IF CARTER READ MY JOURNAL

1. I think I might slap him.
2. I might never talk to him again.
3. I just might forget him and move on.
4. I might never forget him and never move on.
5. I might cry and kiss him.
6. I might cry and kiss him and let him hold me until it doesn't hurt anymore.
7. I might forgive him.

Livvy is a heavy sleeper. I'm dressed and ready to go when I finally shake her awake. She wears my mom's clothes, and those are still big on her. She rolls the baggy jeans up her calf, stuffs a corner of the T-shirt into the band. She can pull anything off, that girl.

We're sitting in my car, still running in the parking lot. My heart is racing.

Livvy looks over her seat. "His bus is here." Then she looks at me. I'm staring out the front windshield. "You okay?"

I nod, not making eye contact.

She places a hand on my arm. "Text me if you need me." She holds her hand there. "I mean it."

"Thank you," I say.

She gets out of my car, and that's when the winds really pick up.

He opens my passenger door and slides in, filling the car with his scent, filling my head with confusion. Because I want to kiss him, but I need to know the truth.

"Quinn?" he asks when I don't speak or look at him. "What's going on, baby?"

Baby? Don't do that to me.

"Yesterday, I found out Destany and Gia had my journal," I say. "Livvy and I got it back."

"Wow," he says, but then he's quiet, because he's confused. "That's a good thing, right? Now you know for sure that I didn't do this."

"Yeah," I say with a sad laugh.

"Then why can't you look at me right now?" He reaches for my cheek.

I lean away from his touch. "Carter, did you read my journal?" I ask, staring out of my windshield.

His hand freezes midair. I can see it in my peripheral. Everything is silent except for my engine humming and the low AC blowing. "What?"

I finally look at him. "You told me you only read the first page."

He drops his hand, searching my eyes. "Quinn, it feels like that happened so long ago."

I gasp. I guess there was a part of me still hoping it wasn't true. That part of me is breaking in two. "How much of it did you read?"

He blinks his eyes to the console between us. "All of it."

I swallow every ounce of hope I had left and press my back against the door.

He leans forward. "But nothing I read changed how I feel about you."

"That's not the point."

"If anything, reading your journal made me like you more."

"That's not the point! You blatantly invaded my privacy."

"And I'm *sorry*! I wish I could take it back. I really do. When I first lied about it, I was trying to spare you embarrassment. But then the blackmail thing happened, and I knew that if I told you, you would think I was the one blackmailing you."

"That's not an excuse."

"I know it's not!" He presses his fingertips into the console. "I'm not trying to make an excuse. I'm just trying to explain." He looks at me, his chest rising and falling. My chest rises and falls at the same rate. "Please come here," he says.

I don't move. I want to, though. I don't want to be mad at him. I want him on my lips. But I know I shouldn't want that.

"Can you just get out?"

He looks distraught. "I know I made a mistake, but you're treating me like I *cheated* on you or something."

My nostrils flare. "I imagine this is what it would feel like to get cheated on. I fell for an idea about you. Now I'm finding out that my idea was wrong. Everything that you've ever said to me, everything we've ever done together is tainted, because you knew! The whole time, you knew everything!"

I shake my head. The truth of my own words is clouding my voice and my chest and my eyes. "You may not have been with another girl, but you did lose my trust. Please get out of my car." He reaches for me, but I push my shoulder against my door. "Please go!"

"I'm so sorry." He pulls away, rips open the car door, slams it shut, then walks through the parking lot with his hands on top of his head.

I crumble. My ribs crack. I pick up my phone and text Livvy: **I need you.**

chapter 23

REASONS I CAN'T LOOK AT YOU

OLIVIA PRIES ME FROM MY CAR. WE'RE MISSING FIRST period. She walks me to Mrs. Henderson's door, then faces me. She wipes under my eyes and all over my cheeks. Thankfully, I didn't waste time putting on makeup today.

"You look beautiful," she says, placing her hands on my shoulders, smiling big. "We'll murder Carter later. Okay?"

I don't want to murder him. I want to surgically remove him from my heart.

She opens the classroom door and pushes me inside. Mrs. Henderson looks up from the board. "Quinn?" She's wondering why I'm late. She's wondering where I've been for the past two school days. She's wondering why I look like I've been crying.

I keep my eyes down and go to my desk in the back. Thankfully, she doesn't press me.

"She's back," the girl in front of me says. "I was hoping she quit school."

"She should be expelled for what she did to Olivia."

"Yeah, poor Olivia."

I look up at the two girls gossiping in front of me. I'd almost forgotten about the *How to Lead a Smear Campaign* list. I stare at their faces without blinking. When they see me staring, they can't hold my gaze. They turn around and shut up, because most of these kids can only talk shit if there's no threat of consequences. But I hold threats in my eyes. Today is not the day to try me.

All class period, I think through everything that happened after Carter read my journal.

That day, when he told me he thought he lost it on the bus, that was a complete lie. He was most definitely flipping through it during first period. Maybe if he'd told me the truth, I would never have tempted the blackmailer to expose my Columbia rejection.

And he had me convinced that he *somehow* knew that my favorite music is '90s R&B, that he *somehow* knew how much I hate Vontae, and that he *somehow* knew about my usage of the term *Oreo*, but all this time it was because he'd read my journal. His uncanny insight wasn't so uncanny after all.

I think about the time he was in my room, how he guessed that I would paint my walls baby blue, how he claimed that he knew it was my favorite color because he was observant. Observant my ass!

What was real? Was anything about him real?

When class ends, Mrs. Henderson calls me to her desk. She asks about my absences. I show her my college-day excuses, and she gives me the assignments I missed.

Calculus is worse. Kids in calculus are still stuck on the Columbia sitch.

"Where are you going to school, Quinn? Austin Community College?"

"She can't get into ACC. Don't be foolish."

I've only made it through two periods, and I'm already tempted to skip again, but I'm so behind. And I'm trying my hardest to show up today, to not be a coward, to not run away like I always have.

I make it through third and fourth period without seeing Carter. I'm grateful because it feels like I'm finally starting to adjust to this new normal. I eat my lunch outside, alone, because Livvy has second lunch.

I stare out into the trees and dive into the only thing that still comforts me—my memories about Hattie, about the one time I did something so brave and careless. The time we drove to the swimming hole despite the dark clouds. It wasn't just a threat of rain. We were on a tornado watch. But I wanted to swim, and Hattie didn't see a reason not to.

She said, "We're here now. Might as well do what we came for." Hattie got out of the Gator and walked to the edge of the creek.

"Wait, Hattie, what are you doing?"

She turned around, grinning. "Girl, I ain't getting in. It'd be the last thing I do if I jump off in that water."

I got out of the Gator and joined her at the edge. The current was slow and smooth. "Get in, scaredy cat," she said, laughing, pushing my shoulder.

"Hattie!" I screamed, jumping back. She was so damn childish. I crossed my arms over my chest. "Turn around."

"Girl, whatever you got, trust me, I had ten times more in my day."

I looked at her tiny stature, doubtful.

"Where you think you get them curves from?"

"Um. My mom?"

She laughed. "Your momma's cute, but she's straight like a twig. You get that butt from me, sweetie." Then she walked past, slapping my ass on her way back to the Gator.

I slipped off my shoes, socks, shirt, and shorts, laying them in a pile on the ground. Lightning struck across the sky. Thunder followed. I looked back to Hattie, sitting in the covered Gator. "Go 'head."

So I ran to the "bendy tree." It was a tree that bent itself over the water, like nature's diving board. Hattie had installed a tire swing in the middle of the trunk that hung over the water. And when it flooded, half the tire swing would be submerged—that was the best, when I could sit and dangle my legs in the water.

It started sprinkling as I crawled across the trunk. I looked down at the water. The wind had picked up, and so had the current. "Hattie, maybe we should just go back!"

"If you're scared, we can go. If you get hurt . . . I can't come save you."

It was true. I was completely on my own. And it's not like we told anyone where we'd be going before we left. Between the two of us, I'd always been the more responsible one. Hattie grew up in a different time, when what didn't kill you made you stronger. So jumping in the rapids below would either take me out or make me stronger.

I looked up at the dark sky, then over to Hattie sitting in the passenger seat of the Gator. Hattie would do it if she could. She wouldn't think twice. I climbed down the rope until I got to the tire at the end. I sat and caught my breath as the rain started falling harder. Then I stood on the tire, holding on to the rope, swinging as hard as I could. "Woo!" I shouted into the wind, catching droplets of rain in my mouth and in my eyes.

I felt like I had life in the palm of my hand, like I couldn't die, not when I wanted to live as much as I did in that moment. Not when I loved life that much.

So I jumped.

When I get to Mr. Green's room, Carter's desk is empty. My eyes instinctively find Destany. She meets my gaze for a second before dropping her eyes again. No smug smiles. Nothing.

When I initially walked away from her, I thought one day we could have a frank discussion about race. I thought eventually I could forgive her. Being ignorant is forgivable. But not this. She and I are completely done.

Auden greets me when I sit down. I look up and force a smile. Then Carter sits next to me silently. His smell assaults me and the hole in my heart.

Mr. Green comes over to our desks. "You three missed a lot." He looks disappointed. "Friday, we watched past screenplays, winners and losers. Yesterday, we picked roles and conspiracy theories and had another quiz. You can either take your quiz today after school, tomorrow morning, or tomorrow after school. After that you get a zero."

"Yes, sir," Auden says.

Carter and I are silent.

Mr. Green lectures for most of the period. I try to concentrate on him and not on the disgust I feel toward Carter. He knew my journal was private, but he had the audacity to read the entire thing. Not just a few accidental pages. The *entire* thing.

For the last ten minutes of class, Mr. Green allows us to write our script. But I can't open my mouth. Carter doesn't either.

"Any suggestions for who should play Kennedy?" Auden looks at the two of us, apprehensive.

We say nothing.

"I think I want to be the government."

I want to ask him, *The entire government, Auden?* but I don't.

"You know," Auden says with a sigh, "I talked to Olivia today."

I pick up my head. So does Carter.

"I let her explain why she rejected me. And, now, miraculously I feel better. My feelings are still hurt, don't get me wrong, but now I know that her rejection had more to do with her past than it did with me."

It feels like he's trying to convince me to talk to Carter, and I don't appreciate it.

The bell rings. We've made no decisions about who will play Kennedy or "the government" and we're still so behind. Auden sighs, gathers his things, and leaves.

I grab my books in a hurry, because I don't want to end up walking out of the classroom with Carter. But even after I beat him out the door, he chases me down in the hallway.

"Quinn," he says, grabbing my arm. I damn near hiss at him for touching me. He puts his hands up. "Sorry." But he continues walking beside me. "I want to apologize. I'm sorry I invaded your privacy and was so careless with your trust."

The hole aches, throbs.

We reach the front, and he hurries to hold the door for me. Then we're walking together toward the parking lot, dodging groups of people on the sidewalk. He keeps up with me, though.

"I'm also really sorry about not trying to understand your feelings, and for trying to downplay what I did to you. What I did was terrible. Not only was it disrespectful, it was cruel, and . . . gross."

That must be why I feel so disgusted.

"But I want to do whatever I can to make it up to you. I want to build trust with you, and I think the only way to do that is with full disclosure."

By this time, we've reached my car. I open my back door and stuff my books and backpack in the back seat.

"I have to get raw and *naked* with you." He hurries to clarify, "Not physically, but emotionally naked, like I forced you to get with me."

My eyes are on the pavement between us. His body is blocking my door. I want to get around him, get in my car, and drive away.

He must read my mind, because he moves and opens my door for me. "Because I realized today that that's what I did to you. I forced you to get naked before you were ready. And I'm disgusted at myself for doing that to you."

My eyes warm. How is he doing that? How is he putting into words exactly what I've been feeling all day? I haven't been able to put my finger on why I'm so angry and disgusted, but that's it. That's exactly it.

"So, I wanna give you this." He goes into the pocket of his sweatpants and pulls out a folded piece of notebook paper. That paper looks dangerous, like everything I don't want right now, but everything I need.

I walk around his outstretched hand, get in my car and shut the door. "Please, Quinn." He taps on my window. "I don't expect you to talk to me after this. You don't even have to read it. Just please take it."

I'm facing the windshield, refusing to look at him. I wonder what it is. He said he wants to get real with me. What on earth could be on that sheet of paper?

I don't need much convincing. As much as I'm resisting, I know I'll kick myself later if I don't take it. I roll my window down, snatch the folded piece of paper, and then roll my window back up before he can say anything else that will make me want to forgive him. My resolve is already softening; I can feel it.

He steps away from my car slowly, shoving his hands in his pockets, then he turns and heads to his bus stop. I watch him in my rearview until my passenger door opens and Livvy jumps inside.

"Hurry, Quinn! Run those bitches down!" She points at Gia and Destany crossing in front of my car.

I smile. I think it's the first time I've smiled today.

"But seriously," she says, turning to me. "When are we taking them down?"

I turn back to my windshield, watching them laugh together. "Soon. First I have to tell my parents the truth about Columbia."

chapter 24

MANIFESTATIONS OF
HATTIE'S ESSENCE

THIS IS GOING TO BE BAD.

My parents have been planning for my life in New York for months. Hell, they've been planning it my entire life.

This is going to be really, really bad.

Livvy holds my hand. I squeeze hers as we walk through the foyer. I notice the Columbia acceptance letter framed on the wall as I enter the living room. Mom has her notes scattered all over the coffee table. She's telling Dad about the case she's working on right now, and he's listening with a glass of wine in hand, sitting on the floor. It's so cute and wholesome and I'm about to mess it all up.

"Quinn, baby, can you bring us that wine bottle that's on the bar," Mom says, motioning to the kitchen. "Oh, hi, Olivia."

And when I get to the kitchen, I notice the congratulations banner still wrapped around the top edges of the walls. My heart races.

"You're a senior, too, huh?" my dad asks her, as I'm coming back to the living room.

"Yes, sir."

"Where are you going to school next year?"

"Texas State," she says.

"Oh, very impressive."

I hand the bottle of red wine to my parents.

"What are you two up to?" Mom asks when we haven't moved from the back of the couch.

"Nothing," I say, nervous.

Livvy looks at me. She spreads her hands, like she's clearing away the bad. "Just say it."

"Just say what?" Dad asks.

"Mom, Dad, I need to tell you something."

Mom's eyes crease with worry. Dad leans forward. "What is it?"

"About Columbia . . . I don't think I can go."

He instantly looks at Olivia, as if she's the devil who convinced me to throw away my future. "Of course you can," Dad says, turning back to me. "We'll take a trip up there next week. We'll lock down an apartment—"

"Dad, I'm not going."

"Yes. You. Are."

Livvy pinches the back of my arm. *Just say it.*

"Dad, I can't go, because I didn't get in."

Silence falls over the entire house.

"What do you mean you didn't get in?"

"We have your acceptance letter," Mom says, pointing to

the frame on the wall.

"It's fake. I made it myself."

"You did what?" Dad stands up. "Where are you going to college, Quinn? What the hell?" He sets his wineglass down on the table and paces back and forth.

"Did you get in anywhere?" Mom asks.

"Nowhere you want to hear about. Even UT wait-listed me."

That takes the breath out of Dad. "Are you kidding me? I thought you were doing well in your classes. And your ACT score, I thought you scored a thirty-four."

"I got a twenty-four."

"Oh my God!" Dad shouts. He bends over, gripping his knees. "We told everyone we *know* that you're going to New York! We printed it on your graduation invitations! We sold Hattie's land so that we could pay for Columbia! How could you do this?"

My blood cools. "Wait. You sold Hattie's land?"

"Do you know how expensive Columbia is? Tuition, books, and New York is about the most expensive city to live in. You know who would have to pay for that?"

"So you *sold* Hattie's land? Did you sell her furniture too? Did you sell her love seat and her rose-petal chair?" My head tilts like it's too heavy to hold up. "Did you sell it at a yard sale?"

He looks confused. "Of course not, Quinn. It's in storage."

My eyelids flutter, grateful. Her furniture isn't spread around in strangers' homes. Her rose-petal chair isn't in

Auden's living room. "You have to get the house back and her land too."

"We already cashed the check, Quinn. The buyer's moving in next weekend."

"When did you plan on telling me?"

"When did you plan on telling us?" Dad shouts back.

Mom stands up, placing her hand on Dad's shoulder. "Maybe we should all take a break."

Hattie's land. Her house. My entire childhood is gone.

"Quinn, take Olivia home. Your dad and I have a lot to talk about."

I stay planted, my hands shaking.

"Go!" Dad shouts.

I grab Livvy's hand and pull her out the front door, down the driveway. "Quinn, slow down." I let her go once we reach my car.

I haven't been on Hattie's property since the day they took her away from me, more than a year ago. And now it's sold, gone forever. "You know what? No. I'm not taking you home." I look at her over the top of my car. "We're going to Hattie's."

FIVE WAYS LIVVY ASKS IF I'M OKAY WITHOUT ACTUALLY USING THE WORDS

1. "Carter's been torn up all day. Do you want to talk about it?"

2. "Might want to ease up on the gas, Quinn. Or I can take over if you need me to."

3. "How could your dad do that to you? You can curse, spit, cry, whatever you need."
4. "I'll take pictures of everything, so you'll never forget what it looks like."
5. "I'm glad you brought me, Quinn. I'm always here for you."

When we get to Hattie's gate in far east Leander, everything comes flying back. We watch the gate swing open, and it feels like a gate inside me swings open too. I creep down the long rocky driveway, remembering every single tree we pass. How some of the curves are so deep, the road looks like it'll disappear, and we'll drive straight into the forest.

When the house comes into view, I don't blink.

Olivia snaps pictures of everything outside her open window. "It's gorgeous."

It is. It's still so beautiful. The cabin-like slabs, the wraparound porch, the brick fireplace on the side.

We get out of the car. Olivia heads to the house, but I shake my head. "Let's go to the trails. I want to show you the swimming hole."

Hattie's garden on the left side of the backyard is just a patch of desert now. The greenhouse door is wide open. The plants are all gone, and so are the birds. It hurts more than I expected, looking at all the emptiness.

The Gator's still parked under the carport, the key in the ignition. It starts right up. Olivia takes her place beside me, holding on to the side handle.

"You sure you're ready for this?"

I reverse out of the carport and then head to the vast tree line over the hill. "No, but I need to do this."

We bump across the pasture fast, the wind whipping away my sweat and my nerves and the knots in my stomach. Olivia is quiet as we cross the threshold into the woods, on a path that I remember like the back of Hattie's hand. The deeper we go, the more my soul feels like it's tearing out of my skin. The smell of oak and cedar take me back to when I was ten and twelve and fifteen. I'm bubbling over with nostalgia, my chest expanding with relief, joy, and sadness all at the same time.

Finally, I see the marker—a tree with an orange ribbon tied around it. "We're coming up to the big bump."

"The what?"

I slow down. As we dip into a giant ditch in the path, I say, "One time I drove through this pothole full speed." I glance at Livvy with a smile. "We turned over. Everything flew out of the back, and my tailbone was sore for about a week."

Olivia laughs, throwing her head back.

"Hattie marked that tree so we'd know to slow down."

The sun can barely get to us through the treetops, but the air is suffocatingly hot. I drive faster to pick up more wind, but then we're coming to the familiar fork in the path. I turn right, and Olivia doesn't question it. While I'm driving slowly, she's snapping photos of the woods.

"This is amazing. Your grandma owns all this land?" she asks.

"She *did*." I swallow hard. "Okay, it's about to get bumpy. Hold on."

She puts her camera down, holding on to the bar on the side of her door. The path gets narrower and much bumpier than I remember. We go over a big bump, and I bite my tongue. "Shit," I hiss, swallowing blood.

"Maybe we shouldn't—" Olivia sucks in through her teeth, her voice shaking like a jackhammer. "Maybe you should slow down."

We come up over a hill, and at the bottom, I spot a family of deer. "Look!"

She gasps. "They're so cute! Can we stop and get pictures?"

"Um, maybe." But I'm going way too fast, and the hill is much steeper than I remember. I try braking, but we're already halfway down the decline, flying. The deer flee for their lives.

"Quinn!" Olivia screams.

I grip the wheel as tightly as I can, my eyes like saucers.

We scream at the top of our lungs as we head to the big curve, the last curve. We fly around it so fast, I can't believe we don't turn over. I slam on the brakes just in time, inches from the edge of the water.

Livvy turns to me, her mouth wide open, her oval eyes as round as mine. Then she starts laughing, maniacally, holding on to her heart. A smile cracks across my lips, and I laugh too.

"Quinn, you took that curve like we were in fucking Mario Kart!"

I laugh harder, choking on my spit.

"I thought I was Luigi, for a second, on Rainbow Road."

I gasp. "Oh, no, no, no! We were definitely in Moo Moo Meadows!"

She turns to me, surprised. "You're totally right!"

I throw my hands to my forehead, catching my breath. "But look," I say, staring out at Hattie's swimming hole, just as clear blue as I remember. The green trees somehow greener, the leaning tree, the tire swing tied to the middle of the limb, it's all there, perfectly intact.

"Oh," Olivia sighs. "This is better than I expected."

I smile as she gets out, turning on her camera. She takes pictures of the water, the trees, me sitting in the Gator. I look up at the sky: no sign of rain. It's kind of disappointing. Swimming in the rain that day with Hattie was the best experience I ever had out here.

After I'd jumped into the water, the water tried to steal me. It tried to drag me under. It tried to pull out my fight. I was scared, but I didn't fight. I let it carry me. And after a while, the water hugged me, cradled me, and lifted me up to the surface. When I was able to breathe, my heart was racing, and I felt more alive than I ever had.

Hattie was standing at the edge of the bank, looking all over for me.

I cried out, "Now who's the scaredy cat?"

"Girl!" she shouted, wiping her face. "I thought I lost you."

"You won't get rid of me that easy!" I wiped the rain out of my face.

With her hands on her hips, she said, "Get on out of there. Let's go home. Your dad'll kill me if he finds out."

She was scared. I could hear it in her voice. And I had never heard that in her voice before. She wasn't scared of my dad. She was scared of losing me.

I swam my hardest, back to the bank, and when I got out, I was exhausted. I sprawled in the dirt in my soaking-wet underclothes, getting pelted by the fat raindrops. Hattie stood in the rain with me.

"Your turn," I joked.

"Li'l girl, I can't believe you did that to me."

I shrugged, wiping my eyes. "I guess I'm more like you than you thought. I won't back down from a challenge."

Hattie shook her head. "*Shit*, I never doubted that you're just like me. I know you are."

Hattie knew. She always knew I was just like her. But I guess, all this time, I'd forgotten about that piece of me that was brave.

As Livvy snaps pictures of the leaning tree, I get out of the Gator. "Did you used to swim here?" she asks, not looking away from the tree.

"Used to?" I rip my shirt off, step out of my shoes and my sweatpants. I walk past her to the leaning tree, wearing bright-pink panties and a navy-blue bra, barefoot and fearless.

"Hell yeah," Olivia says, snapping my picture as I crawl to the middle of the trunk. Then I'm climbing down to the rope, swinging atop the tire like I did that day. "You are a goddess," Olivia says. "A warrior."

She's right. I am a warrior. I faced my to-do list. I fought for my freedom. I stopped allowing Destany and Gia to abuse me. I finally told my parents about Columbia. And now I'm here. I'm back at the place where I first found myself, finding more pieces of who I am.

I dive in and let the cold swallow me up.

WHO I AM

1. ~~A (terrible) liar.~~ Brave enough to take responsibility for the lies I've told.
2. An ugly crier.
3. I always prefer being outside, even when it's raining, even when it's cold.
4. A vegetarian.
5. Socially awkward.
6. ~~A runner, not~~ a fighter.
7. ~~The cowardly lion before he got his courage.~~ A warrior.
8. ~~Not as pretty as her.~~ A goddess.
9. Hattie's granddaughter.

I let Livvy drive back, as I let the wind and the sunlight dry my skin.

"You know, when I used to live in Houston, I would go

to trail rides with my mom. Have you ever been to a trail ride?"

I shift my eyes, confused, motioning to the trail ahead of us.

"No, girl!" She laughs. "A trail ride is a whole event, a whole *sector* of southern Black culture. I'm taking you to Houston. It's trail ride season right now, hell."

I raise my brows. "Okay." I laugh.

"Anyway, my mom used to have this boyfriend, Henry. We'd ride horses down country roads with his family and friends and party every other weekend."

I look at her, wiping a wet strand of hair off my cheek. Her skin is glowing, the sunlight colliding against the beads of sweat on her almond skin.

"Coming through here," she says, motioning to the woods, "it's made me realize how much I miss that. Damn, I miss my horse, Chestnut." She pouts a little, and then turns to me with a smile. "Of all my mom's boyfriends, Henry was definitely my favorite."

"What happened to him?" I ask.

She shakes her head. "He cheated on her, but I mean"— she shrugs—"it was probably the tamest reason she ever broke up with a guy. At least he wasn't a meth head, and at least he never beat her half to death." She turns to me. "Know what I mean?"

No. But I nod anyway.

She continues, turning back to the trail. "Cheating is forgivable. I kinda wish she would've forgiven him."

284

"Do you?"

"Sometimes," she says.

If her mom had forgiven Henry, Livvy might not have ever moved out of Houston. And we might not have ever done this. I might not have ever done this.

"How'd you end up in Austin?" I ask.

"My mom's commissioned by a shop on South Congress to make necklaces and stuff."

"Wow, that's awesome," I say, remembering the jewelry her mom was always making when I came over.

"Yeah, it's pretty cool. It keeps the lights on," she says. "My mom was the one who encouraged me to sell my pictures online."

I can see the fondness in her eyes. They've been through a lot together. I can't even imagine having to deal with a train of men dating my mother, some of them (sounds like *most* of them) turning out to be real shitheads.

She says, driving slowly, "I'm sorry that your dad sold all of this. It really is a treasure."

"Yeah," I say, squinting against the fractured sunlight, breaking through the trees.

"So then . . . why won't you go see her?"

The question is heavy. The answer is heavier. But I don't know, it feels safe here, with her. And I'm still riding a wave of adrenaline. I feel like I can do anything, even talk about Hattie.

"Before my parents decided to admit her to the nursing home, she'd pack up all her things, her clothes, and her pictures—she was always taking pictures off her walls—and she'd load it all in her truck and drive in random directions. It'd take us hours to find her.

"She'd leave the gas on, leave the sink running. She flooded her bathroom. She'd load clothes into the washing machine and never turn it on. Then if she did remember to turn it on, she'd forget to take them out to dry. They'd be covered in mildew by the time we got to them. She couldn't take care of herself anymore."

"I bet that was hard to watch."

I nod to the trees flying past. "I remember my last conversation with her. She asked me to go to her room and get her a blanket because she was cold. She told me to get the blue blanket from her closet, not the one off her bed, because there was a baby sleeping in her bed." I look at Olivia, shaking my head.

"So I checked her bed, and of course, there was no baby. I went and asked her what she was talking about, and she said, 'Baby Quinn.'"

Livvy cringes.

"I said, 'But I'm Quinn.' And she was like, 'Yeah, I know you're Quinn.' She looked so confused. I went to get the blanket, and when I came back, she asked me if I had woken the baby." I bite my lip. "It was too much. I can't even imagine what she's like now."

"I've never experienced anything like that," Livvy says outright. "And I can't pretend that I know how hard it is for

286

you, but I know one thing's for sure—you can't put this off any longer."

"I know," I say. "But it's like the longer I wait, the harder it gets, because I know she hates me for never coming to see her."

"Better to go see her when she's angry than to never get to see her again." Livvy looks at me, then back at the trail. "Besides, if you tell her that your dad is selling her land, maybe she can stop him."

I turn to her, my eyes wide.

She shrugs with a smile. "I know I'd whoop my son's ass if he ever tried to sell something this beautiful of mine."

"Oh my God, Livvy!" I laugh with tears in my eyes. "You're totally right. She'd *kill* him if she knew."

"Yep. Let's go tell his momma what he did!"

We emerge from the woods back into the wide-open pasture. I take a deep breath at the sight of Hattie's house. Once we're parked under the carport, I grab my clothes from the back and get dressed. "Before we leave, can we go inside?"

She looks at me, her brown eyes soft. "Of course."

When we climb the porch, I pause, looking down at the keys in my hand. Hattie's key. I press my hands on the wooden door and unlock it. When the door opens, it still smells the same: like peppermint and tobacco. The armoire with all our pictures is gone. The magazine racks, the fridge, the gas stove, and the Christmas tree saltshaker. The only things left are the bed frames and mattresses in the bedrooms.

I remember how everything used to be. Hattie's chair was by the window, and on the other side was the couch. Right beside the television, Hattie placed the armoire so she could gaze at all our faces—me, Mom, Dad, and Granddad. Dad said she was never the same after Granddad died, but that was the only Hattie I ever knew.

We lock the door back and head to the car. The sun's going down over the horizon as I gaze around the property. I guess this place would be harder to leave if it were still teeming with life, but everything is gone, including Hattie. And even parts of her are disappearing. I don't have much time left. I can't waste another second.

THINGS TO NEVER FORGET ABOUT HATTIE'S HOUSE

1. The curves in her driveway that make it feel like I'm entering Narnia.
2. The creak in the second step of her porch.
3. The sound of rain hitting the tin roof of her carport.
4. The pothole on the trail and the mishaps it's caused.
5. The patches of poison ivy in the woods and the time Hattie showed me how to identify its leaves.
6. The difference between mustard and collard greens, and how Hattie preferred mustards.
7. Me and her, singing in the garden.
8. How the hummingbirds in the greenhouse wouldn't shy away when we were pouring their nectar. The

time one landed on my hand.

9. How to tie a knot as tight as the one holding up the tire swing.
10. The zebra mussels at the bottom of the creek, and just how sharp their shells are when stepped on and cracked open.
11. The fireplace at Christmas.
12. Roasting marshmallows over a gas flame in the summer.
13. White rice in the morning.
14. Ushering in church on Sundays.
15. Her sweet tea recipe.
16. Her lemonade recipe.
17. Her green beans and potatoes recipe.
18. The way she pronounced shit: shet. And how everyone let her get away with saying it as if it's not a curse word.
19. Playing card games and reading books when it was too hot to sit outside.
20. Watching the world spin from her porch swing.

According to Livvy, the nursing home smells, but not as bad as it could.

We go to the front desk and ask to see Harriet Jackson. The receptionist asks for my name and my ID. Livvy has to stay out front, though. "You can do this. You're a warrior."

But I don't feel like a warrior right now. I feel like throwing up.

A nurse shows me down a hallway, keying us in with her badge. The farther we go, the more irregular my steps become. My left foot is taking bigger steps than the right. We come to the end of the hallway, and then the nurse keys us into another. This hallway lets me breathe. It feels less like a hospital and more like a hotel, with carpeted floors and ambient lighting.

The nurse stops in front of door 1243, knocks, and then uses her badge to unlock it. She peeks her head around the corner. "Miss Hattie, you have a visitor."

Then I hear her voice, and my stomach clenches. Her voice sounds different. It sounds weaker. "My son's already been through here."

"Yes, ma'am. Now your granddaughter's here." The nurse opens the door wide for me.

"My granddaughter? Quinn?" Hattie calls. "My Quinn?"

My lungs pump faster, hearing her say my name.

"Yes, ma'am," the nurse answers, nudging her head for me to enter.

I rush inside. She has a huge bed, rounded doorways, clean granite countertops, and a sitting area with a television mounted on the wall.

She's sitting in a chair, her eyes searching for me. She doesn't look the same. She's tiny, frail, her brown skin more wrinkled and darker than I remember, her silver hair thinner too. She's holding her knuckles to the arms of the chair, like she's ready to stand up, but she doesn't look like she can on her own. She looks so small. So, so small.

"Hattie?" I whisper.

"Quinn." She smiles, and I run to her. When I lean down, throwing my arms around her neck, she pats my back weakly.

I pull away, aghast at how weak she is. She could never survive a ride through those woods or bend over to pick greens out of her garden. "I've missed you, Hattie."

"Missed me? We saw each other yesterday, when we went out on the trails." She smiles, but I can't get myself to smile back. She used to be the sanest person I knew, before her brain started wilting. But at least I'm in her made-up fantasies.

Her eyes won't focus on me, or on anything. She looks at the television on the wall, as I take a seat on the couch adjacent to her. I don't know what to say to her, or how to converse with her. She's just watching the world go by, lost somewhere in her memories.

"Hattie," I say. "I need to tell you something." I get up and kneel on the floor in front of her. "Dad's selling your land. Your house. Everything."

She nods. "Yeah, I know. I told him to do it."

"What? Why?"

She shrugs. "I can't take it with me."

I search her eyes, frantically. "Aren't you sad? Your home is gone." *My* home is gone.

"This is my home."

"No, it isn't," I insist. "This isn't your home." How could

anyone let her think this is her home? And how is she so resolved about the fact that she won't ever go home? Not ever. "What about the porch? What about the trails? What about the swimming hole, Hattie? That's your home. That was *my* home. How could you let him sell it?"

"Listen to me, li'l girl." She raises my chin to look in her eyes. "Home is not a place. Home is in here." She pats her hand over her heart. She says, "Don't you fear, I'm right here."

I freeze, searching her dark eyes. She remembers our song? When I'd cry in her garden or at her kitchen table, when I was so worried that my parents were splitting up, she'd remind me that she was with me. I didn't know back then how much I was counting on that to always be true.

I say it with her. "Don't you fear, I'm right here."

I'm full of gratitude that I'm here and that she remembers me. And regret for taking so damn long to face her. I was scared that she'd be unrecognizable, but even though her memories are floating away, everything that remains is still the Hattie who raised me.

MANIFESTATIONS OF HATTIE'S ESSENCE DURING OUR VISIT

1. A basketball game was on the television, but Hattie couldn't stop glancing out the window.
2. I paged the nurse and asked to take Hattie outside, but she said that wasn't a good idea,

because the pollen was especially high today. Then Hattie said in Hattie fashion, "Hush up, girl, and get my wheelchair."

3. We wheeled her through the doors, down the hallways, out front, and Livvy was there waiting. I introduced her to Hattie as my friend, and Hattie looked contemplative. She said, "That's not Destany." I was surprised she could remember Destany. Hattie looked pleased, though. She took Olivia's hand and held it with a smile.

4. We sat in the garden and watched the flowers nod in the light wind, me between Livvy and Hattie, sipping ice water. Hattie grumbled about the food in the cafeteria. She wished she could show those people in the kitchen how to cook real greens—not that canned shit. I told Livvy how good Hattie's greens used to be. Hattie said, "Used to be?" Livvy and I couldn't stop laughing.

5. Hattie started coughing after a while, and I got so scared, I jumped up and tried wheeling her back inside. But she said that she was okay, that she didn't want to go back inside. Her eyes were watering. And I wasn't sure if it was from her allergies or because she really, really didn't want to go back inside. But her coughing got worse, and I had no choice.

6. The nurse gave Hattie room-temperature water

and took us back to Hattie's room. Hattie looked so disappointed when she had to sit back in front of the television. She glanced out the window, then looked at me and ripped my heart in two. She said, "You need to come see me more often, Quinn. Your daddy never takes me outside."

7. I didn't want to leave her. I could tell how cooped up she felt. She never did like staying inside. She's always been too big for indoors. But Olivia was waiting out front, and my parents were blowing up my phone. So I kissed her forehead and promised to be back this weekend. Then she said she loved me. It's been more than a year since I've heard her tell me she loves me. I told her I loved her too and left feeling fractured and healed at the same time.

I should have visited Hattie so much sooner. I should have gone every Saturday. We could have made new memories, and revisited our old ones, and I would have been there to see every grain of sand drift away, savoring all that's left of her.

I wasted so much time living in fear that I thought I was comfortable, but I was writhing in a cage that I didn't know existed, making lists of all my worries with no intent to do anything about them.

Making lists of all my fears kept me from ever facing them.

When we get home, Mom and Dad are coming downstairs. Dad says, "Quinn, where have you been?" Mom looks me over, like she's looking for signs of abuse.

"We went to see Hattie."

Dad's eyes widen, looking between me and Olivia. "You did?"

I nod, looking down to my feet on the tiled floor. "She already knows about the property. It seems I'm the only one who didn't know."

"It all happened so fast," Mom says, stepping around Dad. "We still weren't sure we wanted to sell it when the buyer contacted us."

If Hattie's able to let go, who am I to stop any of this?

"I'm sorry that I lied about Columbia."

Dad's face hardens. Then he shakes his head. "I can't believe you would—"

Mom places her hand on his arm. "Let's take this in strides. For now, go get cleaned up for dinner. Olivia, sweetie, are you staying?"

"Oh, no, ma'am." She mumbles the next part. "Carter's coming to get me."

I turn and look at her, but she avoids my eyes. I say, "Mom, actually, we need to talk to you about something."

She goes over to the refrigerator and Dad turns on the oven. Livvy and I sit at the bar across from them. "How much do you know about cyberbullying?"

Mom spins around. Dad turns to look at us too. I pull out my phone, pulling up the recording of Destany and Gia. "We need your help."

• • •

It's dark outside, but I can see Carter leaning against Olivia's car under the streetlight. I'm peeking out of my bedroom window, from behind my blackout curtains. Livvy comes outside with her backpack, camera around her neck. She goes around to the passenger side, pointing at Carter to drive.

He rubs his hand over the top of his hair and looks up. He sees me, and I freeze. My heart pounds. I almost forget why I'm pissed at him. But then I hurry and turn away, walking to the edge of my bed to catch my breath.

It's been heavy in my pocket since the moment he gave it to me, but now it's burning a hole in my thigh. I have to know. I pull out the folded piece of paper and finally open it.

REASONS I READ YOUR JOURNAL

1. It started out of confusion. I thought your journal was mine at first, but I knew after seeing the list "If I Could Kiss Anyone" that it was your journal, and that it was very personal.

2. I kept going because I saw my name at the end of the list, and I never knew you thought about me like that. I was desperate to find my name again.

3. I didn't respect you. I thought I knew exactly who you were.

4. I was angry because of what happened with your father. I thought you deserved to have your

privacy invaded. I was extremely wrong. No one deserves that.

5. I used to see you write in that journal all the time. I've always been curious to see what you were writing.

6. I was enveloped. The more I read about you, the more I wanted to know. Your imperfections, your mistakes, your desires, everything drew me in. I flipped through your pages, like they weren't pieces of you.

7. Knowing your secrets was like having cheat codes to you.

8. I didn't realize there would be consequences. I thought your secrets would go to the grave with me. I didn't think I'd fall for you.

9. I didn't realize how serious of an offense it was until I saw how much it hurt you.

chapter 25

PROS AND CONS OF
HAVING A LAWYER MOM

PROS AND CONS OF HAVING A LAWYER MOM

CONS:

1. She investigates. I've never been able to fake an illness to get out of going to school.
2. She argues for a living. Winning an argument against her is impossible.
3. She gets in my head. She always knows my next move.
4. She's observant. Lying to her is a full-time job.
5. She's a problem-solver. When problems are presented to her, she's more concerned with solving them than empathizing.

PROS:

1. She's a problem-solver. When problems are presented to her, she solves them.

2. She makes bank.
3. She's an independent bad bitch. (Is it okay to call your mom a bad bitch? Because mine totally is.)
4. If I commit a crime, she'd represent me for free (probably . . . maybe).
5. If someone comes after her child, she comes full speed for their throats.

Principal Falcon has a bronze sculpture of a falcon on the edge of his desk. I stare at it, wondering if it's the sole reason he became a principal. No other office would have held this sculpture so well. Maybe a government office, like Governor Falcon.

I'm sitting between my mom and Olivia. My mom got dressed up and insisted that I dress up too. I didn't, per se, but I'm not wearing sweats. She sits on my left in her attorney clothes—wide-legged black slacks that tie at the waist, silk white blouse tucked in, black pointed-toe stilettos. Her legs are crossed, the bottom foot bouncing.

"I find it interesting that two *Black* students were bullied on school grounds, and you don't seem to think anything can be done."

"Mrs. Jackson, I'm taking this matter very seriously. This"—he points down to my phone—"is grounds for expulsion. I'm only saying there might be pushback."

"And I'm saying there shouldn't be." Mom leans in. "I don't care who Gia's dad is or how much money he donated.

That gives her no right to torment another student. These girls were holding my daughter *hostage*."

"I understand that—"

She leans over and points across me at Olivia. "They ruined this child's reputation a few months ago, spreading disgusting lies, and *vandalized* her work. They've done it twice now, and they'll do it again."

She turns back to Principal Falcon. "Here's the thing: two Black females were harassed under your watch by two white females, one of whom is being protected by a donor. This is a discrimination lawsuit waiting to happen."

His mouth twitches, opening and closing like a fish. I feel so much pride for my mom, it's prickling at my eyes.

"How about we bring the girls in?" He grabs his phone and pages for Destany Maddox and Gia Teller to report to his office. Then he looks at my mother. "I have to ask that you leave the questioning to me. I don't have their parents present—"

"I get it," she says, uncrossing her legs and crossing them the other way.

Then we wait. I look at Livvy, and she looks at me, grinning. She was so excited when I told her my mom was coming. It broke my heart. I imagine she's been waiting for justice for months. She's so strong; she's always made it seem like it never affected her. I can see now how much it has.

The girls come in together. Destany looks scared, but as soon as she sees my mom, she turns terrified. Gia is unbothered. "Yes, Mr. Falcon?"

"Please have a seat."

They pull up chairs, sitting adjacent to his desk.

"Recently, Quinn's journal was stolen, and she was black-mailed by an unknown Instagram account. And Olivia's artwork was vandalized back in January. These girls have reason to believe that you two were responsible for both incidents." He raises his eyebrows, signaling them to speak.

"I don't know anything about that," Gia says.

Livvy scoffs. "Are you kidding me?"

My mom reaches across me and grabs Livvy's hand. Livvy looks into her eyes, takes a deep breath, and sits back in her chair.

"Were you tagged in two lists thought to have come from Quinn's journal?" Falcon asks.

"Well, yeah. Everyone was tagged in the lists."

"But you weren't the ones behind the Instagram account?"

"Nope."

"So you weren't in possession of this journal?" Principal Falcon holds up my red spiral. I wince, seeing his hands stain my cover with yet another set of fingerprints.

"I've never seen that before in my life."

"Interesting," he says. He places the journal back on his desk, then he grabs my phone and plays the recording, starting from when I asked for my journal back, and stopping after Gia threatened to send a message to my father.

Destany's mouth plops open. Gia looks annoyed. "That's not us."

"Both of your names come up," Falcon points out.

"That proves nothing. Can I call my father?" she asks, pursing her lips. "I don't feel comfortable being interrogated and accused for something I didn't do."

"Yes. We will call both of your parents and discuss our next steps."

"Next steps?" Gia asks.

"This offense is punishable by expulsion, Miss Teller. We don't tolerate bullies here."

"Do you know who my father is?" She smiles. "I'm sure he'll love to know that you're questioning us in the presence of a lawyer."

"Mrs. Jackson is here as a mother. Not an attorney."

Well . . .

"Miss Maddox," Principal Falcon says, before Gia can argue. "You've been quiet. Do you have anything to say for yourself?"

Destany looks up at Falcon, then at me. Her nose is turning red, and her eyes are glistening—her sure signs for when she's about to burst. Right on cue, she hunches over, covering her mouth and nose with her hand. "I'm so sorry," she cries.

Gia rolls her eyes up to the ceiling and throws her back against the chair.

"Quinn." Destany looks at me. "You were right. I am a coward."

My eyes start to glisten too.

"I never knew that the . . ." She looks down. "The race stuff, I didn't know it bothered you. I mean, we were all joking. And you were always different. We were never talking about *you*." She looks at me, tears pouring down her face.

She doesn't understand that she can't talk about Black people without talking about me too. She doesn't understand that using the N-word in any context is never a joke. Not for me, it isn't. But she's sorry. She cares. I didn't know she cared. No matter how much she hurt me, there will always be a hole in my heart for her.

"Miss Maddox, did you have any part in this?" he asks her, motioning to my phone and my journal on his desk.

Destany looks at him. Then she blinks up and nods. "I stole the journal."

"And the Instagram account?" he asks.

"I knew about it, but I didn't do the posting." She glances at Gia.

"Miss Teller?" he asks.

Gia crosses her arms over her chest. "Wasn't me."

He nods. Then he looks at my mom. "I'll call their parents now. You're welcome to stay."

"No." My mom stands up, holds her hand out to Principal Falcon. He shakes it. "Let us know your final decisions." Then she faces us. "Girls, let's go."

Falcon hands over my phone and journal. "Do email me that recording," he says.

I nod, following Olivia out of the office. I glance at Destany. She's got her top lip tucked in, watching me go. "Thank you," I say to her.

She slowly closes her eyes and nods. Then she turns back to Falcon, covering her mouth with her hands. Gia doesn't look at us as we leave.

Once the office door is shut, Livvy turns and squeals, hugging me so tight, I can barely pull my arms up to hug her back. Then she runs into my mom's arms. "Thank you so much."

Mom smiles, hugging her back. "You don't have to thank me."

"Yeah we do," I say. "You were awesome, Mom."

Livvy pulls away and nods.

When Mom looks at me, her smile fades. "I just wish I'd known sooner." She shakes her head at me. "I wish I had known everything so much sooner—Columbia, the racism, the blackmail. I can't believe you kept all this from me."

I drop her gaze. "I know. I'm sorry."

She sighs. "Olivia, you can go back to class. Call me if you need anything," she says, looking at her sternly.

"Yes, ma'am." Livvy nods. "Thank you again." Then she turns away, waving at me over her shoulder.

"What about me? I can't go to class?"

"*We're* going to lunch." She leads me down the hallway to the front office.

"Right now?" I ask as she signs me out.

She looks at me with cold eyes. "We have a meeting with one of my friends at UT. You're getting off that wait list one way or another."

We're sitting at a table near the windows, overlooking the porch and decorative palm trees in the distance. It feels like summer in here, like I should be wearing a light dress and sandals instead of these tight jeans and this sweater shirt.

I'm slouching, with my head on the back of my chair. We've been waiting, occupying this table for forty-five minutes, not ordering anything but water.

"Sit up," my mom says, swatting my arm. "She's here."

She's a dark-skinned woman who skirts her heels along the floor. When she sees my mom, she sings, "Wendy!"

"Alorah!" My mom stands and hugs her tight. They rock, humming. Then they hold each other at arm's length.

"Sexy momma," Alorah says, looking at my mom in her office wear.

"Gurrrrl." Mom takes in Alorah's tribal print dress, abundant cleavage, bangles for days, dog hoop earrings, and a vibrant hair wrap tied around the back of her head, her massive pile of curls coming out of the top. Alorah does a twirl as my mom gives her praise. She truly is beautiful. She looks like a queen.

Then she and my mom both stop abruptly. Alorah looks at me over the top of her big round glasses. "Is this the delinquent child?"

I frown and look at my mom.

"Yep. That's her." She motions to me. "Say hello, Quinn."

"Hi." I hold out my hand.

She shakes it as she sits. Then our waiter comes by and hurriedly takes our orders. Once he's gone, Alorah crosses her arms on the table and gets right to it. "Wendy told me about your situation. Pretty messed up what you did."

I shift my eyes, caught off guard by her harsh tone.

"I took a look at your application," she says. "Your GPA and your ACT scores are . . ."

"Bad."

She nods with her teeth bared. "Pretty bad."

I glance at my mom, then down at my glass of water, the condensation dripping down the side. I wonder when we'll get our food. I would like to leave now.

"But then I looked at your essay."

I meet her eyes.

"I guarantee, your essay saved you. It was interesting."

A smile teases my lips. I push it down.

"The prompt was to write about what makes you different from every other candidate," she explains to my mom, then she turns back to me. "You wrote about how good you are at lying to yourself. Ironically enough, your essay was one of the most honest I read in this coming batch." She tilts her head, her curly hair flopping to one side. "Want to tell me about what inspired it?"

"Umm." I don't remember what state of mind I was in when I wrote that essay. It was last minute, early November. "Recently, I've had to face a lot of the lies I've told." I look at my mom. "As much as I lied to you about Columbia, I lied to myself too. My whole life I believed I'd be going to Columbia." I turn back to Alorah. "But I didn't really put in the work, and I don't think I really *wanted* to go to Columbia."

She looks at me with a light smile, the kind that you aren't conscious of.

"I kept all of my truth in a journal so that it could never get out, but once it *did* finally come out, everything blew up in my face. I lied to myself about my friends, that I wasn't offended by their racism. I lied to myself about my grandma, that time would stop for me, and would start back up once I was ready to face her. I lied to myself about my parents."

My mom's chin drops.

Alorah glances at my mom, then back to me. "Lied about your parents how?"

"That anything I did could affect their feelings for each other."

"And when did you stop lying to yourself?"

I smile and shrug. "Today? Yesterday? Literally, at some point in the past three days."

She laughs, turning to my mom. They look at each other for a while, then my mom shakes her head. "Don't start."

"You and Dez?"

Mom looks down at the table. "We're starting therapy."

Alorah tsk-tsks. Then she looks at me. "You know I was your dad's high school sweetheart?"

My face turns horrified, and she laughs at my expression. "I met Wendy at Columbia. I followed your father there."

She shakes her head. "We broke up a few weeks into the first semester."

"Wow." I lick my lips. "So many layers to this story."

She laughs. "I met Wendy in—"

"Women's studies," my mom says.

"Do you know how your parents met?" she asks me.

"All I know is that they met at Columbia."

Alorah smirks. "Wendy was studying in my dorm. I went to do something."

"Shower," my mom fills in.

"And your father came by to drop something off."

"Your sweater."

Alorah smiles. "And what did he say, Wendy?"

Mom rolls her eyes. "*Let 'Lorah know I dropped this off.* But he kept staring at me. He asked me my name and if I would be hanging around more often." Mom smiles. "I said that I would. So he said he'd have to come by and drop off another sweater, then."

I snort. "What? Dad was smooth?"

"Hardly," Alorah says. "Your mom thought he was pretentious. But your mom thought everyone at Columbia was pretentious."

"They were," she says, taking a sip of her water.

"Wendy told me Dez had come by and that he had hit on her." Alorah shrugs. "So I told her she should go for it, but not to get too serious. He was *not* marriage material."

"You didn't care if your friend dated your ex?"

"Girl," Alorah says with pursed lips. "The day your dad and I broke up, I had about ten guys come through my room. I moved on *fast*. He had been my one and only for four years. I was ready for something different."

I nod, laughing. "I see."

"Anyway, this idiot went and married him anyway."

"Hey." Mom laughs. "And we made a beautiful baby girl."

"Yes," Alorah says, smiling at me. "She is gorgeous."

My cheeks warm.

"And smart. Despite the numbers, I can see you have a good head on your shoulders." She pulls her straw from her water, then drops it back in. "You should hear a final answer from the administration by the end of business tomorrow."

I raise my eyebrows. "What does that mean? Does that mean I'm in?" I ask.

"No." She looks at me sternly. "It means what I just said. You'll hear a final answer by the end of business tomorrow."

Mom looks at me with a smile, like she knows something I don't. Or maybe she's still strolling down memory lane. Either way, I smile back at her.

chapter 26

ALL THE TIMES I BROKE
YOUR TRUST

MOM'S ON THE PHONE WITH PRINCIPAL FALCON AS SHE parks in front of the school. "I understand, yes. Thank you." Then she turns to me with round eyes.

"What happened?"

"Gia's been expelled. She won't be able to graduate."

My eyes widen. "Seriously?"

"Destany's only been suspended. She's not allowed to walk, but she'll still receive her diploma."

I nod, dropping my eyes. "That's good for her."

"Is it?"

"Yeah. She should be rewarded for her honesty and for apologizing."

I meet my mom's curious gaze. She smiles and cups my jaw, pulling my face to her lips. "When'd you get to be so mature?"

I laugh a little, the inside of my chest filling up with light and love. "Yesterday?"

She wipes her lipstick off my cheek.

"Thanks, Mom, for your help with everything."

She nods slowly, still disappointed that I kept so much from her. I jump out of her Land Rover wondering what might have been different if I had told her everything from the start, if I hadn't been so afraid to disappoint her and Dad.

When I get inside, sixth period is about to begin. The halls are flooded with people who have already heard about Destany and Gia. I can tell by the way they stare, so apologetically.

I walk through their gazes to my locker. That's where I find him, leaning against the door in blue jeans, a plain white tee, that gold chain and those studs in his ears. My steps slow. I haven't seen him since last night in my driveway, right before I read his list of reasons why he read my journal.

He steps off my locker when I walk up. As I open it, he says, "I don't even know what to say to you right now." He's leaning against the locker next to mine, crowding my space with his height and his warmth and his smell.

I run my hand over my books. I don't remember what book I'm looking for, or what class I have sixth period.

"You told your parents about Columbia, you went to see Hattie, you took down your blackmailers. I'm so proud of you."

A smile teases my lips. It's difficult to fight, because I'm still so full of love from my time with Mom and Alorah. But I push it down because he doesn't deserve to see me smile.

He simmers down, seeing my somber expression. I finally

remember that I'm going to bio this period, so I grab my biology book.

"I got it." He attempts to take it from my hand, his eyes soft on mine.

"I can carry my own books," I say, pulling it out of his reach. I walk past him, heading to Mrs. Yates's classroom.

He follows. "I don't know if you read my note or not, but—"

"I read it," I say, stopping in the middle of the hallway.

He stops, too, surprised.

"It was great," I say, straight-faced. "Now I know why you read my journal. Doesn't make it any better that you read it, though."

"I know."

He looks like he's about to say something else, but I cut him off. "I still don't know who you are." I laugh. "I still don't know if anything between us, if anything you said to me, was real."

He puts his hands out toward me. "*Everything* between us was real."

"Impossible. Not when you were playing, this whole time, with cheat codes." I nod. "Your words. Not mine."

He looks down at the floor, nodding with pinched brows. "You're right. That's why I want to give you this." He wiggles his hand into his pocket and pulls out a folded piece of paper.

I laugh. "Another one? What's this one about, all the times you've ever lied to me?"

He searches my eyes, solemnly. "Yeah, actually." Then he drops the paper atop my biology book and walks away.

I look over my shoulder, my heart wrenching, and he doesn't look back at me. I hate this. I hate fighting with him, but I can't stop feeling sick in my stomach at the idea of what he did.

After I sit at my desk in Mrs. Yates's class, I unfold his note.

ALL THE TIMES I BROKE YOUR TRUST

1. When I read your journal.
2. When I told you I hadn't read any more than the first page.
3. When I told you I thought I left it on the bus. I was panicking. I knew for a fact that I had it during first period, but then it just disappeared. I was hoping that I would find it later and return it to you.
4. When I told you that I don't care about you or your future, that was a lie.
5. When we were on our way to Auden's house, and I said that I wasn't into you like that. I was definitely into you like that.
6. When I invited Livvy to go to Houston with us, I mostly did it because I knew you felt guilty about the smear campaign. I thought it'd be a good chance for you to let that go . . . and I thought you two could become friends. Especially

since, all her life, people have said that she's not Black enough to act as Black as she does. I thought maybe you could relate in a way.

7. "How You Gonna Act Like That" is my favorite song too. That wasn't a lie.

8. When I suggested that Matt was a suspect, I only did it because I was jealous of how much you liked him. Unfortunately, I couldn't stop thinking about all those sexual fantasies you wrote about him.

9. But I never lied about you snoring in your sleep. You do snore. Very loudly.

10. I never lied about my experience at public school, or what happened with Derrick at his pool party.

11. I didn't lie when I said that you were my first girlfriend, or about the reason I've never had one.

12. Imani and I do, however, have a dad, technically. But I refuse to ever speak to that man again. I would love to tell you why.

When I emerge from the classroom, he's standing against the wall, waiting for me. Which is surprising, considering how I chewed him out fifty minutes ago. I thought he was done trying.

I say, "How about when you guessed my favorite color? That wasn't because you read it in my journal?" I'm standing on the other side of the door, against the wall. People are filtering between us, in and out of the classroom. And I can tell he wants to move closer to me, but he doesn't.

"I could have guessed your favorite color the first day in your backyard." He cranes his neck around an especially large group of people entering Mrs. Yates's class. "Your journal confirmed it, but I already knew you loved baby blue."

"Hmm." I look down and slip my hands in my pockets. "And you only brought Olivia to Houston because you thought I needed to let go of my guilt?"

He rubs his neck, avoiding eye contact. "I thought you could apologize, and then you wouldn't feel guilty anymore."

"That's meddling with things that have nothing to do with you." I crinkle my brows, crossing my arms over my chest.

He looks up. "I'm sorry about that. It was none of my business."

I walk past him. "Damn straight."

He follows, not speaking. I know he wants me to ask about his dad, but I'm not ready to appease him or his agenda—as if giving me lists is going to fix everything between us.

We walk silently to Mr. Green's room and sit down across from Auden, who studies us meticulously. He can tell the tension's lessened, but it's not completely gone, either.

Then a body lowers itself on the other side of my desk. I turn and find Matt kneeling by my seat. I tense, because I can feel Carter tense.

"Hey," Matt says. "I heard about Gia and Destany. Why didn't you tell me?"

I twist my mouth. "I didn't want to get you involved. And I didn't want to ruin Destany for you."

"Quinnly, I can't like someone who's racist. I wish you'd told me what was happening to you. I would have helped."

I smile. "I know you would have. Thank you."

Matt looks at Carter behind me for a long second, then he stands up. "I'm glad Gia got expelled. Destany should have—"

"She got what she deserved," I say. "I'm happy with the results."

He looks at me, contemplative, glances back at Carter again, then places a hand on my shoulder before walking away.

During class, Carter and I participate in project planning. Auden gladly accepts our help. After class, Carter and I stay to make up our quiz. Auden already took his in the morning, because of course he did.

We turn in our papers, then Carter walks me to my car in silence. The silence between us is starting to feel comfortable. He opens my back door. I toss my stuff in the back seat. Then he opens the driver's-side door, but I don't get in.

I look up at him, tilting my head. "Why?" I ask.

He raises his brows, caught off guard.

"Why won't you talk to your dad?"

He looks down and back up with a tiny smile. Then he

goes in his pocket and pulls out another folded piece of note-book paper. I purse my lips into an amused smile, shaking my head. He chuckles as I take it and get in my car. I watch him walk to his bus stop, then I unfold it.

REASONS I WILL NEVER SPEAK TO MY FATHER AGAIN (FROM GREATEST TO LEAST)

1. He let me miss my grandma's funeral.
2. I found out she died on Facebook.
3. He didn't tell me she died because he was holding a grudge against me.
4. A grown man was holding a grudge against me, his sixteen-year-old son, because I was suppos-edly ungrateful for all the nice things he's bought me.
5. He agreed to my mom's deal of paying for my tuition instead of child support, knowing that if he paid child support, we might be much bet-ter off.
6. He thinks he can buy my love.
7. He thinks buying me designer clothes counts as being there.
8. He thinks paying for my tuition counts as being involved in my education.
9. He thinks because I'm named after him that I'm at all interested in taking over the family business.

10. *He let my mother name me after him, knowing he wouldn't be around to be my senior. Far as I'm concerned, my name has nothing to do with him.*

Carter Bennett is Carter Bennett II?

I've never felt like I've understood him as much as I do in this moment. His love for Imani and his refusal to let her grow up without a father figure, like he had to. I swear, if my dad let me miss Hattie's funeral, I might murder him. I can't even imagine that pain—missing her funeral. Never getting to say goodbye. My heart hurts for him.

Auden's sitting at Olivia's desk, flipping through the pictures she took at Hattie's yesterday. She and I are sitting on her bed, painting Imani's toenails. Apparently, Carter's out playing basketball with his friends, and Imani didn't want to hang out on the sidelines, so she's here, getting her toes painted pink and purple.

"I want blue nails like yours," Imani says, rubbing her tiny finger over my thumbnail.

"She can have whatever she wants," Livvy says. "Did you see her report card? Exemplary in everything." Livvy tickles Imani's stomach. "She's so smart!"

"That's amazing," I say, smiling. "Wish I had good grades like that."

"You have bad grades?" Imani asks, surprised.

"They're not as good as yours."

"Carter always has good grades," she says, looking at me with pity. "Maybe you should let him teach you."

I smile, finishing up her purple toes. "Maybe I should."

"Livvy, come look at this," Auden says, waving her over.

She puts away the pink nail polish and runs over to join him at her computer screen. As I'm opening the blue polish for Imani's fingernails, I watch as Livvy lets her arm rest on Auden's shoulder. "Audee, this is amazing." She looks at him. "You're such a talented photo editor."

He shrugs. "I'm only good because you are."

I look away, smiling, but then Livvy calls, "Quinn, come look at this."

She takes the blue polish from my hand, and we switch places. I stand next to Auden's chair, staring at a phenomenal photo of me at the swimming hole, swinging on the tire swing. I'm in my underwear, my body, with all its flaws, exposed. My hair is wild and blowing in the wind, mouth open in a smile, one hand on the rope, the other arm spread wide. I look freer than free, as happy as I was when I was with Hattie.

And the way Auden edited it, my dark skin pops against the green trees and the blue water. I'm not muddled in with the background. I pop.

I'm breathless, staring at myself.

"You're going on this wall," Olivia says, motioning to the empty wall behind her bed. I look at the tapestry of her mom and imagine myself as a tapestry.

"You two make a great team," I say, tearing my eyes away from the photo.

"We do, don't we?" Livvy smiles at Auden.

I take the nail polish from her, letting her reclaim her place at his side, and finish up Imani's fingers. Then there's a knock on the door, and before anyone can answer it, Carter steps inside.

"Carter, Carter, Carter!" Imani jumps up and runs to him. "Look at my nails! Queen did my nails!"

Queen. I smile and breathe a laugh through my nose.

He gasps, taking her hands in his. "Beautiful, 'Mani."

"They're blue like hers."

He looks at me and smiles. "Yep. They're gorgeous." He glances at Livvy and Auden huddled together, then back to me. "You ready, 'Mani?"

"Wait, I have to get my stuff," she whines, running around the room, picking things up with the base of her hands, careful to not mess up her nails.

"Okay, baby. I'll be outside." He looks at me and nudges his head. "Can I talk to you?"

I debate it only for a second before I'm following him into the dark hallway. When we get to the living room, he kisses Olivia's mom on the forehead. "All right, Momma."

She nods. "Love you."

"Love you too."

Then he leads me out the front door, and we're alone,

sort of. We're in the middle of the city, so life is bustling all around us, but the top of these stairs feels isolated and private, especially when Carter turns to face me. "Thanks for doing her nails. I know she loved that."

It's dark out, but I can still see him. I go over to the banister, lean on the railing, and inhale through my nose. The air is warm, like stepping into a bath, even though the sun is gone for the day. I exhale and say, "I'm sorry about your grandma."

He's standing behind me, and he's careful to keep his distance. I appreciate that.

"And I'm sorry about your dad. If my dad ever did something like that to me, I would never speak to him again, either." I turn around to face him, hanging my elbows over the banister.

"Thank you." He smiles, running his hand over the back of his head.

We look at each other silently. I try to assess what it is I feel for him. My mouth tastes sour when I think about how many lies he's told and how much he knows about me. But when I look in his eyes, I can see how committed he is to winning my forgiveness. And when I look at his lips, I can feel how much I want to forgive him. Then I look at him as a whole, and my mouth gets sour again.

I look down. Then I say it, because I can't help myself. I tell him about my lunch today and that I might get to go to UT, and he genuinely looks excited by the prospect. I tell him about Alorah and my parents and their history.

He laughs. "Your mom is best friends with your dad's ex?"

"Something like that."

"That's awesome," Carter says. "God, I hope you get in."

I glance up into his eyes. "Me too."

Then Imani walks out of the door with a big plastic backpack on her back. She pauses when she sees us, but then she runs over and hugs my leg. "Bye, Queen."

"Bye, Imani." I run my hand over her braids.

Then she grabs Carter's hand. He follows his sister down the stairs. Looking over his shoulder, he says, "Bye, Queen."

I roll my eyes and smile. When he gets to the bottom, he picks her up, pulling the cutest laugh from her lips. He looks up and gives me a head nod before disappearing around the corner.

chapter 27

REASONS I CAN'T BRING MYSELF TO WRITE ANOTHER LIST

MOM AND DAD ARE HAVING DINNER ON THE PATIO. I GO upstairs, caught in a web of realizations. I have a bio test tomorrow, and in between studying, I'm rereading my journal.

I flip to my *If I Could Kiss Anyone* list and look at Carter's name at the very bottom, Matt's name at the top, and all the famous people in between. This list is so inaccurate now.

I look at all my Matt moments and all my sexual fantasies. I reread every horrifying memory. None of it seems so bad now, and most of the things that I would never admit out loud, I've already admitted.

Then I look at my moments with Hattie. If she's losing all her memories, isn't it my responsibility to hold on to them for her? But maybe none of this matters. Maybe the only thing I need to remember is my name, who I love, and what I love about life. That's all Hattie remembers. Maybe that's all that matters.

I realized on the drive home that I haven't written a new list since I got my journal back. And the thought of trying to write a new list turns my stomach. It doesn't feel safe anymore.

And it doesn't even feel good anymore. Containing my feelings in this journal blew up in my face in the worst way imaginable. It's not that I'm scarred. I'm just different. I don't need it, not since I started bursting. I always thought that the second I was crazy enough to get rid of my journal, I would have proper coping methods in place, but after I lost it, I think I might have developed those.

I flip to the to-do list that started it all.

TO DO BEFORE I GRADUATE
1. ~~Visit the two universities I got accepted into.~~
2. ~~Admit my love~~ feelings ~~for Matthew Radd~~ Carter Bennett.
3. ~~Experience Austin's supposedly incredible night-life.~~
4. ~~Tell my parents I didn't get into Columbia.~~
5. ~~Visit Grandma Hattie.~~
6. ~~Tell Destany the real reason I ghosted her.~~
7. Save for last. You know what you have to do.

I think I might be ready to do the last thing.

The next morning, I wake before the sun. I put on makeup because I'm certain I won't be crying today. I grab a green T-shirt dress that ties at the bottom, cutting me high on my thighs. Paint my toenails orange, slip on a pair of wedge heel sandals, and put on a pair of big hoop earrings, taking a page out of Alorah's book.

When I come downstairs, Mom lights up when she sees me. Dad frowns.

"Change," he says.

Mom flicks her hand across his arm. "She's beautiful and *grown*." She looks at me with a bright smile. "As well as a future UT freshman."

"Wait, what?" My mouth drops open.

"Alorah called. She couldn't wait to tell me."

"Are you serious?" My eyes water. *Damn it!* I blink up to the ceiling. I swore to not cry today. Mom pulls me in her arms, then Dad hugs us both.

He kisses my forehead. "Congratulations."

"You're not mad?" I ask him.

"I'm furious." He looks at me like I'm crazy, but then his eyes soften. "But I'm still proud of you. I know Hattie will be happy to hear the news. You won't have to move so far away from her now."

You see that? That's what did it. A joyful tear drips past the mascara on my bottom lashes. "Okay, I gotta go." I pull away from my parents. Already ruining my makeup, and I haven't even gotten to school yet.

"Quinn, come home right after school," Dad calls after me. "We have to pack up the rest of Hattie's stuff today."

My steps falter, my stomach flipping. It feels too soon. I just got Hattie back, and now I have to say goodbye to a huge chunk of what made us *us*. Dad's eyes apologize when his lips can't. I turn away, grateful, knowing that's a lot more than I would have ever gotten a few weeks ago.

I get to school and spot Carter waiting for me in the parking lot. A defiant smile breaks out across my face. I can't wait to tell him the news.

When I get out of my car, he looks me up and down, his lips parting. "Damn." Then he catches himself. He clears his throat. "Sorry. Uh, let me get your bag for you."

Heat rises up my neck, all the way to my temples. As he's opening my back door, I take a breath, straightening my dress. "Guess what," I say nervously as he's leaning inside my car.

"What?" He glances at me over his shoulder.

An excited smile crosses my lips. "I got in."

He pauses, holding my backpack, looking at me with his eyes wide. Then he slams my door shut. "That's amazing, Quinn!" He pulls me in for a hug, lifting me off my feet. I squeak, not expecting him to break through the wall that's been separating our bodies for three days now.

Then he remembers the wall too. He sets me back down, taking a step back. It's cute, because he can't seem to contain himself today. I straighten my dress with an embarrassed smile.

"Congratulations," he says courteously. "I'm so happy for you."

"Thank you."

Then we're walking side by side to the building, the silence much less comfortable now. The seal's been broken, and now I have this raging desire for him to touch me again.

Between third and fourth periods, I'm leaning my back against the lockers, and Carter's standing in front of me. He hands me a folded piece of paper.

Feeling bold, I unfold it and read it in front of him.

REASONS I CAN'T STOP THINKING ABOUT YOU

1. You made a home in my head, and no matter how many evictions I send, you won't leave.
2. I don't ever want you to leave.
3. Imani won't stop asking about you.
4. Olivia won't stop talking about you.
5. And I can't keep my eyes off you.
6. I can always sense when you're near. My energy shifts to make room for yours.
7. Not even your journal could answer all the questions I have about you.

It's the last item that I keep reading over and over. Because maybe that's a fear that I didn't realize I had—since he's read my journal, he practically knows everything about me, so there isn't a need to get to know me.

Maybe that's why his "meddling" felt so awful. Because

he made assumptions based on what he read in my journal, as if he knew what I needed without talking to me first.

When I look up, I swallow hard. "This is nice. Thank you."

He smiles. "Sure."

After school, he walks me to my car. He asks me how I think I did on the biology test. I tell him "well enough." Then I think about what Imani said about him tutoring me. He reads my mind, because he says, "Next time, we should study together."

I grin to myself. "Yeah, maybe."

After putting my backpack in, he opens the driver's-side door for me. "Congratulations again. We should celebrate soon." Then he pulls another folded piece of paper out of his pocket.

I don't know if I can handle another one of his lists. I take it, timid, deciding to not read it in front of him. I'm not brave enough to let him see me come unwound.

"Think I could call you tonight?" he asks.

My heart rate spikes. I blink and nod before climbing in. He shuts my door and waves before walking to his bus stop. I flip the note between my fingers, watching him in my rear-view. Then I open it.

BECAUSE IT'S OBVIOUS, AND I'M OBSERVANT
1. You haven't written in your journal since you got it back. I'm sure having so many people read

your deepest, darkest secrets ruined it for you.
I'm sorry.

2. You're happy now. I can see it. You're glowing.

3. You know exactly how sexy you are. Don't front.

4. And you know how weak in the knees I get when you smile at me. You should exploit that more.

5. You bite your bottom lip when you're trying to contain yourself. I just wonder what would happen if you didn't try to contain yourself anymore.

I'd bubble over, I'd let myself go, I'd jump out of my car and call to him, like I'm doing right now. "Hey!"

He turns around, halfway to his bus stop.

I stand in the open door of my car, incapable of settling on one thought, one emotion, one directive.

He sees my reluctance and walks back to me, crossing through traffic in the parking lot. When he stops in front of me and I look up at him, I know that I'm ready to talk. I'm more than ready to talk. I need to burst and say every sour word that's been whirling around in my head.

"Definitely call me tonight. Okay?"

He nods, examining my face. "I will."

"And make sure you have time, because I have a lot to say."

He smiles, licking his lips. "Bring it. I got all the time in the world for you."

"Good." I nod, looking down at the ground between us. "That's good."

Then I look up, nervous. I don't know what I want from him, but I don't want him to walk away yet. He watches me attentively.

Then he takes a step closer. My heart races. I don't know if I want him closer. He takes another step, slow, watching my eyes, and stops, his sneakers a foot away from my sandals. He reaches out for my hand. His pointer and middle finger tinker along the tips of mine.

I exhale, looking down at my toes, and wait for his feet to close the gap. I hold my breath for his body to press warm against mine, but instead he takes a step back, extending my arm by the tips of my fingers, and I can breathe again. I look in his eyes, and he's smiling gently. Then he lets go of my hand, turns, and walks away.

My fingers fly up to my lips, astonished that he didn't try to hug me or kiss me. I turn my back to him, then look again over my shoulder. He's looking back at me, too.

When I climb in my car, I try to catch my breath. He could tell how uncertain I was, so he didn't push me. I'm so glad he didn't push me.

I'm driving slowly over the gravel, tiny rocks clinking against the bottom of my Mercedes. A U-Haul truck is parked in Hattie's driveway when I pull up. The front door is open. My dad comes out holding the end of my old twin-size mattress, followed by my mom on the other end.

I get out as they're setting it in the truck. It's hot, and I'm not wearing the right outfit for this. My mom claps her hand over my shoulder, walking me up the sidewalk to the porch. She doesn't say anything. She just holds me close. Dad rubs the bottom of my back as he passes us on the porch steps.

"Now that Quinn's here, we can get these frames," he says.

Mom continues inside after him. But I stop on the porch and hold on to one of the wooden pillars, slipping off my heels, feeling the familiar gritty wood beneath the soles of my feet. I follow my parents into Hattie's bedroom, and even though it's empty, it's hard to not see it how it used to be.

The shelves in the walkway, before you get all the way in the room, were always stacked with blankets and fresh towels. Her old-fashioned box TV, where we'd always watch *Judge Judy* before falling asleep, would sit on the TV stand in the corner of the room, atop a white lace cloth.

Beneath the cloth were shelves full of junk, like that red cup full of nails and screwdrivers, two paper clips, and one pink hair comb.

Her dresser was off to the side, covered in fingernail polish and lipstick, mostly shades of red because Hattie was always bold, even before the red-lipstick-dark-skin campaigns. Her window was on the far wall, with white lace curtains that were really just rolls of fabric tacked to the wall.

Her closet always had Sunday dresses hanging inside and all over the door, cloaked in the plastic bags you get at dry cleaners. She always hung her red suit on the doorknob. She didn't wear it often, but I could tell it was her favorite.

Hattie's comforter, I can't even remember what it looked like. I think it was white, or maybe beige. I remember exactly how it felt, though. Her bed was the most comfortable bed I've ever lain in. I don't know if it was because of her mattress, that soft, heavy comforter, or if it was just lying next to her, but I always slept better in her bed.

None of that's here now. All that's left is her bed frame. Dad's standing against the wall at one end of the frame. Mom is standing closest to me on the other end.

Dad says, "Quinn, have I ever told you about when Hattie first met your mom?"

I shake my head, intrigued.

He leans his back against the wall, stroking his beard, and Mom takes a seat on the edge of the bed frame.

"Your mom went back to Chicago for the summer after our freshman year, but when she got there . . ." Dad suddenly looks uncomfortable.

But Mom picks up her head and says, "I didn't have a home to go back to. My mom was out on the street. No one knew where she was, or if she was alive. And my family wasn't exactly welcoming, so the angel herself, Hattie Jackson, invited me to come live here for the summer."

She looks at Dad. He says, "We flew her out and she stayed in your old room."

"Really?" *How am I just hearing this story?*

Dad nods. "Your mom cried for about two weeks straight.

She was afraid of being a burden—"

"And scared, because what if things didn't work out between me and Dez? Where would I go?"

"I tried to reassure her that no matter what, she would have a place to go. But—" Dad shakes his head. "Finally, your mom was crying herself sick. Hattie called her to the kitchen, and out of nowhere, she taught Wendy how to cook green pinto beans."

"I'd never had green pinto beans before." Mom laughs. "But Hattie could *throw down* in the kitchen."

I smile. Hell yeah, she could.

"Helping her cook the beans took my mind off things, and made me feel like I was actually contributing, so I stopped crying, then she offered me a job at the feed store."

"You know Granddad's old feed store?" Dad asks me.

"Of course." Granddad used to own a feed store in town. By the time I was born, though, Granddad was gone, and Hattie couldn't keep it up on her own, so she sold it.

"So, all summer I earned my keep in the feed store. I paid rent." Mom smiles. "And every Tuesday, Hattie would reward me by cooking my favorites: green pinto beans, fried chicken, or smothered pork chops.

"Then she and I would sit down, just me and her, and watch soap operas together. She loved soap operas, and I started to really like them too. Honestly, sweetie," Mom says, leaning forward with glistening eyes, "I never knew what it felt like to have a mom until I stayed here with Hattie."

Then she looks at Dad with a tilted head. When she turns back to me, she's crying. My lips tremble. I can't watch her cry. I cannot. I walk over and hug her.

Dad watches us with crossed arms and a smile. I wipe under Mom's eyes. She says, "I love, love, love you so much, and I hope you never question that."

"I never have."

We all take a breath, and then we take our places at the edges of the bed frame. "We'll have to turn it on its side to get it out of the door," Dad says. Then he looks at me across from him. "Quinn, I was hoping you'd bring your boyfriend with you. We could have used the extra manpower."

My eyes shift, and my mouth opens slightly.

Mom snaps, "Desmond."

"What?" he says, confused. "It's not like it's a secret. I'm the one who walked in on them kissing. You didn't have to see that."

My mouth opens farther. This is so embarrassing.

"Dez, Quinn's an eighteen-year-old girl. Just because she kissed a boy, that doesn't make him her boyfriend." Then she looks at me with her chin high. "Am I right?"

I roll my eyes and sigh. "Yeah."

"Things have changed," Dad sings.

Mom purses her lips at me. "They haven't changed all that much."

Once we get all the bed frames in the back of the truck, Mom and Dad work on driving the Gator onto the ramp. I head across the yard in my wedge heels with my journal in hand. In the far edge of the backyard, there's a patch of ash like a hole in the green grass, where Hattie burned leaves and brush and things she didn't need anymore.

That's the attitude I'm trying to summon right now. I have a lighter and a tiny stack of limbs and a shit ton of paper that no longer serves me. I rip out my first to-do list, the list that started this all, and set it ablaze. Complete. And now that it's complete, I have so much room on my shelves for all the things this new Quinn's going to do.

Like all the new memories I'm going to make with Hattie every weekend. And all the new things I'm going to try with my new friends. Because without this journal, I won't have a bunch of lists dictating who I am. Maybe my new favorite color will be green or red or maybe it'll be blue forever. I'll decide on the fly. And all the new fantasies I have about Carter. But this time I'll do what I can to make them real.

I throw the burning to-do list on the pile of sticks and watch them catch fire. Then I gaze down at the red spiral in my hand. I squeeze it tight, knowing that without it, I'll have so much room to burst. It contained my feelings when I didn't know how to express them out loud, but now I can't do that anymore. I cannot be contained. I'm too big for this journal.

So I throw it in the fire without allowing myself to over-think this moment. I watch it burn, my hand over my mouth. I almost want to run in and stamp out the flames, because it feels like my memories are fading before my eyes. When did I first write down my ugly cries? When were the best days of my life?

I take a step back, though, shaking away those questions. I know who I am. I'm the girl who got rejected from Columbia. I'm the girl who's terrible at English but good at writing funny captions. I'm the girl who learned to stand up for herself. I'm the girl who faced all her fears.

My red cover turns to black. I turn on my heel and say goodbye to what's left of Hattie's property as the ashes of yesterday's fears rise high in the sky.

chapter 28

IF CARTER HADN'T LOST
MY JOURNAL

"SORRY I WAITED SO LONG TO CALL YOU. IMANI WAS IN
rare form tonight."

"It's okay."

"Are you in bed? Did I wake you?" he asks.

"I'm in bed, but I wasn't asleep."

We're quiet. He's waiting for me to start, but I'm not sure
how. I've been practicing in my head, but now that he's here
on the line, I'm freezing up.

"Carter," I say. It's a heavy start—his name. I don't think
I've said it in days.

"Yes, Quinn?"

I take a deep breath. "So, walk me through it. You were
about to study for history. You opened the last section of
the journal and saw my 'If I Could Kiss Anyone' list. Then
what?"

"After that, I knew it was your journal and not mine. But
I couldn't help but read the whole list. Then when I saw my

name at the bottom"—he takes a deep breath, speaking on his exhale—"I started flipping pages, looking for my name. I didn't realize what I was doing at the time."

"You didn't have feelings for me back then."

"I didn't know you. The only thing I knew was that you were beautiful."

"Okay," I say, letting that settle. "You decided to lie to me about reading it because . . . ?"

"Because I was ashamed. And because I knew you'd be embarrassed. At the time, I thought I would give you back the journal and be done with the whole thing. You would never have to know that I'd read it."

"Because you had no plans of pursuing me?"

"Well . . . I never had plans to make you my girlfriend, no."

I gasp. "You were gonna take me to bed and that's it?"

He laughs. "Quinn!"

"The audacity! I am a *lady*." I smile.

"If you were down, I was down, is all I'm saying."

I wonder if I would have. I can't imagine only wanting him for sex and nothing else.

"Okay, back to the matter at hand."

"Yes, ma'am."

I flip over onto my side, resting his voice between my head and my pillow. "Why were you so mean to me that first day at my house?"

He sighs. "I misjudged you as a stuck-up rich girl. And an Oreo. I wasn't your biggest fan at the time."

338

"But that didn't change the fact that you wanted to—"

"Smash?" He laughs. "Hell no. I mean, I wasn't blind."

I nibble on my bottom lip. "Hmm. Okay. So, you were helping me with the list. We went to Houston, and you took the liberty of inviting Livvy, because you thought it'd be a good opportunity for me to apologize . . ."

He's quiet.

"You know all that meddling I've been talking about?"

"Uh-hmm."

"You know why it pissed me off?"

He pauses. "Why?"

"You assumed you knew what was best for me. Just because you read my journal, that doesn't mean you know everything about me."

He sputters, "I never thought I knew everything about you."

"Good. Because you don't. There are things about me that you won't get from reading my journal."

"I know, Quinn. Like I said, I want to get to know all of you. Not just what you thought was interesting enough to write on your lists."

I chew on the inside of my bottom lip. "Well, I guess that should be easier now that I've burned it."

"What do you mean you burned it?"

"That was the last thing on the list—to get rid of the journal for good."

He breathes, and I listen for any hitches. "Wow, I would have never guessed."

"You would have never guessed that I could be so brave?"

"No, I know you're brave. I would have never guessed that the last item would be so . . . evolved. And before you take that the wrong way—"

"I wasn't *going* to," I say, smiling.

"Hmm," he hums, unconvinced. "Well, what I meant was, burning the journal is such a self-developed thing to do. You knew that it was a bad habit, and you intended to stop."

I listen to the AC blow through the air vent in my ceiling. I listen to him turn over in his bed.

"Carter?" I ask.

"Yeah?"

"You read my most horrifying memories, right?"

"I did."

"Even the one about when I was in kindergarten?"

"Yeah." His voice is quieter.

"What did you think when you read that?"

"I was a little surprised, but it was nothing compared to reading your sex fantasies. You put so many details in . . . you should write erotica."

I laugh. "Okay, never mind. Next topic."

"I'm serious! You could make a career out of that."

"Next question," I say, grinning.

He calms down, then he croons low in my ear, "What's your next question, bae?"

Tingles spread throughout my middle, down to my thighs. "Did anything happen between you and Emily Hayes?"

"Are you serious?" He laughs. "You believed that bullshit rumor?"

"Well, I wasn't sure. She's a pretty girl."

"She's not my type, like, at all."

"What *is* your type?"

"You." He lets that word stir me up. Then he says, "Obviously."

I smile, riding the wave of a thousand butterflies. I try to force it away, but it's like the exact opposite of my ugly cry. I've completely lost control over my face muscles. I say, "Okay. Next question."

Dad's back at work. Mom's still getting dressed when I come downstairs. I grab an apple from the bowl, tired from staying up all night on the phone with Carter, but amped to see him today.

I walk outside, feeling confident and excited until I see a girl standing in my driveway, hands in the pockets of her sweatpants, hair in a high ponytail. "Hey, Quinn," she says, weakly.

"Destany?"

We're sitting on the curb. I thought about inviting her inside, but I didn't want to contain the tension between us. It's too much.

She bends over to hug her knees to her chest. "Quinn." She sighs, looking up at the morning sun. "I was mad."

My mouth opens. I almost rip into her, because *I was mad* is never a good excuse, ever, but I hold my tongue.

"You weren't talking to me, and I thought you were throwing away our friendship because of a stupid boy. So I took your journal. I wasn't going to read it. I was just going to . . . hold it captive until you talked to me. Gia was the one who started reading it. It was her idea to do the blackmail. And, I don't know. She convinced me that you cared more about Matt than you did about me. I was stupid. I'm sorry."

I look down at my hands in my lap. That feels a little better.

"It's been really hard knowing that you think I'm a racist. You know I never thought less of you because of your skin color, right?"

I look across the street at the Johnsons' house, their empty driveway, the sprinklers spraying their green grass. "I think you were trying to be color-blind."

"Yes, exactly. I always forgot you were Black. You know? Like, it's not something I thought about."

I look at her and her makeup-free face. "That's not a good thing."

She bunches up her brows.

"When you think of me, I want you to remember that I'm Black. It's a huge part of my identity."

"You want me to constantly think about how different we are?"

"I want you to be able to celebrate our differences. I need you to be aware that our differences will get us different outcomes in life. And I need you to know that just because I don't fit into your stereotypes, that doesn't mean I'm any less Black." I grind that last sentence out. If she doesn't walk away hearing anything I've said, please at least let her hear that.

"Quinn, I was just joking about the 'practically white' thing."

"But you understand how that's not funny? And how inappropriate that joke was in that moment? Gia was repeatedly using a racial slur, and that *hurt* me. That word *hurts* me."

"I didn't know that. I mean, we've used that word before, and you never said anything. I wish I knew. I wish you'd told me."

I look down with a sigh. "I just wish I didn't have to tell you. I wish I didn't have to have this conversation with you. It's exhausting."

She looks offended. "I'm sorry. I just wanted to talk. I wanted to understand."

"I know that." I tilt my head. "And I appreciate it. I just hate that it has to be explained. But, Destany"—I turn to her—"please don't stop asking questions. I'm glad you care enough to ask. And I'm willing to talk, if you're willing to listen."

"Of course I am. We've got a few months before I move to Dallas. Where are you going to school, by the way?"

"UT."

"Oh?" Her eyes smile. "That's great."

"Thanks."

She stands up and offers me a hand. "I'll call you later?"

I blink a couple of times, thinking. I'm not sure that I'm ready to have another conversation like this so soon. "Maybe I can come over next weekend?" I take her hand and let her lift me up.

She nods with a smile, stepping backward toward her car. "It's a date, then. Hope Carter doesn't get too jealous."

I smile, too, hoping that by then I'll be ready to talk. I thought after finding my journal at her house I would never speak to her again. How could I? Our relationship has always been laced with toxicity, but if I don't give myself this chance to explain my pain, then it will always be that way. And I'm so done with letting pain take the wheel. Now it's time to let love drive.

"Quinn, you have to sit still."

"But Carter's texting me." I bite down on my grin, looking at my phone. He says, **What are we doing after the mall? I want more time with you.**

"Head up," Livvy sighs, doing her best to gather all my hair between her hands.

I type: **Whatever you want. I want more time with you too.** "Okay, I'm done." I reach back and place my phone on my desk.

She brushes the front of my hair into her hand, then drops the brush in my lap. I close my eyes and relax into her closeness. It's been two days since I burned my journal. The desire to write lists still visits, but it never comes inside. It looks in through my windows and watches me burst and laugh and live my life. I've been so busy living that I've barely missed my journal.

But I tend to think in lists. Like, when Livvy stayed over last night, I thought of all the things we could do together. Then I realized that they were all things that I would do with Destany, so I scrapped that list. I let her decide what we would do instead.

She wanted to swim, so afterward, we washed and deep conditioned our hair, watched movies, and ate snack cakes.

She starts to tie a band around my hair, letting it all flow over my forehead, but when my phone vibrates, I reach for it without even thinking.

"Quinn!"

It takes two hours for us to get ready. Livvy does my makeup and picks out a short spaghetti-strap black dress that I haven't worn since I was at least ten pounds lighter, showing all the twists and turns in my body. But at least she doesn't make me wear heels with it.

As for Livvy, I style her natural, shoulder-length, curly hair, parting it down the middle and tying it up in two pig-tail top knots. She wears a white lace see-through top with a black bra underneath and black high-waisted shorts. *We look extra hot.*

So when we're coming down the stairs, smelling like vanilla and shea butter, my dad shakes his head in the kitchen.

"Change. Both of you."

Livvy looks at me, eyes wide.

Mom comes to our rescue from the living room. "Dez, leave them alone. They're adults."

"Uh, honey. You're not seeing what I'm seeing."

Then she comes around the corner with her reading glasses on the tip of her nose. When she sees us, she cringes. "Yeah, no. Go change."

"Mom," I whine, tilting my head.

She tilts her head, too, eyes skeptical. "At least put on a sweater."

I look at Olivia. Then we turn to my mom, in agreement. "Okay, sure."

We toss the sweaters in my back seat and peel out.

The boys are waiting for us in the food court. "Okay, Quinn. Chin up. Shoulders back. Strut," Livvy says when Auden and Carter come into view. They're sitting together at a table, and they haven't caught sight of us yet.

Livvy struts, and she's damn good at it, her golden-brown skin free and exposed. I don't often get to see her natural hair. She doesn't like to keep it out of her microbraids for long, because she hates taking care of it, but it's gorgeous. *She's* gorgeous.

Auden's jaw drops when he sees her. He nervously runs his fingers through his curly hair, not looking away for a second.

Carter notices and turns, following his gaze.

I try strutting for about three steps, but I feel like a fish out of water. I'm walking as normal as I can, but I don't know what to do with my hands.

Either way, Carter is entranced. He rubs his hand over his mouth and down to his beard. Then he stands up abruptly and hurries toward us. He's got a black baseball cap on backward, with a graphic tee and blue jeans. Simple, but so sexy.

He's hurrying through the crowd, forgetting his manners. When he reaches us, Livvy stops in front of him. "Hey, Carter."

He barely pauses. "Move!" He swerves past her to get to me.

"Rude," she gripes, heading over to Auden.

He stops right in front of me, pulling his bottom lip into his mouth, eyes dropping to my thighs, both hands adjusting the cap on his head. Then he meets my gaze. "Queen Jackson, I am not worthy."

I cover my smile with my hand. He reaches over and pulls my hand away from my lips, then he kisses the top. "Ready to pick out a graduation dress?" he asks, taking a step closer.

"I guess." He swings my arm around his neck, resting his hands on my hips. I swing my other arm around his neck, looking up into his eyes. "I don't really care," I say. "It'll just be covered by my gown, so what does it matter?"

"True." He glances down at my lips, but then he looks away, exhaling. We haven't kissed again. Not since we started "building trust." We've both wanted to, but it hasn't felt right. The sour taste in my mouth still lingers, even after the nasty words have gone. It's taken a minute for it to fade back to sweet desire.

Instead, he pulls me against his chest. "But it's a big deal. We're graduating."

"Yeah," I say, losing myself in the warmth of his neck.

"Carter Bennett, release her this second. If you mess up all my hard work, I'll kill you."

Livvy and Auden stand behind us, waiting.

"Okay!" Livvy claps her hands once we've pulled apart. "Let's go."

I join her at the front, while the boys follow behind. She grabs my arm and whispers in my ear, "Auden was literally speechless when I tried talking to him."

"I bet he was. You look sexy as hell."

She bites her lip. "I think I'm gonna ask him out today."

"Are you ready for that?"

She shrugs with a bubbly smile. "Yeah, I think so."

I bump her side, giddy. She and Auden would be so perfect together.

Once we get to the first store, she rushes over to the clearance rack, while I hang back, mindlessly flipping through crop tops near the front doors. Carter comes over and watches me for a second. I meet his eye.

"Wanna try any of that on?"

"Oh, no, I'm good. I'm not a huge fan of this place. Not my style."

He looks over my curves and hums. "Come here," he says, grabbing my hand. I glance over my shoulder. Livvy's tucking Auden's head through a hanger, draping a slinky dress over his body. She laughs, and he laughs too.

I smile as Carter leads me out of the store. He pulls me against the wall, out of the way of traffic, turning to face me. There's purpose in his eyes, like he has something to say.

"What is it?" I ask.

He holds both of my hands in his, making a sort of bridge between us. "I'm sorry, Quinn, for hurting you."

My eyes sink. "I know."

"If it weren't for me, your journal would have never gotten lost, and none of this would have happened."

"Yeah, so maybe it's a good thing it got lost." I look down between our arm bridge. "If you hadn't lost my journal, I know for a fact I would have never faced that to-do list."

"I don't believe that." I look up, and he's shaking his head. "You're strong. You would have done it on your own."

"Yeah?"

He nods.

I try to imagine what my life would have been like had he not lost my journal. I don't know if I would have ever had a conversation with Olivia, or Auden, or *him*. Maybe I would have had the courage to do the list on my own, but I wouldn't have had nearly as much fun as I did conquering my fears with my friends by my side.

"I wish we would have started talking earlier," I say. "Like, after that English project sophomore year."

"Me too," he says, smiling.

"And I could have known you sooner. You and Olivia."

"And Auden," he says.

"And Imani," I say, raising my brows.

He smiles, showing his teeth. "She wanted to come with us, but"—he shakes his head—"I wanted you to myself today. I'm excited for our date after this. I'll give you the exclusive tour of the east side." I watch his eyes sparkle as he lists all the places he wants to show me, and I feel so lucky to have the chance to know him. To know him *better*.

"The art is incomparable, and so is the food. I promise you're gonna love this."

"Carter"—I take a step closer—"where does your mom work?"

I can see the surprise in his expression. "She has two jobs. She does hair at a shop on MLK, and she's an overnight stocker at Target."

I take another step forward. "Is that why your hair always looks good?"

He smiles. "I guess." Then he pauses. "Wait, why?"

I look down at the space between our shoes. "Because I have as many questions about you as you do about me."

He's looking down at me, speechless. Then he cradles my cheeks between his palms. "Quinn." This time he says my name like it's part of his foundation.

"I have something for you." He releases my cheeks and digs in the pockets of his blue jeans. He pulls out a piece of notebook paper folded in quarters.

"Another one? Carter, you don't have to keep doing this."

"Just trust me. Open it."

CARTER'S TO-DO LIST BEFORE COLLEGE

1. Share my most horrifying memories with Quinn— the things I could never admit out loud.
2. Tell Derrick the real reason I ghosted him.
3. Attempt to make amends with my father.
4. Finally ask him where my grandmother is buried.
5. Visit her.
6. Tell my mom that I'm moving out in the fall, and not in two years like she thinks.
7. Save for last; you know what you have to do.

"I was hoping you'd help me do mine," he says.

I look up, my eyes watering. "What's the last item?" I ask, my voice scratchy.

"You'll see."

I laugh, holding his eye. "Of course I'll help you with your list. I would love to." My smile widens. It grows and grows, like a plant that you water every day, like a scar that heals from patience, like the time you take to make sure you feel okay. So big and so bright.

"It's a deal?" Then he holds his hand out.

"A handshake?" I ask, tilting my head.

He tilts his head, too, smirking. "How else should we seal the deal?"

I grab his hand and place it on the small of my back,

stepping up close, bathing in the warmth emanating from his body. He places his other hand around my back as my hands crawl around his neck. I play with the brim of his hat, standing on the tips of my toes.

"Are you sure you're ready?" he says, looking down at my lips.

"Yeah." I lean in. And at the feel of his mouth, I take a deep breath.

Kissing Carter feels like I'm right where I need to be. Like everything happened just so that I could end up here, free of lies and fear and guilt, with friends who understand and respect me, and a boy who isn't perfect, but who's patient and whose light shines over all my darkness. Like *finally*.

acknowledgments

Ugly Cry's journey all started with my magical agent, Brianne Johnson. Bri, you don't realize how thoroughly you changed the course of my life with your email back. Thank you for actively sifting through your slush pile and making not just mine, but so many authors' dreams come true.

My editor, Alyson Day, thank you for believing in this book, for falling for Quinn and Carter just as hard as I did, for being open to my ideas and helping me mold this book into something I can be proud of for years to come. Thank you, Aly and Eva Lynch-Comer, for answering all my panicky, newbie emails and for helping me to breathe.

Thank you to everyone at HarperCollins. Maya Myers and Laura Harshberger for catching all the things I missed. Molly Fehr for the beautiful cover design and the lettering and Mlle Belamour for bringing Quinn and Carter to life with your artistic genius. I love, love, love this cover!

Thank you to everyone at Hot Key Books! You guys won my heart right off the bat with the sheer amount of effort you put into everything you do. I can't express how grateful I am to be working with you. To my editor, Carla: your emails are always the highlight of my day. You don't understand how comforting it is to have you on my team, because you care so much—for Quinn and Carter, for Black readers and Black representation, and for me. I can't thank you enough. And to Sophie, the designer of this amazing cover, thank you for the care you put into getting it just right. Thank you to the immensely talented Sarah Madden for the beautiful illustration. I love my UK cover so, so much!

Thank you to everyone at Writers House: Cecilia De La Campa for this amazing title. GURL. Everyone who heard the title fell in love instantly. Cecilia and Alessandra Birch for your amazing work talking this book up to folks all around the world. I could not have imagined the reception we received. Alexandra Levick for taking such good care of me and all the behind-the-scenes stuff.

This book went through so many rounds of revision. Thank you to all my beta readers and critique partners.

Jenevieve Gray: I found you in a random group on Goodreads, and I'm so glad I did. You read two different versions of this book, and I thank you so much for giving me some of the most useful advice and comments anyone ever took the time to give. You were really hard on Carter, and I'm so thankful. He used to be so toxic!

Noni Siziya: I'm so grateful that you didn't hold your tongue, especially when it came to Quinn. Your eyes were especially valuable, because you gave me notes on the Black reader's experience. I remember, in your comments you said that you never realized how much you needed to read about a Black couple until now, and that doing so had made you ridiculously happy. That stuck with me and kept me going. I hope I can do that for all my readers.

Thank you, Mrs. Shevlin, my fav English teacher, even though I hated English more than anything. You were more than a teacher for me. You were my counselor, my therapist, my friend when I really needed to talk through all my debilitating angst. Thank you so much for being there for me, and for so many of your students. I love you!

Thank you to my Kia bosses, Adam and Aaron, for letting me take book calls during work hours.

Thank you, Mom, for coming up with random character names and whatnot on the fly. For answering all my celebratory calls and acting just as excited as I was about every little piece of good news. I called you crying so many times. I'm sorry, but it's not stopping here.

Thank you, Blake. You put up with me locking myself away for hours. You believed in my capabilities when I doubted myself. You pushed me to press send on my query letters. And thank you for letting me talk at you about my ideas, and for being the best brainstorming partner a writer could ask for. You the real MVP.

Lastly, thank you, Francis Mae Harden (A-May), for the memories you gave me and my sister at your house, at your church, in your garden, and in the back of your red Chevy Blazer. Love and miss you so much.

joya goffney

Joya Goffney grew up in New Waverly, a small town in East Texas. In high school, she challenged herself with to-do lists full of risk-taking items like 'hug a random boy' and 'eat a cricket,' which inspired her debut novel, *Excuse Me While I Ugly Cry*. With a passion for Black social psychology, she moved out of the countryside to attend the University of Texas in Austin, where she still resides.

HOT KEY BOOKS

Thank you for choosing a Hot Key book.

If you want to know more about our authors
and what we publish, you can find us online.

You can start at our website

www.hotkeybooks.com

And you can also find us on:

We hope to see you soon!